To Patrick

Enjoy,

ALL BECAUSE OF HANNAH

DANIELLE PATARAZZI

AMETHYST & HERKIMER BOOKS

Published by Amethyst & Herkimer Books

Printed in the United States of America

First Printing, 2018

ISBN-13: 978-0-692-13804-5

ACKNOWLEDGMENTS

I offer my heartfelt thanks to my family, friends and colleagues throughout the long process of writing this book.

The staff at Red Adept Publishing for helping me through the first editing process of my book and making it that much stronger: Lynn McNamee, Stefanie Spangler Buswell, and Laura Koons.

David L. Miller, DO, FACOI, and Mary Kathleen Lockard, MD, FAAP, for helping me with all the medical procedures and jargon.

John Erb, attorney, for his legal input regarding malpractice lawsuits.

Melody De Meritt for proofreading the final draft.

Iain Rob Wright for teaching me about self-publishing and helping me with formatting.

My friends that read various drafts of my book and provided valuable feedback: Micki Hein, Alison Solotoroff, Stephanie

Elliot, Dave Wesolowski, Elizabeth Pasillas, and Leana Stemwedel.

My literary friends who guided me through this new process of writing and publishing: Renee Rosen, Tasha Alexander, Andrew Grant, Javier Ramirez, and Brian Wilson.

To my parents, Caesar and Mary Patarazzi, for always supporting my writing career since I was nine years old, and my brother Chris Patarazzi who never stopped asking, "When are you going to get your book published?"

And of course, to my baby brother Michael. Without you, this book would have never been written.

In memory of Michael Patarazzi
1982-2011

PART I

2003

Chapter 1

JILLIAN

If this were a scene in a movie, a romantic drama perhaps, it would be depicted as a joyous occasion: a family of three at the hospital eagerly awaiting the arrival of the fourth member. They would argue playfully over baby names. The husband would stroke his wife's hair and hold her hand through the contractions. Their excited twelve-year-old daughter would sit in the waiting room, surrounded by grandparents and close friends, nervously waiting as her mother pushed her new brother or sister into the world. They would hold their breath when the new dad enters the waiting room dressed in scrubs to announce the baby's healthy birth, then hugs and kisses when it's confirmed that mom and baby are just fine. And, nurses would gladly snap photos of the new-and-improved family of four.

Instead, the mood in my hospital room was somber, as if we were waiting for the results of a CAT scan instead of the birth of our second child. Nathan sat in a chair turned toward the TV, quickly flipping through the channels to find something to focus on other than his laboring wife. Caroline was over by the window, her head dropped down, hair tented over her phone. I lay in my hospital bed wearing a starchy gown, while the nurse hooked me up to a fetal monitor.

"How far apart were the contractions when you left the house?" The nurse asked.

"Six minutes." I pulled my knees to my chest as the nurse checked my cervix.

"Only four centimeters," she said. "You've got a few hours before there's any action."

Caroline wiped her eyes and yawned as she propped her feet up on the windowsill. I had imagined her here with me, witnessing the birth of her sibling, solidifying a bond between them. But now, as I rolled on to my side to face her, I wondered if watching her mother squeeze a baby through her vaginal canal might be more than a bit awkward for her. I told her she could sit in the waiting room.

"No, I wanna stay here," she said, fumbling with the silver charm bracelet Nate and I had given her on her twelfth birthday.

I was content with her refusing the get-out-of-jail-free card. She hadn't taken the news well when we'd told her she was going to be an older sister. Nate hadn't been too thrilled, either. After all, we were both thirty-seven and had given up on having any more children. But as the baby grew inside me, so had their reluctant acceptance of its inevitable arrival.

"What are you going to name it?" Caroline asked.

"Either Hannah or Aubrey works for me. Owen for a boy. Or Jacob." Nate turned to me. "It's your call, though."

Caroline sat up. "Owen's a cool name for a girl, too."

Their attitudes slightly shifted in a more positive direction compared to the ones they'd had the last time I'd brought up baby names. Going into my fourth month, I had convinced them it was time for a family night out at Chen's, our favorite Chinese restaurant. We sat in uncomfortable silence after placing our orders when I broached the subject of the new baby's name. Caroline was completely disinterested, muttering, "Whatever." And Nate had noted that we had another five months to decide on names, then quickly changed the subject to the Blackhawks.

Hearing them initiate the subject voluntarily was like an

epidural easing my labor pains, which, I noticed at that moment, seemed to have stopped.

I glanced at the clock. "What time was my last contraction?"

Nate shrugged. "Five minutes ago?"

I shook my head. "It's been longer than that." I looked down at my belly as if it held the answer.

"Maybe they just slowed down," he said.

"They're not supposed to slow down."

Dr. Stewart arrived a few moments later, wearing wrinkled blue scrubs with sweat stains under the arms. "Good morning, Mrs. Moore." He pushed his glasses up the bridge of his nose and reviewed the monitor feeds. "How are you feeling?"

"I think my contractions stopped."

"Well, let's take a peek." I pulled my legs back again for Dr. Stewart. "Still four centimeters. Let's go ahead and break your water and see if that speeds things along."

He unwrapped a sterile amniohook, which looked more like a crochet hook than an instrument used to break the amniotic sac. I closed my eyes as he inserted it into my cervix. I felt some pressure, then a light snap; water spilled out of me, spraying my legs with droplets. Dr. Stewart pulled off his latex gloves and said he would be back to check on me in about an hour.

"See?" Nate said. "He wasn't too concerned." He turned to Caroline, who still had her nose to her phone. "Hey, Care-Bear, you hungry? Wanna check out what kind of crappy food they have in the cafeteria?"

As she and Nate walked out, I told Caroline to make sure she didn't just load up on carbs and to include some protein in her crappy meal.

Counting the ceiling tiles was a perfect distraction while I waited for the next contraction. By the time I got to twenty, my mind shifted to the list of names we were considering, and I began matching them with potential middle names we still had yet to choose. As I sat up and grabbed my purse from the nightstand to dig for a pen, another contraction drove up my spine, and a sharp pain stabbed me in the stomach causing me to drop the pen. It was a welcome discomfort. How long had it been since the last one? Fifteen minutes?

There was a soft knock at the door, and a new nurse popped her head in. "Hi, Mrs. Moore. How are you feeling?" I recognized her from our church. Her name was Rebecca Russert, and she was active on the fundraising committee that I'd volunteered for in the past.

"Much better now that I had another contraction," I told her.

She smiled. "Breaking the water seemed to help." She read the monitor then checked my cervix. "You're still at four centimeters, though."

"Where's Dr. Stewart?"

"He had to go back to his office, but he'll be back shortly."

Once she left, I reached for the remote. And as I flipped through the channels I relived the last time I was in the maternity ward almost thirteen years before. My labor pains had gone from twenty minutes apart, to ten, to five, and then I'd pushed for almost two hours. When they placed the beautiful baby girl in my arms, still moist from my womb, I whispered in her ear, "I'll make mistakes, but I'll do the best I can."

I continued to channel surf, until I got lost in an episode of the *Golden Girls*, but when the show ended, I was back in the present, alone in a room on a hospital bed. The monitor beeped in short intervals, a subtle reminder why I was there. I hadn't had another contraction.

"Something's not right," I told Nate when he and Caroline returned. Caroline was already preoccupied with texting.

"Why do you say that?" He pulled the chair up to the bed.

"Because I can feel it. The contractions are slowing down." I told him the nurse hadn't seemed very concerned.

"Honey, don't worry about it," he said. "We're in a hospital. If anything happens, they'll know what to do."

Nate had aged so nicely, with his light-brown hair fading at the temples and the laugh lines around his smiling eyes. I'd told him he had smiling eyes the first time we had lunch at Hardee's in the student union where he'd followed me after listening to me give a pro-life persuasion speech in class.

By the time Kate stopped by, the sun had broken on the horizon, casting an orange glow across my room. "Well, good morning, Mama. How are you doing?" She wore a faded red plaid sweater vest over a light pink turtleneck and brown plaid pants. Her dishwater hair was tied back in a loose ponytail with a rubber band that I was sure she had pulled out of a junk drawer.

Kate and I had first met in first grade, but we hadn't become friends until we were lab partners in sixth grade. She'd thought I was stuck up. I'd thought she was just plain weird. I still did, but in a more endearing, appreciative way. Kate loved being the center of attention, even if that attention was negative. She would burst into a room at a high volume, walk up to any stranger she spotted, and start chatting him up. After twenty minutes, she would know his life story. Sometimes, she could be embarrassing, like the day she'd worn head-to-toe mismatched paisley to our friend's daughter's bridal shower. But she had a heart of gold and was always there for me and my family.

Nate greeted her with a hug and told her she looked ridiculous.

"This is my favorite sweater vest," she said as she hugged Caroline. "I've had it for over twenty years, since right before my mom died. I always get compliments on it."

"They're probably being sarcastic," I said.

She laughed and leaned down to kiss me. I told her about the slowing contractions.

"Oh, that's normal." She reassured. "My sister's contractions slowed down, then sped up again. Then she popped out an eleven-pound boy. Don't worry about it." She reached into her purse and pulled out a stack of magazines. "I brought you some trashy tabloids to take your mind off of things."

I perused the covers of *Us Weekly*, *InTouch*, and *People* then tossed the magazines aside.

Kate stayed until around eight-thirty, then offered to take Caroline home who was getting restless and wanted to go back to bed. At that point, I didn't want my daughter there anyway. I wanted to shield her from the noticeable angst that had overtaken me.

Nate paced the room trying to stay busy and, most of all, stay positive. Around eleven, he announced that he was going for a cup of coffee. I watched the nurses at their station right outside my room, chatting and laughing, relaxed. *If they're not worried about my baby, should I not worry?* Nate always told me I tend to overreact. *Or should I be listening to my gut?*

The monitor beeped, loud and piercing, as if it were giving me an answer to my desperate question.

Nurse Rebecca came in and surveyed the monitor. The baby's heart rate had dropped below the normal fetal heart rate during labor. "It's not getting enough oxygen, which means you aren't, either." They hooked me up to an oxygen machine and had me lay on my side. I again asked her where Dr. Stewart was.

"Still at the office," she said. She waited as I inhaled the oxygen, and the baby's heart rate slowly climbed.

"Everything is going to be fine," Rebecca assured me. She had strawberry-blonde shoulder length hair pulled back in a ponytail and kind green eyes. "Do you have names picked out?"

"I want a C-section," I said through the mask. "Can you call Dr. Stewart and tell him? Right now."

"I'll let him know. But try to relax. We want to keep the baby's heart rate normal."

The next few hours crept by without contractions. I knew it couldn't be false labor since the doctor had broken my water. I had no idea what was happening because no one would tell me anything. I lay in bed, wiping the tears from my face, waiting for someone, anyone, to tell me what to do. Nate wandered in and out, feeling helpless. Each time he went to the nurses' station and drill them, he got no answers. Rebecca continued to check up on me, trying in vain to keep me calm as I demanded to see my doctor—or any doctor.

I waited. I prayed. I poked at my large tummy to see if the baby would react. Nothing moved.

"Hey." I poked again, the tears filling my eyes. "What are you doing in there?" I pressed on my right side, where just yesterday, I'd seen a foot sticking out. "Give me a sign that you're still okay. Please."

The tears spilled over and onto the sheets. "Please, please, baby. Show me a sign."

~

DR. STEWART finally arrived around three o'clock, looking disheveled and exhausted, with bloodshot eyes and a sweaty forehead, as though he'd just come from the gym.

"Mrs. Moore. I'm so sorry to keep you waiting. We had a couple of emergency C-sections. Is everything going okay?" He said that last part to my chart rather than to me.

"Okay?" I sat up. "Where the hell have you been? I've been asking for you for hours."

He didn't respond and instead turned to Nurse Rebecca who filled him in on the details, when the last contraction had been, and that the fetal heart rate had dropped.

Dr. Stewart reviewed the heart monitor and scanned the papers that spat out results like a register receipt after a shopping spree. He checked my cervix. "You're still only four centimeters. I think it's time to consider a C-section."

"Consider? I've been requesting one all day. No one was listening to me."

"Mrs. Moore, I assure you that while I was tending to other patients, you were in good hands. The baby will be fine, but we need to get it out quickly."

They wheeled me into a cold OR and quickly prepped me for surgery. A chill ran up my spine right before they inserted the epidural needle. A nurse wrapped a blood pressure cuff around my arm and clipped an oximeter to my finger to measure my blood oxygen levels. I squinted at the bright lights above me as the nurses put up a sterile drape to hide my belly from me. I heard instruments clanking and gloves being snapped on. I felt the cold sterilization solution being swiped onto my stomach. Nate stood beside me and held my hand as I prayed silently.

Hail Mary, full of grace. The Lord is with Thee. A tear slipped from the corner of my eye, down my temple, and into my ear.

Blessed art thou among women. I heard squishing noises, organs being dug into and pushed aside. *And blessed is the fruit of thy womb, Jesus.* I felt tightness in my abdomen, then cramping, as Dr. Stewart reached in and pulled out my baby. *Holy Mary, Mother of God, pray for us sinners.*

"It's a girl," he announced. He handed her over to the nurse. I caught a glimpse of her right arm, her tiny fist with her pinky finger sticking out like a graceful little lady. They rushed her out of the room.

"What's going on?" I called out. "What's wrong?"

"Why isn't she crying?" Nate asked.

Dr. Stewart pulled off his surgical mask. "She's not breathing."

Now and at the hour of our death.

Amen.

Chapter 2

JILLIAN

The news that I was pregnant at thirty-seven was not positively received by anyone—not even me. Our original plan was to have at least one more baby after Caroline, but after three miscarriages within two years, we had accepted that she was going to be an only child.

I was ten weeks pregnant the first time I miscarried. It was a late spring morning, and I'd felt light cramps while I was scrambling an egg for Caroline, who was almost three. Knowing that cramping wasn't unusual during the first trimester, I didn't panic and popped two Tylenol. After breakfast, the cramps got stronger, enough for even Caroline to notice that I wasn't feeling good, and her face twisted in concern. Her snub nose crunched up, and her tiny forehead furrowed. "It's okay, baby," I said. "Let's go out and play."

Caroline pulled off her sandals that I had just strapped on her and ran across the dewy yard to the sand box. She jumped into the sand and giggled at how it stuck to her damp feet. I sat at the patio table and watched her build a little town in the sand. "Our house." She pointed to each mound of sand. "Store... school...park..."

As I watched Caroline construct Santa's house in the North

Pole, something gushed between my legs. I jumped up from the table, startling Caroline.

"Mommy?"

"Honey, stay here, okay? Don't move. Mommy will be right back."

A warm liquid trickled down my legs as I waddled inside. I called Nate, who was still upstairs sleeping after a night out with friends. Kate rushed over to watch Caroline while Nate took me to the hospital. The ob-gyn on call who examined me broke the news that we had already suspected. I had lost the baby.

I cried myself to sleep that night, mostly from guilt for not protecting my baby, for not keeping it safe, and for not getting a real chance to bond with it. I waited until after the six-week recovery period before telling Nate I was ready to try again. Three months later, I was pregnant. It never crossed my mind that another miscarriage was possible. I'd chalked up the first experience to bad luck and wasted no time preparing for the birth of our second child. I announced my pregnancy to our family and friends. I started suggesting baby names to Nate, who was a bit more hesitant.

"Let's get through the first trimester before we...you know," he'd said.

"Before we get too attached?" I asked. "Should we just pretend I'm not pregnant for another three months?"

I miscarried halfway through my second month. I pushed my resentment toward Nate to the back of my mind, as if his hesitation to celebrate the pregnancy somehow caused this. We put child making on hold, not because we were giving up, but because we needed a break from the emotional course we had been on for months. I told Nate I was going back on the pill, and he didn't argue. We didn't start trying again until a year and a half later, and I got pregnant immediately. This time, we held our excitement in check, telling no one, not even our closest friends. We left the spare bedroom crammed with boxes of Christmas decorations and unused furniture.

I almost made it through my second trimester.

Nathan and I began accepting the probability that Caroline would be our only child.

It was a painful dose of reality. Would she be too spoiled as an only child? Lonely? Would she know how to share and be compassionate? Nate was ready to accept the challenge, telling me he was done sitting by as another baby leaked out of me.

Life went on. Nate thrived in the creative department at a PR firm. I continued my career in advertising at the Foster Group, working various accounts until landing the Senior Account Director position on the Lady Luster hair care account. As our careers blossomed, we appreciated having only one child. Caroline turned out to be a wonderful little girl—always caring, friendly, and outgoing, and never selfish or spoiled as I had worried she might be. We raised her to be independent, free spirited, compassionate, and grateful. I naively thought she would stay that way throughout her teenage years.

THE MORNING I found out I was pregnant was the day of the big business pitch to Corbin International to renew our Lady Luster retainer. There were rumblings that Corbin was considering other shops, agencies that had an edge and were more versed in online marketing than an old-world agency like the Foster Group. For weeks my team and I prepared to prove them wrong: researching the competition, reviewing past promotions, and analyzing the effectiveness of the Lady Luster website. I was handling most of the pitch, but I made sure the rest of my team had the chance to contribute. Jorie, the account supervisor, would present the competitive analysis, while Sydney, the account executive, would present an overview of the past promotions we had developed and executed. The day before the pitch, we locked ourselves in the main conference room to go over the details of the strategic analysis and the brand positioning statement, making sure we understood the annual plan from start to finish, dress rehearsing for the pitch. We ordered Chinese for lunch. We ordered pizza for dinner. At eleven-thirty that night, I finally crawled into bed next to Nate.

The next day, I should've waited.

I'd worked my butt off over the last three years on that account, building brand awareness, retaining the brand loyalists, and bringing back customers who had switched to Pantene.

I should've waited, but the symptoms weren't going away.

The morning of the pitch, after Nate left for work, I peed on a stick. I was determined not to get distracted by the positive sign that appeared in the tiny window. I needed to focus on the pitch and the key promotion we were proposing, which included a grand-prize trip for four to New York City during Fashion Week. I tossed the stick in the garbage and left for work. As Jorie and Sydney ran around the office, taking care of last-minute details before we drove out to Corbin's headquarters, my mind kept veering back to the morning discovery. When it came time for the presentation, I stood at the head of the table in front of my team, my boss, and five people from Corbin. *Focus*, I told myself. *We need to retain this account.* I stood up straight and steadied myself. But I zipped through my sections of the presentation as if I were high on caffeine, too preoccupied with what was growing inside of me to focus on selling shampoo.

The next day, we were eliminated from the running after the first round and lost the account. I knew what was coming next. A week later, Jorie, Sydney, and I were laid off because of revenue cuts, along with six other people throughout the agency.

I went home that day and told Nate the expected had happened: I'd lost my job. Then I told him the unexpected: I was pregnant.

He paused as he was pulling out a bottle of Pinot Noir. He looked down at the bottle, staring at the label for a long time. He carried the bottle over to the counter, pulled open the drawer, and dug for the corkscrew.

I wasn't sure why I'd waited until then to tell him what I had already known for a week. After the pitch, I'd been too focused on how mediocre the presentation had gone after all my team's hard work. I worried about what would happen if we lost the account—if I lost my job. I'd been focused on the immediate issue: my career being in jeopardy. And maybe I was expecting to miscarry anyway, so then I wouldn't have a reason to tell Nate in the first place.

Nate and I were raised Catholic, and we chose to bring up Caroline in the church. Although Nate was more of a lapsed Catholic, I still had a little faith and tried to instill some of the Catholic teachings into our lives. I dragged my husband and daughter to church a couple Sundays a month. We'd baptized Caroline when she was a month old and celebrated her first Communion when she was eight. I taught her to pray every night before bed. I was aware that none of this religiousness would've happened without my influence. So when Nate uncorked the bottle, poured himself a glass, and told me that we had options, I wasn't surprised. But it still grated on my nerves.

"What options?" I asked.

"I'm just saying," he said, spreading his hands. "It's legal."

"Not according to the Catholic Church," I said.

"Yeah, well, the Catholic Church frowns upon premarital sex, but that didn't stop us."

I winced at the retort I'd known he would throw in my face. He'd made the same argument when we'd first started dating, before we even slept together. Nate sipped the Pinot and held up the bottle to me. "Are you not having any then?"

I shook my head. Filled with nervous energy, I grabbed the sponge and wiped the countertops.

Nate sat down at the table, staring down at his glass as he swirled it. "I'm sorry. I didn't mean to sound callous. I just want you to know that we have options, and I'll support you no matter what you decide."

I scrubbed at a caked-on smudge on the countertop. I picked

at it with my nail until it loosened then wiped it clean. "I'm not thrilled about this either, Nate. But I'm not getting an abortion."

"I didn't say I wanted you to get an abortion." He rested his head in his hands. "Right when you lose your job. How are we going to afford this?"

"I have my severance package. And I can file for unemployment. So we'll be okay for a little while." I sat down next to him. "After the baby is born, I'll start looking for another job."

It felt like a moment to reach across the table and grab his hand, like characters do in romantic dramas after a tense scene. But I kept my hands in my lap, afraid of his rejection or his limp hand-holding, which would be more of an obligatory gesture than a sincere show of affection.

Chapter 3

JILLIAN

The nurse dimmed the lights, but they were still too bright. I blinked, straining to open my eyes wider than a slit. The bare recovery room was quiet. The effects of the medication the doctor had given me were kicking in. I gripped the sides of the mattress to keep from feeling as if I were floating way. Far away from the nightmare I was about to endure. Instead, I needed to stay lucid enough to replay the incidents of the day through my clouded mind. Something had gone wrong. But when? Should I have pushed to get a C-section sooner? Didn't I try to warn everyone that something was wrong with the baby? And where the hell had Dr. Stewart been all afternoon?

And Nate. I tried telling him that something was wrong, but he thought I was being paranoid. I wondered how he was feeling now, his smiling eyes probably veiled with regret, as he followed the ambulance that carried our newborn daughter downtown to Children's Memorial Hospital.

I thought back to his less-than-thrilled reaction upon finding out I was pregnant again. Later that same night, as Nate snored next to me, I'd thought about Lindsey Hobbs, my college roommate.

Lindsey and I met when we were placed together as room-mates freshman year. We became close friends, and by junior year, we had rented a tiny house off campus. She was dating a basketball player named Paul and had fallen hard for him. They'd been dating for five or six months when one day I arrived home from class, and Lindsey was sitting cross-legged on the couch, crying as she folded laundry. She told me through hiccupped sobs that she was pregnant but afraid to tell Paul because she thought he would break up with her. I tried to reason with her, reminding her what a great guy Paul was and that he wouldn't do that to her. But she kept shaking her head, her face contorted in sorrow and worry, as she wiped her tears with a washcloth from the laundry basket. She said she was going to get an abortion anyway, so she saw no point in even telling him. I didn't try to talk her out of it. Her decision was made, and I didn't want to push my beliefs onto her. Then she asked me to go with her to the clinic. I hesitated. If I went, would that mean I was pro-choice? If I didn't go, I wasn't supporting my friend. In the end, our friendship was more important than my personal beliefs. She needed me. That was the bottom line.

We went to the nearest Planned Parenthood clinic, which was forty-five minutes away. Outside, a small gathering of protesters stood hollering, holding up posters of aborted fetuses. I avoided the gruesome images as we pushed our way into the clinic. In the waiting room, I held her hand and embraced her when her name was finally called. An hour later, she came out looking tired and gaunt, as if much more than a fetus had been sucked out of her. She clutched her purse to her vacant tummy as we walked back out through the protesters.

She didn't say a word during the ride home. I made her some tea when we got back and asked her if she wanted to lie down. She shook her head and asked me to sit with her and not talk about the details of the day. For a few days afterward, she was a little down. But after about a week or so, she returned to her usual upbeat self, bouncing in from class, asking if I wanted to go to happy hour in town.

I didn't think I would ever be able to rebound like she had. I tried to picture myself in her situation. Lying on the surgery table in a paper gown, legs up in stirrups, blinking back tears as I stared up at the florescent lights. I imagined the cramping procedure followed by the hissing and sucking noises, like a wet vac cleaning up spilled soup. I shook the evil thought from my mind, instead remembering the blissful day of Caroline's birth and the joy it had brought into our lives.

I had naively believed that the birth of my second child was going to be the same.

I couldn't blame Nate. I thought of him sitting beside me as they'd cut me open, wiping the tears from my face, softly tugging on my earlobe. "Cute earlobes," he'd whispered. I turned to him then, picturing him fifteen years younger, like he'd been when we'd first met. His eyes still smiled but were softer around the edges.

HE WAS such a pest when I first met him. Persistent. After I'd finished my pro-life persuasion speech in public speaking class, he came up to me, his backpack slung over his shoulder, his fraternity cap backward on his head. He was a charmer. Or at least he thought he was. I was adamant to not let his charms work on me.

"Hey," he said to me. "That was an okay speech."

"Just okay?" I asked as I gathered my books.

"Yeah, you made some great points, but I'm afraid you still failed me in the persuasion part."

"Why is that?" We walked out of Simpkins Hall into the rush of students hurrying to their next class.

"I can understand your view, about life starting at conception, but what's it to you?"

"Excuse me?" I glanced over my shoulder at him as he hurried to keep up with me.

"I mean, if a girl gets an abortion, what impact will that have on your life?"

"That's not the point. A fetus is a living thing."

"It's inside a woman's body. Therefore, she should be able to decide whether or not to keep it, right?"

"It's a little more complicated than that."

"How?"

I picked up my pace, weaving in and out of the throng of people, hoping to lose him. When I arrived at the student union, he was still on my heels. I entered Hardee's, deciding if I had a taste for a cheeseburger or a fish sandwich.

"Wouldn't it bother you if the government told you what to do with your body?" he asked.

"No one has a right to murder an innocent baby."

"Ah." He held up a finger. "But the question is, is it really a baby that early in the pregnancy?"

I rolled my eyes. "Isn't that what I said during my speech?"

"Yes, but if it's a baby, wouldn't it be able to live and breathe on its own outside of the womb? A fetus can't do that at eight weeks."

I stepped up to the counter and ordered a cheeseburger and a small Coke.

He came up beside me. "And I'll have a double cheeseburger, large fries, and a large Coke." He reached in his back pocket, pulled out his wallet, and threw a twenty on the counter. "For here," he told the server behind the counter.

As the lady placed a tray on the counter, I turned to him. "You're presumptuous."

"No, I'm Nate." He smiled. "And you're Jillian, right? Can I buy you lunch, Jillian? This way, we can finish our discussion."

I laughed. "What makes you think I want to finish it?"

He smiled as he grabbed the tray after the order was fulfilled and walked to a two-seater. I reluctantly followed.

"So," he placed the tray on the table and sat down opposite me as he shoved fries in his mouth.

"Listen"—I held up a hand—"I appreciate your opinion, and I'm really, truly sorry I wasn't able to persuade you to switch sides. But I really don't give a damn."

"Hmm. I see." He picked up his burger and took a large bite.

"And since you won't ever be able to persuade me, what's really the point of all this?"

He shoved more fries in his mouth while watching me. His eyes seemed to smile at me. At the time, it irritated me. "What?" I said.

"You have cute earlobes." He reached over the table and tugged lightly on my right ear.

"Okay," I said. "That's a new one."

"New what?"

"Pick-up line."

"It's not a pick-up line. It's a compliment."

"Thanks. I've always wanted someone to notice my dainty earlobes."

He followed me outside after we ate and walked beside me as we headed toward my house. On the doorstep, as I fished my keys out of my purse, he invited me to his fraternity's spring party on Saturday, and I agreed after some hesitation. But when he picked me up on Saturday, he surprised me by taking me to dinner at Carmine's, the only fine-dining restaurant in town. Until then, most of my first dates had been greasy burgers at the pub in the town square. Nate's charming disposition that he'd displayed at Hardee's was gone from our dinner at Carmine's. His wore his vulnerability like a security blanket as he told me about how his mother had died of breast cancer when he was five. Just a year later, his dad decided to marry Nate's third-grade teacher. Then when Nate was seventeen, his dad and step-mom both died in a car accident, forcing him to live with an aunt until he finished high school.

"That's unbelievable," I said. "How did you handle going through all that loss?"

"What else can I do but keep moving forward?"

I admired his bravery, and his willingness to tell me about his childhood put me at ease enough to tell him about my family life. I was an only child with a functioning alcoholic for a father and a helpless co-dependent mother. I told him about the numerous times throughout my childhood that I'd hid the vodka bottles or dumped the contents down the sink, knowing that my father would simply think he had finished it all himself because he was too drunk or hung over to remember otherwise. My mother would drive to the store to buy him another bottle when he was drunk, telling me it was safer than letting him get behind the wheel. She would reason with me and explain that his alcoholism was a disease that we couldn't change. *Only he can help himself,* she would tell me. *But he's set in his ways, and we have to accept that.* My mother was old fashioned in that way, believing her duty as a wife was to be by her husband's side, supportive. *Supportive of alcoholism?* I thought. I was too young to understand what co-dependency meant, but I would not be complacent like my mother. Dad died of cirrhosis the year after I graduated high school. Mom believed she'd done everything she was supposed to do, right up until she'd died of a heart attack a month after Caroline's birth.

Nate and I didn't talk politics on our first date. We didn't get into the abortion debate. After dinner, we went to the Delt party. As his fraternity brothers did beer bongs and keg stands, Nate stayed relatively sober, only sipping on a couple of beers throughout the entire night. He stayed by my side, protecting me from his rowdy, drunken friends.

We dated the rest of our college years and got engaged a year after graduation. Nate landed his first copywriting job at Leo Burnett. I got a job at a smaller agency, so the timing was right for the next logical milestone. Caroline was born two years after we were married. Life progressed with very few bumps in the road.

Until now.

≈

THE DOOR to my hospital room creaked open, and Kate stuck her head in. "You awake?" She approached, holding a bouquet of pink and white flowers, a sad attempt to make things a little better. But flowers couldn't make me smile. Neither could Kate's ludicrous ensemble of a yellow polka dot button-down shirt and bright-red capris.

She placed the flowers on the windowsill and sat on the edge of the bed.

"She was grey," I said to her. "The baby was grey. I knew something was wrong. No one would listen to me."

She leaned down and dabbed my face with a Kleenex. "Did you get any sleep?"

"No, Nate's supposed to call."

"I'll wake you when he calls. "

"I didn't even get to see her," I cried. "They took her away."

"They're taking good care of her. Children's is one of the best pediatric hospitals in the country."

It was a switch in the roles of our friendship. Since grade school, I'd been the one who could calm Kate, who tended to over dramatize every situation. The tables had turned. As Kate poured a glass of water for me, she persuaded me to take the sleeping pill the nurse had left in a small paper cup on the nightstand.

I wanted to keep my head clear enough to retrace my steps. I needed to keep playing the events of the day over and over in my mind until I came to some conclusions. Kate listened as I told her every detail through weakened sobs.

"Where's Caroline?" I asked.

Kate got up to close the venetian blinds in the room, blocking out the late-afternoon sun. "She's at Courtney's. I called and told her she had a baby sister." She smiled.

"What did she say?" A lump swelled in my throat. "Did she sound happy?"

"She said she couldn't wait to meet her."

I'd been eager to see Caroline's face when she first met her new sister. I pictured her walking into the room with Nate while I cradled a bundle in a pink hat swaddled in a blanket wearing one of the hospital-issued pink hats. I would watch her face light up as soon as I placed her baby sister in her arms, and all the doubt would evaporate.

"Will you go get Caroline for me?" I asked, my voice groggy. "I need to see her. I need to see my daughter."

Kate agreed, but only if I would take the sleeping pill when she returned. After she left, I closed my eyes and began drifting. I was back in the OR, hearing Dr. Stewart murmur things to the nurses. I saw a nurse take the baby from Dr. Stewart's hands and rush away. *Cry, baby*, I remember thinking. *I just want to hear you cry.*

"Mom?"

I opened my eyes and saw my beautiful Caroline looking down at me. I reached out and pulled her to me. My sweet baby girl. I held tightly to my firstborn.

"Mom, where's the baby? Can I see her?" she asked with wide eyes.

"Not yet. She had a little trouble breathing, so the doctors are helping her. But she'll be okay." I added those last words to reassure us both. "Say a prayer for her, okay?"

She nodded. "What's her name going to be?"

I paused. Since her birth, I hadn't thought of the name. I'd been so consumed with worrying if the doctors could keep her alive. It seemed so long since I was lying in my hospital bed, pairing first names with middle ones.

I remembered the glimpse of my baby as they pulled her from my womb and her tiny pinky sticking out as if she were sipping tea from a porcelain cup like a graceful little lady. "Hannah Grace," I said.

Caroline smiled. She had the same smiling eyes as her father.

"Come lay down next to me." I attempted to scoot over to make room. She crawled into the bed and curled up by my side like she had when she was little and would climb into our bed after a bad dream.

I wrapped my arms around her like a security blanket, and moments later, without the help of the sleeping pill, I was asleep.

Chapter 4

CAROLINE

I was a little more than disgusted when I found out my mom was pregnant, which obviously meant that my parents were still having sex. I also didn't like the idea of having a younger sister or brother. When I was little, I'd asked Mom if she would have another baby. She would give me the usual, "We'll see," which really was her way of telling me no. As I got older, I realized how great I had it as an only child. My best friend, Courtney, has a younger sister and two younger brothers, and I hated going to her house. Her bratty sister, Stephanie, was always butting in, tagging along, or eavesdropping. Her hyperactive brothers, Caleb and Jon, were always playing pranks on us. The bathroom was always occupied. And when it was available, there was always pee on the seat. We couldn't watch what we wanted on TV because the others would whine. So we spent most of the time at my house, where we had everything to ourselves.

Being an only child had its rewards. With a new baby in the house, that would all change.

When the baby was born, I was almost thirteen—an appropriate age to start babysitting. My parents had timed it perfectly for a built-in babysitter. And they probably wouldn't even pay me.

So not only would I not be able to hang out with my friends, I wouldn't even be earning any money.

And what about when I get my license? My annoying sibling would want to hang around me every time a friend came over or tag along on trips to the mall. I could picture the little brat throwing a tantrum until my parents pleaded with me to take him or her with me. *Just this once,* they would promise.

These were the selfish things going through my mind during the first few months of my mother's pregnancy.

Be careful what you wish for, I thought to myself.

"What are you thinking about, hon?" Kate was standing next to me, holding a pan of macaroni and cheese. In the days after Hannah's birth, she came by to help out while Mom was still in the hospital and Dad was going to and from Children's to see Hannah. I didn't know much about how sick Hannah was. No one told me anything, except that she wasn't breathing well when she was born.

Kate's hot pink and turquoise bracelets clanked as she placed a heaping bowl of macaroni and cheese in front of me. "It's your favorite. Your mom told me you like it with peas and Corn Flakes mixed in. Although you didn't have any Corn Flakes, I found Raisin Bran in the pantry, so I added those. I just picked out the raisins." She waved a bejeweled hand.

I dug in and shoved forkfuls of macaroni into my mouth. "Did you talk to my dad?" I asked between mouthfuls. "Is Hannah going to be okay?"

Kate scooped a spoonful of the pasta onto her own plate. "Don't forget to eat some salad." She pointed to the bowl in the middle of the table. "The dressing is homemade. It's my grand-mother's recipe. Comes all the way from Scotland."

"Kate?"

She avoided my eyes and shoved food around on her plate. Her cheap plastic headband held her dishwater-blond bangs back from her face, making her blue eye shadow stand out. "Sometimes when babies are born, they have trouble breathing, but the doctors will work with her until she gets better. Then she can come home. She's going to be fine."

I put my fork down and pushed my plate away. I'd overheard Kate talking on the phone in the kitchen that afternoon. I was in the family room, straining to hear what she was saying and only made out a few words from the conversation. I pieced together what I had heard and concluded that Hannah wasn't breathing and had been rushed to Children's Memorial Hospital in Chicago.

I excused myself and went up to my room, where I spent most of my time. Mom called it my cave because I usually kept the shades drawn so it stayed dark. The house was unusually quiet. The TV wasn't on. Mom wasn't chatting on the phone. The sound of dishes clanking as Kate loaded the dishwasher was the only noise. I dialed Courtney's cell, but got her voice mail, which wasn't surprising. I hadn't told her yet that I had a baby sister, and I wasn't sure if I should mention that she was sick.

I sent Courtney a text: *It's a girl!* She was probably out with Chloe McAllister, Polly Bonner, or one of the other more popular girls she'd recently started hanging out with. She never invited me to go. Not that I wanted to, anyway.

I lay back on my bed and scanned the posters on my wall: Pink, Beyoncé, and Justin Timberlake. If I had their financial freedom, I would just pack up and leave. I could go on a long vacation to Bali and not care about school or friends. I would use all of my money to pay for whatever Hannah needed to get better so she could come home. And then my parents would be happy.

The landline rang, and a moment later, Kate knocked lightly on my door and stuck her head in. "Sweetie, your dad's on the phone."

I reached for the phone. "Daddy?"

"Hi, Care-Bear," he said. "I miss you."

"When are you coming home?"

"I'm not sure yet, baby," he said.

"Daddy"—I swallowed back the tears—"what's wrong with Hannah?"

He paused and took a deep breath, taking time to form an appropriate answer. "She was having trouble breathing. So now the doctors have her on oxygen until her lungs get stronger."

I nodded, too afraid to utter a word until I'd swallowed my emotions.

"Caroline?"

"Yeah."

"I love you. She'll be okay," he said. "I promise."

I smiled even though I knew they were just words. Nobody could promise that. I wasn't even convinced I was going to be okay.

My phone buzzed shortly after I hung up with Dad. Courtney had responded to my text. *OMG! So excited it's a girl! Can't wait to meet her!*

Then the next text came through.

You'll never believe what Chloe did! It was hilarious! Call me later!

I tossed my phone aside and lay back down, hoping sleep would come easily that night.

Chapter 5

JILLIAN

I sat up slowly in my bed. My abdomen was still sore, my mind still foggy from the pain meds. I needed to use the bathroom, but I refused to buzz the nurse. I swung my legs over the side of the bed. Carefully, I stood up and took small steps toward the bathroom.

I'd felt paralyzed for the last two days, confined to the hospital bed. I tried to stay focused on the moment, waiting for the phone calls from Nate about Hannah's progress.

Rebecca Russert, RN, was my new best friend. From the moment Hannah was born until the transport team from Children's Memorial arrived more than three hours later, Rebecca squeezed air into Hannah's weak lungs at five-second intervals. Because Ferndale Hospital wasn't equipped to care for Hannah long term, we were forced to wait anxiously for a resident physician and a nurse from Children's to be available to drive up to transport Hannah. For hours, while we waited, Rebecca hovered over my baby, spoke gently to her, and whispered prayers while keeping her alive.

She also stayed by her side in the ambulance for the journey downtown. She'd stopped by my room after returning, hours after the end of her shift, after turning Hannah's care over to the staff at Children's. She stood at the edge of my bed in her street clothes and asked how I was feeling. I answered with the slightest shake of the head. She'd told me what she knew. Hannah was stable. Her oxygen level was low, and she was on a ventilator. The doctors would know more the next day.

"What happened?" I asked her. "Why couldn't my baby breathe?"

She brushed the hair behind her ear. "It was most likely meconium aspiration," she said, "due to fetal distress."

"Meconium? Like feces?"

She nodded. *My baby inhaled meconium?* My body heaved as I gasped in between sobs, gulping for air like my baby had inside my womb.

Rebecca handed me a box of tissues that was sitting on the side table.

"I baptized her," she said as I mopped the tears from my face.

"What?"

"I recognized you from church," she said. "Immaculate Conception. I'm a member, too. I thought you'd want to know that I baptized your baby. I hope that's okay."

She told me how, during the ambulance ride to the hospital, she'd made a tiny sign of the cross with her thumb on Hannah's forehead and whispered those sacred words, "I baptize you in the name of the Father, the Son, and the Holy Spirit. Amen."

My heart swelled. When I was little, my mom told me the story of how my great-aunt Martha, who was a nurse in Italy during World War II, had baptized a newborn boy right before he died. The Catholic Church allows a civilian to baptize someone in an emergency, Mom had told me, "So he could get into heaven."

I got one step closer to the bathroom before Nate walked in, followed by Kate and Caroline.

"Honey, you shouldn't be doing that on your own," he said.

"Hi, Mom." Caroline reached for me, and I held her as tightly as I could, despite my weakness.

"Nate, what are you doing here?" I demanded. "You're supposed to be down with Hannah."

"I came home to change into some clean clothes and to check up on Caroline. I'm on my way back down, but I wanted to stop in and see you."

"I'm fine." I continued the trek to the bathroom. Nate grabbed my arm to support me. I shook it off. "You should go back down. I don't want her to be alone."

When I returned from the bathroom, they helped me back into bed.

"She's still stable," Nate said. "But her oxygen levels are increasing slowly."

My head sank into the pillow, and I closed my eyes. *When her oxygen levels get to the normal rate, she can breathe on her own, and then they'll release her.* "Did they say how long until we can take her home?"

Nate shook his head. "Probably a few more weeks. Listen"— he sat down at the edge of the bed—"I called a lawyer."

"What? What lawyer?"

"He's a general lawyer," Kate said. "The one my cousin used after her car accident."

"I just wanted to talk to someone," Nate said, "to get an opinion." He'd told the lawyer everything that had happened, and the lawyer had advised us to contact a medical malpractice lawyer.

"Jillian." Kate walked over to the side of the bed. On any other day, I would have smiled at the silly paisley-dotted button-down she was wearing over a yellow dickey. "Maybe you should start writing things down. Everything that happened. You know, just in case."

Just in case Hannah doesn't pull through. In case something's wrong with her because she inhaled her own feces. In case this is much worse than we could've ever imagined. Rebecca baptized Hannah just in case.

I didn't want to think about it. I didn't want to have to rehash the experience of the last two days. The loneliness. The crying.

The pleading. The anguish. I wasn't ready to think about lawyers and lawsuits. I just wanted to see my baby. The unexpected surprise that I'd carried for nine months was lying in some scary hospital, and I hadn't even met her. Nate had taken some pictures and showed me two-dimensional snapshots of our little girl on a small digital-camera screen. She had dark hair like Caroline had when she was born. She had my button nose and Nate's square chin. My own daughter was not quite a stranger, but someone I had never met.

Nate sat down in the chair beside the bed. "Honey, write down anything you remember while it's still fresh in your mind. What time the labor pains stopped. What time the doctor first saw you. How long it took for him to check up on you again."

What time I first raised concern but was ignored. I pulled the sheets up to my chin and turned to Caroline, who was sitting on a chair by the window, watching us, taking in every word. "Sweetie, you know there's a gift shop downstairs. They have a lot of neat things. You want to go down and check it out? Daddy will give you some money."

"I don't want to." She picked at her cuticles.

"You can buy yourself anything you want, and you can buy a little present for Hannah, too," I said.

She shook her head. "Why can't I stay here?"

Nate pulled a twenty from his wallet and handed it to her. "Go on. Kate and I need to talk to your mom. It's adult time."

Her mouth twisted into a sneer. "'Adult time'? Isn't it family time? Aren't I part of this family anymore?"

Nate's face hardened. "Caroline, don't argue with me!" he snapped.

Her sneer faded, and she glared at him, holding his gaze for a few seconds. Her mouth tightened into an angry pout. She snatched the money from his hand and stomped out of the room.

"Do you think you can recall all the details?" Kate asked.

"How could I forget? I don't want to remember." I turned over on my side, my back facing the two of them, but I still felt their eyes boring into my back. "Do I have to do this now? I'm really tired."

"You don't have to do it right now," Nate said. "But write down everything soon, before you forget. It could be very useful to us."

"It's a precaution," Kate said.

Just in case.

CHILDREN'S MEMORIAL HOSPITAL was a large complex in the middle of a trendy neighborhood on the north side of Chicago. It employed the best pediatric staff and had the latest life-saving equipment and technology that most suburban hospitals didn't have.

From one hospital to the next, I thought as I stepped out of the car and gazed up at the imposing structure that had kept my daughter alive for the past five days. As Nate and I rode the elevator, I wondered if I would get that instinct when I first laid eyes on her, that tinge deep in my bones like when a lioness is reunited with her cub. As I pulled on the yellow, sterile visitor's gown, I prayed that I hadn't missed the chance to form a bond with my newborn daughter.

Her incubator was decked out in pink flowers cut from construction paper. Someone had made a sign with her name on it and taped it to the foot of the incubator. I stepped up and held my breath as I peered down at a smaller version of a newborn Caroline. Hannah's face was round and pink, like a little apple, and she had a tiny dimple in her right cheek. She took a deep breath and sighed as though she were relieved to see me. Wires and tubes snaked out from her as if she were electronic. The pacifier tumbled from her mouth when the nurse picked her up.

Her eyes opened wide as I took her into my arms. "It's me," I said to her, a smile splitting my face. "It's Mommy." I kissed her lightly on the forehead, careful not to pull the oxygen tube from her nose. "I'm here. Mommy and Daddy are here."

I held her close to my chest, imagining us sitting at home in the rocking chair Nate and I had bought for the nursery, instead of the cold, clinical hospital room.

When I got home that afternoon, I sat at the kitchen table with a cup of tea and a notebook. I wrote all the details from the day Hannah was born—from the time I felt the first contraction early in the morning, to the time they pulled her out of me at 3:29 p.m. I blinked back the tears as I recalled each painful moment. I imagined the possible excuses that Dr. Stewart could have for being gone all that time and leaving me alone in anguish. He'd said he was performing emergency C-sections. *But shouldn't the nurses have done something? Contacted another doctor? Wasn't my situation considered an emergency?*

Dr. Stewart had to have a reasonable explanation. Maybe he would provide one at the follow-up appointment I so desperately wanted to avoid. While in the hospital, I had begged them to remove the stitches from my operation so I wouldn't have to keep my appointment with Dr. Stewart. But they'd told me they weren't responsible and that, legally, I was still under Dr. Stewart's care.

I had no choice but to face him. Maybe it was a chance to get some answers.

~

I LIFTED my shirt and studied the stitches.

When Caroline was eight, she'd fallen and hit her forehead on the corner of the end table and had needed ten stitches. I remembered taking her back to the doctors after two weeks and watching as the nurse gently cut the plastic threads with tiny scissors and pulled them out with tweezers. *How hard could it be?*

I wanted answers from Dr. Stewart, but was afraid to hear them.

I poked at my stitches then dug at the thread with my fingernail to see how loose it was. The wound was closed and still a bit swollen, but didn't look infected. I got a pair of tweezers, manicure scissors, and rubbing alcohol from the bathroom medicine cabinet. I lay on the bed and dabbed at the closed wound with an alcohol-soaked cotton ball. After wiping the tweezers and scissors with the alcohol, I snipped underneath the knot at the end and carefully pulled out the first few stitches. As soon as I did, blood seeped through the wound. I dabbed at it with the cotton ball, but the bleeding didn't stop. I grabbed a tissue from the nightstand and held it against the wound.

"What are you doing?" Nate was standing in the doorway.

"It's nothing. I just need a Band-Aid."

"Are you out of your mind? You can't remove the stitches on your own."

"Nate, I don't want to see him." I tossed the blood-soaked tissue and grabbed a fresh one.

"You have to let a professional take them out. Let me see." He examined the lesion, where the blood still trickled out.

"There's a Band-Aid in my purse." I motioned toward the dresser where my purse sat. Nate dug through it and pulled out a standard-size bandage.

"This isn't big enough." He disappeared into the bathroom and returned a few moments later with a larger bandage. He gently applied it to the wound. "I know you don't want to see him. But you could get an infection if you try removing them yourself."

"I want to know why this happened." I wiped my nose with one of the dirty tissues.

"Maybe he can give us an answer."

I nodded, realizing the curious side of me wanted to see how he would react when he saw me. Maybe I would even get an apology from him.

Nate came with me to the office, and as we sat in the waiting room, I checked out the framed artwork on the walls that I had become familiar with over the last nine months. One in particular, a contemporary abstract print of a living room, always reminded me of the inside of Barbie's Dream House. The pastel colors were happy, and a sunny blue sky peeked through the window in the background. While waiting for my prenatal appointments, I would look at that painting and remember my childhood, playing with my Dream House and pulling Barbie up to the top floor by the strings of the yellow elevator. I'd thought of the child growing inside of me, wondering that if it were a girl, maybe she would enjoy playing with a Barbie Dream House, like Caroline had.

But now as I waited for the follow-up appointment, the picture brought me back to the days before Hannah's birth. When I was eagerly awaiting the baby who would bring so much joy to our lives. When I had naively thought I was in good hands and that nothing could go wrong. When she was still healthy living inside me, a normal fetus that I'd watched during an ultrasound as she brought her tiny hand up to her mouth to suck her thumb.

A young woman sat across from us. She had a solitaire bridal set on her left hand, which rested on her round belly. She stared at the TV as she waited for her name to be called. It wasn't too late for her. Her baby was still safe inside of her. She still had time to switch doctors. *I could warn her.* When her name was called, I watched her get up and disappear through the door.

"We shouldn't be here," I said to Nate.

"It'll be over quickly. You don't even have to say anything to him if you don't want to."

A few minutes later, the nurse came out and called me in. She led me to a room in the back and told me to change into the gown. I waited anxiously for ten minutes, sitting on the paper-covered examining table, until a technician came in and introduced herself. When she pulled open my gown, she saw the bloodstained bandage. "What happened here?"

I didn't say anything as she gently pulled off the bandage.

"Did someone try to take these stitches out?"

"Yes."

The nurse blinked. "Who?"

"Me."

"Why on earth did you do that? You could've caused an infection."

I said nothing and let her admonish me as she reached for the sterilized tweezers and scissors. She snipped the threads, and I felt the stitches slide out of my skin. As she dabbed at the wound with alcohol and covered it with gauze and medical tape, a wave of hope come over me. *Maybe I won't have to see Dr. Stewart after all.* The technician told me to switch the gauze twice a day and to keep the wound clean.

I sat up. "Can I get dressed now?"

She was writing something in my chart. "Oh, no. You still need to see the doctor. He'll be in shortly." She left the room.

I sat on the edge of the table, swinging my legs and reminded myself why I was really there. I was finally going to get an answer. An explanation. An apology. He was my doctor, and doctors have a genuine concern for their patients. Maybe he'll even have some reassuring advice about Hannah.

Dr. Stewart knocked on the door then popped his head in. His face was damp and blotchy as if he'd just gone for a run. He greeted me as he ran a shaky hand across his sweaty forehead. He sniffed as he perused my file, then dropped it on the desk. "So, how's that baby boy of yours?" He looked at me with a smile plastered on his face.

An awkward pause surrounded us. I couldn't find my voice. My eyes narrowed as I waited for him to correct himself. Did he seriously not remember removing a limp baby girl from my uterus?

His forced smile began to fade the longer I stared. He glanced down at my file and fumbled with the pages. I gazed at him, waiting for his expression to show a hint of recognition of who I was.

He rubbed his nose and sniffed. "Uh... so... why don't we take a peek and see how you're healing?"

Chapter 6

CAROLINE

I hate hospitals. I know everyone does. But I *really* hate hospitals. Ever since I was nine and sneaked down to the family room after my parents were asleep and watched *Night of the Living Dead*, I've had this fear that the bodies in the morgue will rise up and attack us all—an irrational fear, as my mom put it.

I was excited to finally meet my baby sister, but I also knew I was going to see other children while visiting Children's Memorial Hospital. Ones who'd survived horrific car wrecks wrapped in bandages like mummies. Kids who'd been pulled from burning buildings, their skin blistered and raw. Or with cancer, walking around with skeletal frames for bodies. I remember when Melissa Greenberg's little brother had leukemia. I saw him at school one day with his bald head and sunken cheeks. I would steal glances at him and wonder how it felt to go out in public with everyone staring at him. I was going to a place full of people like Melissa's little brother. And my sister was one of them.

The lobby of Children's Memorial Hospital looked the same as any other hospital, except for the Mother Goose murals lining the hallways and the framed paintings of clowns inside the elevator. The doors opened on the third floor to a little boy in a wheelchair in the middle of the hallway. He wore a hospital gown with Batman on it and his nose and mouth were covered with a mask. He laughed as the man standing in front of him performed a magic trick.

As we walked down the corridor, I glanced into each room. A kid whose entire head was bandaged except for his eyes and mouth sat in a chair as a nurse held a straw to his mouth for a drink. I heard sobs coming from inside a room where the door was slightly ajar. Other than that, I didn't see much of what my vivid imagination prepared me for. No mangled and battered bodies walking around. No children clinging to life, shuffling down the hall, fanning the flames of my irrational fear.

We were required to put on starchy, yellow hospital gowns before entering Hannah's room. I fumbled with the tie on my gown as I followed my parents into a room with four incubators. Hannah, it appeared, was the only girl, judging from the pink bunnies and flowers that decorated her incubator.

"Look who came to see you, Hannah!" the nurse sang when she saw us enter the room.

Mom walked up to Hannah's incubator and waved me over. She rested her hands on my shoulders as I peered inside Hannah's plastic home. I saw a tiny baby that looked a lot like me when I was born, except that she was mostly bald. A tuft of brown hair on the top of her head was all that was left after her head was shaved so they could hook up the wires for tests.

I stared at her. This tiny thing born from the same parents just three weeks before. She'd swam in the same womb. This was the baby I worried would one day read my diary, stick her grubby little hands in my makeup, and stomp her feet until I let her come with Courtney and me to the mall. She was dressed in a pink onesie dotted with daisies that Kate had bought and yellow booties my great-aunt Joan had knitted. A thin tube ran from her nose to a humming oxygen tank nearby. Her eyes were barely open, but they shifted around as if she were trying to figure out where she was.

"You can hold her if you want," the nurse said.

They pulled up a rocking chair, and I sat down as the nurse gently lifted Hannah out of the incubator and handed her me. "Remember to hold her head."

"Watch the tube," Mom added as she pulled the camera out of her purse.

Hannah smelled like a mixture of talcum powder and Band-Aids. Her chapped lips formed an "o" as if she were delighted to meet me. Her arms lay by her side, not flailing around like most newborns do when they're awake. When her eyes opened a little wider, I noticed that they were dark, like little Hershey's Kisses. "Can she see me?"

"It's a little blurry for her," the nurse said. "But her sight will develop over the next few months."

Her forehead was warm and damp when I kissed it. She sighed softly, and her breath smelled stale. Here she was—the sister I had always asked for as a child, but didn't really want anymore. I reached for her hand and unfurled her tiny matchstick fingers, wanting to see if she would wrap them around my index finger like babies do. But they were limp and unresponsive.

I leaned down to whisper in her ear, careful not to let the others hear my first words to her. "I'm sorry."

Chapter 7

JILLIAN

Bringing home a newborn takes adjusting. Every parent in every part of the world goes through a learning curve the first few weeks after their baby is born. Schedules are rearranged. Sleep is almost nonexistent. Showers become a luxury. It was everything I had already experienced almost thirteen years before, when we first brought Caroline home.

Bringing home a baby born with complications adds a new level of intensity to the adjustment.

We brought Hannah home from Children's when she was just over a month old, once the doctors had pronounced her lungs strong enough and she was able to breathe without the oxygen tank. She was doing well, but as for her future, all the doctors could tell us was that we wouldn't know the extent of the brain damage, if there was any, until more tests were performed when she was older. It was a promising prognosis. There was still a possibility that she would be completely normal. Or maybe she would be a little slower than her peers and would need tutors to get by. Several more tests would keep track of Hannah's progress in the coming months, starting with an appointment with the pediatric neurologist in a few weeks.

The day we brought Hannah home was a joyous one. Friends

and family stopped by bearing gifts of little pink outfits, toys, onesies, and diapers. Neighbors brought over casseroles, lasagnas, and baked macaroni and cheese to stuff into our freezer. The whole day, guests were in and out of the house. Caroline, whom I had expected to hide out in her room all day, was by my side, watching as I changed Hannah's diaper, fed her, and rocked her when she fussed.

Nate, too, was supportive, but more on the housekeeping side. He threw in loads of laundry, made sure lunch was made, and took phone messages. Our spirits were up, and the atmosphere was thick with hope. The subject of the lawyer hadn't come up again since that day in the hospital. We focused all our attention on Hannah.

The final guest left just after eight that evening. Caroline was exhausted and went upstairs to bed.

"Do you want anything to eat?" Nathan asked, inspecting the choices in the freezer. "Didn't Judie Mosley make this casserole when Mr. Koslovsky died? I remember eating it and wanting to vomit. I think she puts potato chips in it."

"Caroline will eat it," I said, shifting Hannah from one shoulder to the other. "Can you fix a bottle for Hannah?"

"Don't you want anything?" He pulled out the formula and mixed it with water in a bottle.

"I'm not hungry."

I didn't have much of an appetite. Hannah had barely slept that day, and I was hoping at that point that she would be tired enough to sleep through most of the night, like Caroline had at that age. I placed Hannah in the bassinet and stuck a pacifier in her mouth while Nate heated a bottle of formula on the stove. I'd tried pumping while Hannah was at Children's to stock up on breast milk until she came home, but I wasn't producing enough to feed her, so we switched to the formula Hannah had while she was at Children's.

"I think I'll cook this lasagna." Nate stared down at an

aluminum pan covered with foil. He lifted a corner to peek at its frozen contents.

"Now? It's after eight. It'll take an hour to bake. I'll make you a sandwich instead."

"I can do it," he said, sticking the lasagna back in the freezer.

"It's okay. I'll make one for me, too. I don't want to wake up in the middle of the night with a growling stomach."

When I brought the two ham sandwiches into the family room, Nate was sitting on the couch with Hannah cradled in his arm, sucking on the bottle. He was watching her intently, his face beaming.

"It's been so long since I've done this," he said. "I'm a little rusty."

I sat next to him, wrapping an arm around his waist. We both stared at our daughter and listened to the soft noises she made as she ate. Her eyes were growing heavy, and I knew she would be asleep before the bottle was empty. "Thanks for all your help today."

"I didn't do much." The answer was rehearsed, what a husband was supposed to say to his wife, but I took it. I leaned in and kissed him on the cheek. We hadn't been alone together in a long time. At that moment, a closeness came between us that felt comfortable but foreign.

Hannah stopped sucking on the bottle. Her eyes opened wide, and she stared past us. Her head jerked sharply to the right. Her eyes swept up and to the left, and her face twisted into an eerie grin.

"She's seizing." I took Hannah from Nate's arm. "Get the timer."

"I have my watch." Nathan looked at the face of the Fossil watch I'd bought him for his thirty-second birthday. "Fifteen seconds."

Hannah held her cockeyed gaze, the right corner of her mouth twitching up in a smirk. To a regular person, she seemed to be smiling like any newborn trying to focus her developing eyesight on new surroundings. That was what I'd thought the first time I'd witnessed Hannah seizing at the hospital, until a nurse had told me what was happening.

Hannah's frequent seizures were another byproduct of being a brain-damaged child. Her doctors had prescribed Phenobarbital to stop them from occurring so often, but they'd told us that the tremors would still break through occasionally.

"One minute," Nathan called out. "Should we call the doctor?"

Dr. Isaacs, her pediatrician, had instructed us to call if the seizure lasted more than three minutes. Our eyes were on Hannah.

Caroline came downstairs. "What's going on?" She saw Hannah lying stiffly, like a doll. "What is she doing? What's wrong with her?"

"She's having a seizure," Nate said. "One minute, thirty."

I kept my eye on the baby as she lay motionless, a crooked grin frozen on her face. "C'mon, baby. Come back."

Hannah blinked, turned her head forward, and sighed. Back to being a regular baby, she kicked her legs and whined.

"One minute, forty seconds," Nathan announced.

I stuck the bottle back in her mouth, and she settled down again. "Maybe the dosage of Pheno needs to be increased. I'll call Dr. Isaacs in the morning."

"Why was she having a seizure?" Caroline asked. "Is she all right?"

The doctors had warned us that babies born with brain injuries often suffer from seizures, but for how long and how severe those spells would be, they weren't able to say yet. Not until she got older. Not until we saw how she progressed. *How do I explain this to a twelve-year-old without worrying her?*

"The doctor said she'd have seizures sometimes, but they'll eventually stop when she gets older." I held Hannah out to Caroline. "Do you want to feed her?"

And then Hannah projectile-vomited all over Caroline's shirt.

~

AS THE DAYS WENT BY, more incidents occurred, like fate dropping us hints, gently reminding us that our baby was different. In addition to the seizures, Hannah started throwing up the formula. At first, I'd thought we were feeding her too quickly, so we slowed down, breaking every ounce or so to burp her. This seemed to help for a while, but not long. Dr. Isaacs suggested switching to another brand. But she immediately projectile-vomited after the first try. We tried soy-based formulas, organic formulas, and store-brand formulas. She kept nothing down. We tried feeding her Cream of Rice, but that didn't work. Kate suggested trying donated breast milk. Our neighbor Karen Colson, who at the time was breastfeeding her second son, Charlie, offered me some of hers. But Hannah didn't keep that down, either. So I brought her back to Dr. Isaacs.

"It's most likely because her esophagus hasn't developed normally," he said. "As she gets older, it will develop more."

"But what do we do until then?" I asked. "How is she supposed to eat?"

"Keep trying different things until you find something that works," he said. "She's probably keeping some of it down, which explains why she isn't losing weight."

"What else can we try?"

"Try some pureed fruits and veggies. They may work."

But of course, they did not. She threw up the plums. Peaches made her wheeze. Bananas were a little better, but not much. We continued to try different produce, like strained peas, carrots, and squash. The doctor was right—she seemed to keep some of it down, but she still threw up most of it.

Then Sasha, a friend of Kate's, suggested that we try chestnut flour. Sasha, a vegan with a porcelain complexion and a svelte but sculpted figure, told me that she ate chestnut flour when she had the stomach flu because it was the only thing she could keep down. At that point, I was willing to try anything, and Sasha's healthy lifestyle gave her credibility. I bought a one-pound bag at Whole Foods, brought it home, and cooked it in water, since we had already determined that Hannah was allergic to milk. It made a creamy cereal like the others we had tried, and right away, I had doubts. If she threw up Cream of Rice and Cream of Wheat, she would probably throw up cream of chestnut.

Nate held her while I fed her small spoonfuls of the warm cereal. After a few bites, we paused for several minutes, waiting to see if she would regurgitate. We waited until she grew impatient, squirming and whining for more food. We fed her more, little by little, giving her a couple of minutes in between to digest, until she'd finished the whole bowl. She kept it all down. Dr. Isaacs was pleased, telling us chestnut flour is the best thing we could give her because it was full of protein.

We were able to get back into the normal routine of raising a newborn baby. Nate went back to work after taking off three weeks. Caroline fell back into being a normal teenager, spending her summer vacation hanging out at the beach or the public swimming pool. Hannah was growing steadily, only having the occasional seizure, which we kept track of in a notebook.

Chapter 8

JILLIAN

The Indian summer afternoon had turned into a chilly autumn night. I closed the window in Hannah's bedroom after laying her in her crib. After two hours of fussing, she'd finally fallen asleep in my arms.

As I was walking out of her room, I spotted the baby book Caroline had given me before Hannah was born. It was propped on the bookshelf, forgotten. The next day was Hannah's first appointment with the pediatric neurologist, and we were eager to hear promising news, to close this chapter in Hannah's life, and start a new, healthier one. Feeling inspired, I pulled the book off the shelf, wiped the dust from the cover, and sat in the rocking chair. I switched on the Mother Goose lamp and turned to the first page of the baby book, ready to catch up on the last four months of Hannah's life and look forward to all the upcoming milestones. I still had the lingering worry that some of these milestones would occur later for Hannah than they did for other babies. I shook the thought from my mind and filled in the general stuff. Name: Hannah Grace Moore. Birthday: May 10, 2003. Time: 3:29 p.m. Weight: 8 lbs. 3 oz. Place: Ferndale Hospital.

The page labeled zero to five months listed the typical "firsts" for a baby in that age group: date baby first rolled over, date baby first sat up, date baby first crawled. I read through it, with nothing yet to write. I'd hoped I would have more progress to record a little later, maybe on the six-to-twelve-months page. *The neurologist appointment should bring more answers.*

Date baby first smiled. Hannah was always smiling and laughing, despite her prognosis. She'd smiled for the first time when she was about two months old. She'd been sleeping in her crib, and I snuck into her room to check up on her. I stood and watched her as she slept. Her perfectly round face was soft, and her full lips were so pink, as if she had just finished eating a cherry popsicle. She stirred, opening her eyes a crack. She gazed around, blinking. She noticed me as if she were saying, "Oh, what brings you here?" And then she smiled. She cooed and kicked her chubby legs. I grinned at the memory as I wrote down "two months" in the book.

I peeked in the crib. Hannah was asleep on her tummy with her legs tucked up under her. I crept out of the room and into ours, where Nate was already sleeping, or at least pretending to be to avoid any unnecessary conversation. I climbed into bed and switched on the lamp next to me.

The next entry: Baby's favorite foods.

I clicked the pen and wrote "chestnut flour, diluted formula" in the baby book. With the chestnut flour as her main diet staple, she'd been able to keep down a little bit of diluted formula as a supplement.

I'd tasted the chestnut flour once. It tasted bland, but I'd guessed breast milk and formula were, too. At least she was eating.

I flipped ahead to the upcoming months of Hannah's early life, staring at the blank pages, trying to foresee the words that I would write on them. By the time we got to the page listing the accomplishments at two years old, would she be caught up? Would we capture her first full sentences or the first day she went potty in the toilet? Or would we still be waiting for the doctors to give us a prognosis, holding on to the hope that she will be a normal little girl?

THE WAITING ROOM at the pediatric neurologist's office was about the size of a classroom and was filled to capacity. I held Hannah as we waited for our ten o'clock appointment. She fussed in my arms, despite having gotten plenty of sleep the night before, only waking up at four o'clock for a feeding. Maybe she knew something I didn't. Maybe she already knew the results we were about to get.

The other patients waited anxiously, finding ways to occupy their time until their name was called. A boy who was about two years old with a swollen head and crossed eyes wobbled while taking a few steps as his mother held his hands. Another woman was cradling her sleeping baby who was probably about the same age as Hannah. A girl around four or five sat in a special wheelchair, a long cord of drool hung from her chin that her mom wiped with a cloth diaper. I held Hannah tighter. She didn't look like any of these kids. We were there to get a positive diagnosis, and this would be the last time we ever visited this office.

Hannah finally stopped fidgeting and fell asleep in my arms around eleven. I placed her in the car seat and covered her with a blanket. I laid my head back and closed my eyes for a minute, trying to relax and manifest positive outcomes. At eleven thirty, the nurse finally called us in and led us into a room, where I had expected to wait another hour. Thankfully, Dr. Jerome Greenwald came in twenty minutes later. An intern followed him, carrying a clipboard.

"Good afternoon, Mrs. Moore." He shook my hand. "This is Matthew Britten. He's an intern and will be observing today."

He leaned down to Hannah, who was still in her car seat. "Hi, Hannah, how are you doing today?" Hannah stirred, opened her eyes, looked up at Dr. Greenwald then yawned. He lifted her out of her car seat and laid her on the examining table. "This is a typical case of microcephaly due to meconium aspiration syndrome," he said to the intern. He measured Hannah's head with a small measuring tape. "Her head should be at forty-six centimeters, but isn't because of the injury."

The intern nodded as he scribbled down notes. "What's the prognosis?"

"Severe cerebral palsy."

I turned to him, waiting for him to add an addendum or to clarify. He said nothing. "But she'll catch up when she gets a little older," I added.

Dr. Greenwald looked at me, his forehead furrowed. "I'm sorry?"

"That's what they told us in neonatal," I said.

"They told you that?"

A feeling of dread seeped into me. "Yes. They said we weren't going to know how severe the injury was until she was old enough to go to school."

Dr. Greenwald's face dropped. He placed Hannah back in her car seat and sat down next to me. "Mrs. Moore, I'm sorry, but the way your daughter is right now is the way she will always be."

A din filled my ears like I was suddenly under water. His voice sounded far away.

"What are you talking about?"

"Her brain is never going to grow. I can't believe the doctors in neonatal didn't tell you this."

He had to be mistaken. "Wait a minute," I said. "They told us there was no way of knowing anything until she was older. That there was a possibility that she would catch up to other kids her age. Or she might have learning disabilities. That's what they said."

"I'm very sorry." His voice softened. "I have no idea why they would tell you that."

"No." I shook my head. "You're wrong."

"Hannah is permanently brain damaged," he said. "This is the way she's going to be for the rest of her life."

"Stop saying that!" I looked at my daughter sleeping in her car seat, helpless and clueless. "It's a mistake. That's not what they told me. Why would they tell me something different?"

"I don't know," he said. "It was highly irresponsible of them to tell you something they weren't certain of. Again, I'm very sorry."

"What are you talking about?" My voice got louder. "Didn't they talk to you? Isn't it written in her file what they told me?" He was wrong. He was just another doctor who didn't know what he was talking about. I kept shaking my head, my vision blurring with tears.

Dr. Greenwald pulled a few tissues from a box and handed them to me. "Do you have a lawyer? If not, you should get a good malpractice one."

The words stabbed my heart, and my chest tightened. I placed my face in my hands, imagining lawyers, court dates, and "he said, she said." No. Dr. Greenwald had to be wrong. He was being dramatic. Doctors could get that way.

"I would be more than happy to testify if you need me to. I've done it before." Dr. Greenwald stood up. "I'm so sick of these careless doctors getting away with this sort of behavior."

On the drive home the roads blurred behind my tears as I searched for the words to tell Nate. I stepped on the gas and passed cars that had the gall to drive only seventy-five. I weaved from one lane to the other, cutting off an old man in a Cadillac. Hannah giggled from where she was strapped in her car seat in the back.

"No." I kept saying the word aloud to myself and pounding the steering wheel with each syllable. "No. No!" I had done everything right. I ate healthy food. I didn't smoke. I took good care of myself. Why was I being punished?

Why, God? Why was this happening to us? What did I do to deserve this? What did Hannah do to deserve this? I went to church on a regular basis. I raised my child according the church's doctrine. I did the best I could to be a good Catholic. And it had all been for nothing. What was the point in having faith when life was going to rip out your heart? When your beautiful child is sentenced to a life of helplessness and discomfort?

I noticed a squad car ahead of me and started to slow down, then changed my mind and stepped on the gas. *Let him arrest me. Throw me in jail.* This screwed-up world was full of idiots, and because of that, I had a damaged child, and I had no idea how to take care of her.

It would be so easy to swerve the car into the median. Just one quick turn of the steering wheel and it would be over. Hannah and I wouldn't have to face the dark reality that lay ahead of us. It would numb the pain that was pumping through my body, and it would save Hannah from a future of misery. And then Nate would have to take care of Caroline.

Caroline.

How different everything had been for us when she was born. I remember when she first learned to dance when she was eighteen months. I think a Spin Doctors song was playing on the radio. All she knew how to do was twirl and jump around at that age. But she had laughed so heartily that her pigtails bounced while I'd held the video camera.

I smiled through the tears at the memory, and I heard Hannah giggle again from the backseat.

And then I slowly eased up on the gas pedal.

Chapter 9

JILLIAN

This was a law firm with a solid reputation, Nate had told me. As we walked through the glass double doors, I could tell by the way the mahogany tables gleamed and the buttery-soft leather waiting room chairs that this wasn't the office of a lawyer who advertised on the sides of buses. We sat down on the sofa, and the receptionist offered us something from the espresso bar.

After our appointment with Dr. Greenwald, the anger for Dr. Stewart that I had tucked away came rushing back to the forefront. For the last four months, I had stayed focused on the positive, watching Hannah grow and slowly develop, holding on with hope and anticipation to her uncertain future. But her future had been determined, and I had nothing to hope for. All I had left in me was festering hatred for Dr. Stewart.

We were out of options. We had nothing left to give Hannah, except to keep her comfortable. A few days after the dreadful appointment with Dr. Greenwald, Nate obtained the name of a highly regarded malpractice firm in Chicago.

Leventhal, Dole, Marquart & Simon was one of the leading personal injury law firms in Chicago. Their website boasted a list of cases won, including an obstetrics malpractice suit that awarded $20 million. Mark Leventhal himself was named one of the best personal injury lawyers in the United States by *Town & Country* magazine in 2001. *Chicago Magazine* named him Illinois Super Lawyer in the Field of Plaintiff Personal Injury in 1998. In 1994, he was ranked by the Leading Lawyers Network as One of the Top Personal Injury Attorneys in Illinois. Satisfied with the firm's credibility, we called and made an appointment.

Nate sat beside me, quiet but fidgety. He kept smoothing his pant legs as if he were about to go into a job interview. I sat stoically, staring ahead at the Renoir on the wall, my mouth pressed into a straight line.

"Mr. Leventhal is ready to see you now," the receptionist said. She motioned for us to follow her down a long hallway to a large corner office. Inside was a large mahogany desk with the Chicago skyline behind it. Two men were seated in the office. The man behind the desk stood up and buttoned his jacket. He had to be six and a half feet tall and had broad shoulders. His dark hair was greying at the temples, and his teeth were bright against his olive skin tone. He held out his hand.

"Mr. and Mrs. Moore, I'm Mark Leventhal. Please, have a seat." He gestured to the man sitting in one of the guest chairs. "This is my associate, John Marquart. Did my assistant offer you anything to drink?"

"Yes," Nate said. "We're fine, thank you."

He sat back down, reviewing his notes on his desk. "So, why don't you start by telling me everything that happened? From the beginning."

Nate reached for my hand as I rehashed the day of Hannah's birth. Leventhal and Marquart nodded as they listened, interrupting at times to ask pointed questions like, "Did you smoke or drink during your pregnancy?" and "What time did you first ask for a C-section?" Leventhal was particularly curt and brusque, leading me to wonder if we'd picked the wrong firm. Whose side were they on, anyway? I continued with the details as Leventhal occasionally jotted down notes on a yellow legal pad.

After I finished, he put down his pen. "Well, we believe we

have a case. But before we can be certain, we'll need to get all the records to review. From Ferndale Hospital and Dr. Stewart's. We'll have to review the fetal heart monitor tracings for decelerations, to determine when Hannah's heart rate first dropped, when the doctor should have ordered a C-section." He flipped through his notes. "We'll also get all the files from Children's Memorial and Dr. Greenwald to see what we have. We'll look at the whole picture and then determine for sure if we have a case."

I nodded. Nate handed me his handkerchief with NM embroidered on it. We'd received a matching set as a wedding gift. I hadn't seen mine in years.

"After we review all the records," Marquart said, "if we agree that we have a solid case, we'll file the complaint. Have you written everything down? Everything that happened that day?"

"Yes, I wrote down most of it a few days after it happened."

"It's important that we have the details, because their lawyers will ask about every element," Marquart said. "Go home tonight and read through your notes. Make sure you've captured everything. Every small detail."

I nodded. "What happens after you file the complaint?"

"There will be interrogatories, questions for you to answer from the opposing lawyers," Leventhal said. "And there will be depositions that you'll need to attend, Mrs. Moore."

"Will I need to attend them, too?" Nate asked.

He shook his head. "Not right away. Technically, it's your wife that will be filing the lawsuit. She was the one that was neglected. Then the doctors and nurses will be deposed. After that, we'll depose friends and relatives. Possibly even your older daughter."

"Caroline?"

Leventhal nodded.

"Why would she be deposed? She's only thirteen."

"Hopefully, it won't get to that point," Marquart said. "It's only a possibility at this point. We try not to depose someone that young unless we absolutely have to."

I leaned forward in my chair. "Mr. Leventhal, I don't know

how this happened. I did everything right. I asked for a cesarean several times over the course of the day, and no one would listen to me." Saying the words was like an additional release. I needed him to hear it from me, even though I was sure at that point that he was already on our side.

"I know," he said. "That's what we're going to prove to the judge, and that's why we'll make sure Dr...."—he glanced down at his notes—"Jeffery Stewart will pay the consequences."

Chapter 10

CAROLINE

According to the Child Development Institute's website, an only child usually exhibits certain characteristics: being pampered or spoiled, feeling incompetent because adults are more capable, expecting to be the center of attention, being self-centered, and being used to getting their way.

Geez. They make it sound like I was a total brat. Sure, I enjoyed being an only child. But I always loved having friends over. I shared my toys with them. I let Courtney borrow my Barbies. I cooperated and played nice, as my mom always told me. For my tenth birthday, I had a slumber party with my five closest friends, and even though it was my birthday, I let Marcy Millinger sleep in my N*Sync sleeping bag and let Cami Stole eat the last piece of pizza.

My parents raised me to be my own person. But at the same time, they taught me to be compassionate, giving, selfless, and thankful. I knew how to balance both worlds.

I read what appeared on the computer screen: "The oldest child may respond to birth of second child by feeling unloved and neglected. Strives to keep or regain parents' attention through conformity. If this fails, chooses to misbehave. Strives to please."

I thought back to visiting Mom in the hospital a few days after Hannah's birth. Dad had snapped at me for wanting to stay with them in the room instead of going down to the gift shop. Neither of them had ever reacted toward me that way. Of course, they occasionally yelled at me when I misbehaved, but they'd never dismissed me with such irritation. I remember looking to Mom that day, hoping she would provide some sort of comfort. But I saw in her vacant eyes how preoccupied she was with her own hell. Later, while I browsed the shelves of the gift shop and the stinging of my ego subsided, I understood why. Hannah had to be much sicker than they were telling me. And things were going to be very different. At that moment, I knew my childhood was over.

I turned away from the computer screen and rubbed my eyes. My parents had run out of the house that morning to go to their first meeting with the lawyer, leaving me alone with Hannah. Kate was supposed to come over and watch her, but at the last minute, she'd called to cancel because her ex-mother-in-law was sick. *Who takes care of their ex-mother-in-law?* So my parents moved on to their built-in backup babysitter—me.

I protested. I had plans to meet Courtney and Chloe at the mall. They didn't include me often, and I was so excited to get out of the house.

"This is important," Mom said as she gathered her purse and jacket. "You can go to the mall another time."

She called out feeding instructions to me as she and dad hurried out the door. "Feed her five ounces of chestnut cereal. Remember how to do it? Mix it with the warm water." She pulled the door closed.

Of course, Hannah started crying as soon as they pulled out of the driveway. I picked her up out of the baby swing and walked around with her, bouncing her lightly like I'd seen Mom do. But she wailed louder, so I fixed some chestnut cereal and fed it to her until she stopped whining. Then I changed her diaper and laid her in the crib, where she cooed happily with a full belly and a dry booty. Soon, she fell asleep.

Sitting in front of the computer, I wondered what I would be doing at that exact moment if Hannah had never been born. Mom and Dad wouldn't be at the lawyer's. I would be out with Courtney and Chloe with a twenty in my pocket that Dad would've given me to spend on whatever I wanted. Mom would still be working at the agency. Dad wouldn't be so stressed. Status quo.

I was the oldest now. For the first twelve years of my life, I'd been an "only." That was who I was used to being. *Who am I now?* If things were different, if Hannah wasn't sick, she would've looked up to me. She would've envied me because I'm older and smarter and I get to do more things like stay out later and date boys. I would be driving by the time she turned three. I would go away to college before she turned five. But in truth, that didn't matter because we wouldn't have much of a childhood together. After that one doctor's appointment months ago, when Mom came home sobbing, clinging to Hannah, I knew the truth. Dad came by my room later and told me how the doctor had said that Hannah's illness was permanent and that she wasn't going to get any better.

I am the oldest. But does that mean anything anymore?

I got up from the desk and tiptoed upstairs into Hannah's room. She was lying on her back, staring at the ceiling.

"That was a short nap," I said to her. Her chest was rising and falling quickly. "Do you have the hiccups, Hannah-Banana?" I took a closer look. Her lips were puckered and they were an unusually dark shade, as if she were wearing lipstick. I flipped on the light. Hannah's lips and face were a sickly shade of blue.

"Oh my God, Hannah?" I picked her up. She gazed past me as she wheezed.

What do I do? What do I do! "Oh my God. Oh my God. Oh my God." I ran to the phone in my parents' room to dial Mom's cell phone, but I couldn't remember the number. I had never memorized it because I had it programmed into my phone. I ran back to my room, searching frantically for my phone. "Fuck!" *Call some-*

one! I picked up the landline. I hesitated. *Should I call Kate? Dr. Isaacs?* Hannah gasped. I dialed 9-1-1. I frantically told the operator my sister was not breathing.

"What's your address?" she asked.

"Um... um..." Hannah was still in my arms, gasping. "It's..."

"Honey," she said calmly, "I need your address. What is your address?"

"It's... um..." *Address, address, what's our address?* I spun around, searching for something that would give me answers. I shut my eyes and focused until the number came to me. I barked out our address to the operator.

"Okay, someone is on the away," the operator said. "Until then, I want you to stay on the phone with me, okay? Is she conscious?"

"Yes."

"How old is she?"

"She's... um... ten months? She was taking a nap, and I came and checked up on her, and her lips were blue and—"

"Are you home alone?"

"Yes."

"Where are your parents?"

"Out. They had a meeting."

"How old are you?"

"Thirteen," I said. "Almost."

"Can you put the phone on speaker? I want to walk you through CPR while we wait for the paramedics to get there."

I managed to find the speaker button on the handset, dropped it on the floor, and laid Hannah down next to it. The operator walked me through the steps as I breathed tiny pockets of life into my sister. *Please, God. My parents will never forgive me if she dies.* Her eyes met mine as I bent over her. They were full of peace, as if she had faith that I was going to save her. Either that, or she was ready to die. The operator continued to coach me. The minutes went by slowly as I fought to keep Hannah alive. "Where are the fucking paramedics?" I yelled.

"They're coming," the operator said. "Keep giving her CPR. You're doing great."

I heard loud banging on the front door. *Fuck!* I'd locked it after my parents left. I ran downstairs, swung open the door. Two paramedics burst in carrying medical boxes and equipment. I pointed up the stairs. They ran up and immediately took over CPR, barking medical lingo to each other. They strapped an oxygen mask on Hannah's face and carried her downstairs. Somehow, I managed to be in the right frame of mind to grab my jacket and cell phone before following the EMTs out the door. A small crowd of neighbors watched from the sidewalk as the EMTs loaded her into the ambulance.

In the ambulance, I sat next to an EMT, a friendly looking man named William. He talked to me calmly as he and his partner worked to keep Hannah stable until we got to the hospital. Someone seemed to have pressed fast-forward on my day. Minutes ago, I'd been researching my new birth order on the Internet, and now I was in the back of an ambulance, watching my sister struggle to stay alive.

The air being pressed into her lungs brought color back to Hannah's cheeks. She relaxed as her eyes swept across her surroundings. She gazed up at William and giggled.

"What are you laughing at, silly girl?" William asked. "Are we going for a ride?"

Hannah laughed through the oxygen mask and kicked her legs.

At the hospital, the nurse told me to stay in the waiting room as they rushed Hannah to the ER. "What's your parents' phone number, sweetie?" she asked me.

"What?" I stared at her blankly.

"Your parents' phone number," she repeated. "I need to call them."

I pulled out my cell phone and stared at it. The bright, colorful application buttons shone up at me, waiting for me to decide which one to push.

"Do you want me to find it for you?" the nurse asked.

I handed her my phone. She managed to find "Mom Cell" in my contacts and called her.

"They're on their way," she told me. "Do you want me to bring you something to drink? A Coke?"

"Is my sister going to be okay?" I asked.

"You did the right thing. She got to the hospital just in time," she said. "You did a good job calling 9-1-1."

The words were little comfort to me at the time, but I thanked her anyway and told her I wanted a Sprite.

The waiting room was empty and lonely. No emergencies except for the one I'd caused. I paced the floor with my hands tucked under my armpits to keep them from trembling. Maybe I shouldn't have put Hannah down for a nap so soon after feeding her. Maybe I didn't burp her enough. *How long are my parents going to be mad at me for this? Will they ever trust me with Hannah again?*

Mom and Dad raced through the entrance several minutes later. They barked something at the nurse behind the desk then disappeared through the ER doors. Mom glanced toward the waiting room, but she didn't notice me. I had to be okay with that.

This was my new life.

I was now the oldest.

Chapter 11

JILLIAN

I left the meeting with Leventhal feeling high with hope. Someone was finally on our side, not just supportive friends like Kate, but people with as much power as Leventhal and Marquart, who saw the whole picture and were determined to do something about it. Empowerment surged through me as I walked out of that office with Nate trailing behind me. For the first time since Hannah's birth, I saw a light at the end of the tunnel. I saw justice and a more stable future for my daughter, and for us.

But as Nate drove up the Edens Expressway toward home, a dark thought entered my mind. Why was I assuming we were going to win the lawsuit? Stewart might win. The judge could think we were money-hungry opportunists. My good mood deflated, and I fell back down to earth with a thud. Anxiety twisted inside me. I watched Nathan as he drove, peering at his rearview mirror before switching lanes without turning on the signal. Then I got the call from Ferndale Hospital.

I snapped the phone shut after speaking with the nurse and ordered Nate to drive straight to the hospital. The entire ride up, I cursed our decision to leave a twelve-year-old with a sick baby.

"What the hell were we thinking?" I said. "Caroline's not ready for this. We shouldn't have left them alone."

"We didn't really have a choice," Nate said as he turned into the fast lane and stepped on the gas.

We rushed into the ER, calling out Hannah's name to the nurse at check-in. She pointed us in the right direction. Behind a curtain, the doctor and nurse bent over Hannah, a stethoscope to her chest, an oxygen mask over her face. The sight that was already becoming too familiar. I blurted out a list of Hannah's allergies to the doctor—eggs, dust, dust mites, peaches, corn, milk, and grass.

"Did she ingest any of those foods?"

"No, she doesn't eat foods."

The doctor gave me a confused look.

"I mean, she only eats chestnut flour and a little formula," I said. "She has cerebral palsy. She needs a shot of adrenaline."

"We'll need to contact her pediatrician. What's the name?"

"What? Why?" Nate asked.

"We have to contact the pediatrician before we can do anything to this child. Name?"

"Dr. Howard Isaacs," I said as one of the nurses ran out to make the call. "But you have to give her the adrenaline now. She can't breathe."

"Is she allergic to any medications?" the doctor asked.

"No," I said. "Not that we know of."

"Albuterol?"

"No, she's taken Albuterol before."

The nurse who'd left to call Dr. Isaacs was back moments later. "Called the pediatrician. He said to give her a shot of adrenaline."

I rolled my eyes. "Hurry. Please."

The nurse pulled out a needle, inserted it into a small vial, and pulled out the liquid. She tapped the syringe before injecting it into Hannah's arm. Hannah didn't even flinch. Her labored breathing slowly eased, her tense expression softened, and the color returned to her face.

The doctor released Hannah with orders to let her rest. *As opposed to what?* I wanted to ask. *What else would we do with a ten-month-old who spent a good part of the evening struggling to breathe?*

I cradled Hannah in my arms as we checked out. Nate said he would pull the car around and check up on Caroline, who, until that moment, I'd completely forgotten about.

When we piled into the car, Caroline leaned her head against the window and closed her eyes. I reached over and touched her leg, but she was sound asleep.

THAT NIGHT after falling into a deep sleep, I dreamt of my daughters.

Blurred visions of them swam in my subconscious. Hannah was lying in her crib gasping for air, as Caroline stood off to the side, frozen like a mannequin, her arms bent upward in helplessness and a look of anguish plastered her face. I startled awake, gasping for air like Hannah in my dream. My damp nightgown stuck to my body as I kicked off the comforter for air.

Nate's side of the bed was still empty, the sheets still tucked on his side of the mattress.

I sat still in my bed, waiting for my heart rate to slow.

Last night hadn't been the first time Hannah couldn't breathe. She would continue having seizures and breathing problems. Would we always be prepared to save her? Would the paramedics get there on time? Would we always be close enough to a hospital?

I found Nate sprawled on the couch in the den, sound asleep, the remote resting on his belly, rising and falling with each breath. I nudged him awake.

"It's after midnight. Don't you want to come to bed?"

He sat up, focused on what was on the television, then started flipping the channels. "I'll be up in a little bit."

I sat on the couch next to him and stared blankly at the TV as he changed the channels, finally settling on *Die Hard 2* on TBS.

A few weeks ago, while I was at the grocery store with Hannah, I ran into our neighbor Karen Colson and her baby, Charlie, who was about the same age as Hannah. I bent down to say some words of endearment to him, and he reached out and grabbed my nose. I backed up, staring at Charlie, who was watching me with eyes so full of knowledge and curiosity. He held a small stuffed toy in his little hands. I looked at Charlie and pictured Hannah, her face framed with curls, her big brown eyes searching for answers. Karen asked if I was all right. I mumbled something about being late for an appointment and ran out of the store.

Nate sat up and cleared his throat. "Did you check out the website yet?"

I didn't respond right away.

Nate looked over at me, waiting for a reply.

"Yes," I said.

"What do you think?"

Nate had first heard about Misericordia, a home for mentally challenged children and adults, several years ago from his coworker, Chad, whose seventeen-year-old nephew, Gary, had lived there since he was five. He was first admitted after a few perilous incidents at home. Once, he tried to give his baby sister a bath, and she'd almost drowned. Another time, he tried to light the fireplace and almost burned the house down. Although Gary had cerebral palsy like Hannah, he was higher functioning and was able to walk and communicate. "I remember when Chad first told me about Gary," Nate had said the first time he mentioned Misericordia. "I remember thinking how lucky we were that Caroline was healthy."

He'd broached the subject a few months ago about Misericordia being a suitable option for Hannah. I wasn't ready to discuss it then.

Caroline would've never forgiven herself if Hannah had died last night, and I never would have forgiven myself for leaving Hannah in her care. How could we give Hannah the proper care she needed in an unsafe environment? She would need a wheelchair when she was older. How were we going to carry her upstairs to her room when she got bigger? I didn't want to hear it then. I didn't want to think about Hannah as a non-walking toddler, a teenager who couldn't speak, or a grownup who couldn't drive. But I also didn't want to be responsible if something went terribly wrong. She needed twenty-four-hour care. She needed to be in a sterile environment where she would be monitored around the clock.

Misericordia opened in 1921 and was originally a home for unwed mothers. It was run by a nun under the guidance of the Chicago Archdiocese, but the facility accepts anyone from any religion. The campus spans thirty acres and includes fifteen homes for residents with various needs. Currently, about five hundred fifty people with disabilities from mild to profound lived at Misericordia. I'd scanned the website, looking at pictures of happy residents painting, dancing, and baking a cake. I read about the fundraising that friends and families of residents do every year—dinner dances, Halloween parties, and festivals. The only thing left to do was to pick up the phone and call them.

"It sounds like a great place, Jillian," Nate said. "Chad says it's amazing."

"Chad didn't have to make this decision," I pointed out. "It was his nephew. Not his child."

Nate brushed his hands through his hair. He went back to watching Bruce Willis fighting terrorists. I grabbed the remote and shut off the TV.

"This isn't an easy decision for me to make," I said.

"It's not an easy decision for *us* to make, Jillian. But it's still the best decision. Unless you want to hire a full-time nurse. But even then, we don't have the equipment and the accommodations to fit her needs."

"We could move."

"Where?"

"To a ranch house. Everything all on one level."

"Okay. So we still would need to have twenty-four-hour nursing care to look after her. We can't afford it."

The decision seemed so easy for him, and I hated him for it. I hated that he was right. I hated that he didn't appear to be stressing over this or feel like as much of a failure as a parent as I did. It seemed that since day one, when I'd told him I was pregnant, he hadn't been one hundred percent behind the whole baby thing.

"I know what you're thinking," he said.

"What?"

"About me suggesting you should get an abortion. You don't think I feel guilty about that?"

We sat quiet for a minute.

"I love Hannah," he said. "I wouldn't trade her for any healthy baby in the world. I feel like the bad guy for mentioning abortion. I look at Hannah now, and I can't imagine not having her in our life." He looked down at his hands and started picking at his cuticles. "Now I'm feeling like the bad guy again because I think we should put her away in some facility. If there's a way we could keep Hannah at home, I'd be all for it. I'd do it in a heartbeat. But we have to be realistic. We'll never forgive ourselves if something happens to her and we're not prepared to save her."

I felt the urge to punch him in the face and kiss him at the same time. I tossed the remote on the floor. It skidded across the hardwood and the batteries tumbled out from the bottom. I jumped up from the couch. "Then you call them. Tomorrow." I went upstairs to bed, hoping Nate wouldn't follow.

He didn't.

Chapter 12

CAROLINE

It happened during social studies class.

I felt a warm liquid running between my legs while Mrs. Hanwell was teaching us about major metropolitan cities. At first I ignored it, thinking I was imagining it. But as class went on, the dampness spread to my thighs. I looked down under my black-corduroyed butt to see if anything was on the seat. Then I reached down and discreetly rubbed my fingers there, pretending to scratch an itch. My fingers were lightly smudged in red. *Oh, fuck me.*

I looked over at Courtney. She was staring at the teacher but I could tell she wasn't listening to a word. I tried to get her attention, but I didn't know what to say. And besides, even though I trusted her, I was paranoid about it getting out. Last month, when Lizzie Ward had her period, the whole seventh grade found out about it, and all the guys started calling her Queen Crimson. So I couldn't go to the nurse's office because everyone would definitely find out.

Having their first period seemed to be a momentous occasion for some girls, a turning point. I'd read *Are You There God? It's Me, Margaret* a couple of years ago. All the girls in the book were so desperate to have their first period, and they made it sound like a special bonding moment between a mother and daughter. I couldn't imagine my mom and me going to Walgreen's, where she would teach me about the different feminine products and which ones she liked best. Mom had been so preoccupied with Hannah lately that I wasn't sure I even wanted to bother her.

But I had another worry. *How do I keep the blood from getting all over the chair?* I checked to see how much of a mess I'd made, but didn't see anything. I had to get to a bathroom and see what was going on. Luckily, my pants were dark enough that the blood stain wasn't visible. In the girls' bathroom, I locked myself in the last stall and checked the damage. My underwear was entirely soaked. *Fuck.* I had to go to the nurse's office. It was only 11:30 in the morning. I couldn't spend the rest of the day wearing damp, bloody panties.

The nurse's office was thankfully empty of students, and Mrs. Hernandez was sitting behind her desk when I walked in.

"Hi, Caroline. Is everything all right?"

The compassion in her voice mixed with my raging hormones made me burst into tears.

The chair scraped against the floor as Mrs. Hernandez got up and came to my side. "What is it, sweetheart?" She rested her hand on my back. "Is it your sister?"

I shook my head. Mrs. Hernandez went to our church, so she knew all about Hannah. She handed me a Kleenex, and I blew my nose. She'd been the school nurse since before I was born, and all the students treated her like a surrogate mom.

"Here, sit down." She motioned to the couch.

"I can't," I whispered, thinking about the huge bloodstain that would be left on the chair. "I got my period."

Sympathy washed over Mrs. Hernandez's face, and she pulled me into a hug. "Oh, honey, come with me." With her hands on my shoulders, she led me to the bathroom and told me to wait there. She left for a moment and came back holding a maxi pad. "This is your first time, isn't it?"

"Yeah." I tore off a piece of toilet paper and wiped the tears from my face.

"Did you bleed a lot?"

"My underwear is ruined," I wept, "and it's all over my pants. I can't sit down, or I'll get blood everywhere, and everyone will know."

Mrs. Hernandez rubbed my shoulders, telling me everything was going to be all right. "Did your mom have a talk with you about menstruation?"

I shook my head, thinking back to a time when my mom would've even brought up the subject. But I doubt it ever crossed her mind recently.

A look of pity draped her face. "Why don't I call your mom and have her come pick you up? Menstruation can be very uncomfortable and even painful at times. So I'm sure you'd like to go home and go right to bed." She patted me on the back. "Put on this pad, and I'll give you an old towel you can sit on during the car ride home. You can throw it away afterward."

She left to call my mother while I attached the pad to my soaked underwear. I thought about how nice it would be to get home, soak in a warm bath, change into my pajamas, and curl up on the couch. Mom will make me lunch. Maybe she'll even sit with me, tell me about her first period. I lay on the couch, and Mrs. Hernandez gave me a warm water bottle for my tummy, even though I wasn't feeling any cramps. I relaxed, knowing that no one was going to find out about this. Mrs. Hernandez would send a message to my teacher saying I'd gone home sick.

Ten minutes later, I heard the clicking of pumps coming toward the office and the clanking of plastic bracelets. Kate walked in wearing head-to-toe neon green.

"What are you doing here?" I asked. "Where's Mom?"

"She's busy with Hannah, so she asked me to come get you."

I wondered if Mrs. Hernandez mentioned to my mom on the phone that I'd had my period. Or maybe she'd told her that I wasn't feeling well to be discreet. Because Mom would've definitely come to get me herself if she knew I'd had my period.

Kate gave me a hug. She smelled like garlic. "I remember when I first had my period. My mother announced it to the whole family that I had become a lady. I was mortified."

Mrs. Hernandez laughed. "My mother cried tears of joy and took me to Baskin Robbins."

"Could we go now?" I snapped.

During the car ride home, I said very little as Kate tried to make conversation. I was sure Mom felt bad for not being able to come get me herself. She probably stayed back to make me soup or draw me a bath.

When I got home, Mom was sitting at the kitchen table, with stacks of papers spread in front of her. She had her head down, focused on a brochure.

I dropped my backpack on the floor, but she didn't look up. I picked it up and dropped it again. Still nothing. "Mom?"

She jumped. "Oh, Caroline, you startled me. Did Kate leave?"

I nodded. "She had a doctor's appointment."

"Oh." Mom got up and pulled me into a hug. "How are you feeling?"

"Fine. Tired." I peered over her shoulder at a pot simmering on the stove.

Mom stood back from me, keeping her hands on my shoulders. "I know this is a confusing time for you," she said. "Do you want to talk about it?"

I shrugged.

"Do you have any questions you'd like to ask me?"

I thought about the morning I'd had. The stained underwear. The soaked pants. The uncomfortable wetness between my legs as if I'd peed my pants. I wondered if that was how my period would be every month for the rest of my life. *How will I know when to expect it? Will a maxi pad even be enough to hold all that blood? Will I always have to wear dark pants in case I have an acci-*

dent? My stomach ached. I lowered my hands to my belly. Mom turned away and looked down at the table covered with papers.

"I was reading over some information about a place for Hannah when Mrs. Hernandez called." She picked up a brochure and glanced at it, then dropped it back on the table. "Sorry I couldn't come get you myself. I didn't want to wake her. She fell asleep about an hour ago. She didn't sleep much last night and was fussy all morning."

I wanted to ask her why she didn't have Kate stay with Hannah while she came and got me. After all, I'd just had my first period. Wasn't that important enough? I scanned the papers on the table. *Misericordia*, one of the booklets read, *A Community for your Loved One with Special Needs.* Several of the other documents had the same heart logo with a cross down the middle. I'd heard Mom and Dad arguing the other night over whether or not to put Hannah in a home. Dad was all for it, but Mom wanted to keep her at home. Had she changed her mind?

"Are you hungry?" Mom walked over to the stove and stirred whatever was cooking. She tapped the wooden spoon on the side of the pot, and I noticed something white and creamy drip from it.

"Is that Cream of Wheat?" I asked. Mom always made it for me when I wasn't feeling well. Sometimes, she drizzled hot maple syrup on top.

"No, it's Hannah's lunch," she said, as I caught a whiff of chestnut cereal. "Do you want me to fix you something?"

"No." I turned to go upstairs. "I'm not hungry."

In the bathroom, I drew a bath and stripped off my clothes. I dumped the ruined pants and underwear in the garbage and lowered myself into the tub, inch by inch as the hot water drew in my body. I kept going until I was fully submerged, and I stayed underwater, holding my breath for as long as I could.

Chapter 13

JILLIAN

They led us into the room where Hannah would live for the rest of her life. Room 214 was similar to a hospital room in the pediatric ward: cold and sterile with three steel cribs lining the walls.

"These are Hannah's new roommates," Claire, Hannah's Certified Nursing Assistant, or CNA, said. "This is Jacob, and that chubby little guy over there is Juan."

Nate walked up to Juan's crib and started cooing to him. I stood in the middle of the room and held Hannah tightly, inhaling her scent, memorizing it. I wanted her home with me, where I would be the one to change her diapers and feed her when she cries, instead of the staff. My eyes stung with tears.

The entire ride down to Misericordia that morning, Nate kept repeating. "This is the best thing for Hannah," as if he were trying to convince himself more than me. After calling and setting up an initial meeting, we met with the administration, toured the campus, filled out the paperwork, and got put on a waiting list. Four months later, Hannah was admitted when one of the beds opened up in the McAuley Residence. Which meant that a current resident had died. It all happened so quickly—too quickly. *Wait a minute*, I wanted to yell, *let's think about this some more*. But if we hadn't accepted the spot, it would have gone to the next child on the list. Nate stressed the importance of letting Hannah live in a place where she would be safe. She would have all the care she needed. And we could bring some normalcy back into our lives.

But my mind still went back and forth, weighing the pros and cons of keeping her home. No matter what, it always went back to Hannah's safety. Keeping an eye on her twenty-four/seven was impossible at home.

But she was my baby, and I was abandoning her. I had failed her.

I looked at the doorway. I still had time to change my mind. *If I walked right out of here with her, I wouldn't be breaking any laws.*

"We're all excited to have a girl moving in," Claire said. She had such a presence in the room. She stood about six feet tall, was large boned, and had smooth skin the color of dark chocolate. Blond highlights streaked her dark-brown bob. And her bright, wide smile made it hard to be in a bad mood. After meeting Claire during our walk-through of McAuley Residence, I'd felt a little better.

The sight of Hannah's crib made me wonder about the baby who used to sleep there, whether it was a boy or a girl, and what the parents were going through. I squeezed Hannah tighter. *This is the right thing to do.* I'd continuously told myself that throughout the night as I'd lain awake. We couldn't possibly care for Hannah at home. Even if we hired a nurse full time, where would she stay? We didn't have any extra bedrooms. Plus, we didn't have a room on the first floor where Hannah could stay once she became wheelchair bound. *God, I can't even think of that yet.*

Hannah drew her head back, sneezed, then dropped her head back down on my shoulder. Except for the fact that she couldn't hold her head up, she wasn't obviously disabled. Not like Jacob, who had a large head and twisted teeth, or Juan, who had a tube running from his throat to the oxygen tank. Hannah wasn't like them. She was normal. She had a perfectly shaped head full of beautiful brown curls that dangled past her ears. When her eyes opened wide, she gazed around the room as if she were enthralled with everything in sight. She kicked her legs and flailed her arms when she cried in her crib. When the tip of a spoon touched her mouth, she opened wide to eat the cereal. She laughed. She cooed. She was perfect. *Why does she have to be here?*

"Hi, my beautiful baby boy," someone said from behind me.

I turned to see a woman about my age walk up to Jacob in his wheelchair. She wiped the drool from his mouth then covered his face with kisses. Her blond hair was pulled back into a low ponytail, and she wore jeans and a Northwestern Wildcats sweatshirt. Claire introduced us. Her name was Abbie Fishman.

"How long has Jacob been here?" Nate asked.

"A year and a half. He's five now." She watched me cling to Hannah like a security blanket. "She'll love it here. The staff is phenomenal."

I nodded and attempted to smile.

"Well, Jacob, are you ready for your walk?" She pushed the wheelchair toward the door then she turned back to us. "I've been in your shoes. If you ever want to talk, give me a call." She handed me a business card before walking out. *Abbie Fishman, Owner, Jacob's Crumbles.* She lived in Lake Bluff, not far from us.

"Hannah's probably starting to get hungry," Claire said. "I'll go get her chestnut cereal ready."

I sat down in the rocking chair next to Hannah's crib. Nate stood beside me as I pushed the curls from her forehead and covered her with kisses. I wondered if she realized we were leaving her here or if she would even notice she wasn't at home in her own crib. Would she cry for me when I left like other babies do when their mommies leave the room?

"Tell me again why we're doing this," I whispered to Nate.

He knelt beside me. "Because we can't take care of her."

"We're her parents."

"As her parents, we have to do what's best for her," he said. "She'll be safer here."

I laid Hannah in her steel crib and covered her with a blanket I had gotten as a gift at my baby shower, back when I never would've thought things would turn out like this.

"We can always take her back home if we want," Nate said.

I knew he'd only said that to make me feel better. We couldn't take her home. Hannah wasn't ours anymore. She never had been.

THE NEXT MORNING, Nate let me sleep in while he got Caroline ready for school. I curled up in the fetal position, pulled the covers over my head, and let my mind fall back into unconsciousness. Occasionally, I opened my eyes, still half asleep, the topic of my strange dreams still playing in my mind. I blinked in the sunlight, willing myself to crawl out of bed and do something useful. I glanced at the clock, but the digital numbers meant nothing and I drifted back into sleep.

At noon, I was conscious enough to drag myself out of bed. I pulled on Nate's sweatshirt that was lying on the floor and went downstairs to make coffee. I threw a load of laundry in the washer without even bothering to separate the whites and unloaded the dishwasher. I ordered a sub sandwich for lunch. At two-thirty, I fell asleep on the couch watching *Judge Judy*.

The sound of the back door opening woke me a few hours later. Nate was home after picking up Caroline from soccer. I greeted them and asked them how their days were, but I didn't pay attention to the answers. I threw dinner together that night. Not entirely certain of the contents, I pulled plastic containers out of the fridge and heated them up in the microwave.

I climbed into bed at seven-thirty and fell right to sleep.

The next morning, I followed the same routine. Nate patiently let me sleep away the morning while he got lost in the distraction of his job. I got up at ten and forced myself to do some housework. I vacuumed the upstairs hallway, spending extra time pushing the machine back and forth over the same spot in front of Hannah's closed bedroom door. I made Caroline's bed, which I hadn't done since we'd taught her to do it herself when she was six. I dusted and cleaned mirrors. By one o'clock, the couch was calling me, and I napped.

Someone shook my shoulder, jostling me out of my slumber. "Well, it's a good thing you don't have a job anymore," Kate said. "Makes it easier to mope around the house all day."

I blinked. "What time is it? What are you doing here?"

"It's four-thirty." Her orange lipstick had stained her teeth. "I came to take you out of the house."

"Why?"

"It'll be good for you." She pulled back the blanket. "C'mon. You don't even have to change out of those grubby clothes."

I didn't argue. And I didn't ask where she was taking me. I let her drive us through town, past all the people who were grocery shopping for their complete families, past mothers pushing their toddlers in strollers. Kate pulled into the parking lot of Kentwood Beach and cut the engine.

"What are we doing here?"

"C'mon." She grabbed her purse and a grocery bag from the backseat.

"Kate, we're not dressed for the beach." I looked down at my stained Bulls T-shirt and workout shorts.

"No one will notice," she said with a wave of her hand.

She was probably right. The morning showers had left an overcast sky in the afternoon, and Kentwood Beach had been neglected by the city of Ferndale. Instead, the local government poured money into renovating Cloverdale Beach a few miles south, where most of the residents spent their summer days. Kentwood was more of a place to come for some solitude or to simply watch the sunrise.

We walked through the damp ravine along an old stone path.

The scent of moss and rain hung in the air. In the distance, waves crashed on Lake Michigan. Kate walked ahead of me, her fuchsia leggings stretched over her wide bottom. She wore a pastel striped shirt and a wide-brimmed hat even though the sky was overcast with clouds. The contents of the grocery bag she was carrying clinked with each step she took.

We arrived at the beach and sat on a concrete block that existed for some unknown reason. It had been there for as long as I could remember. As teens, we'd sat on top of it and drank beer after the beach closed.

Kate pulled out a liter of vodka, a half-gallon of orange juice, and two plastic cups.

"I don't think we're allowed to have open alcohol at the beach," I said.

"Then don't tell anyone," she whispered as she poured me a screwdriver. "Here."

I waited as she poured herself one, then we toasted to nothing in particular. She'd made my drink too strong, but I gulped it anyway. The humidity lifted, and the summer afternoon grew cool. I wished I'd brought a light sweater.

I waited for Kate to say something, to tell me life would get better and that I wouldn't feel this pain forever, or some other lecture to try to lift my spirits. Instead, she stared straight ahead at the horizon and sipped her cocktail. The sound of the waves crashing was soothing. The late afternoon sun was behind us, casting an orange glow in the east.

After an hour of drinking and no words spoken, Kate drove me home.

Chapter 14

CAROLINE

Dad told me Hannah's new home was built with money raised from fundraisers, and it had state-of-the-art equipment and amenities that severely developmentally disabled people like Hannah needed. She was going to have the best around-the-clock care, he assured me as we entered the lobby of McAuley Residence. The first thing I noticed was the shiny wood floors. They were so glossy that I was afraid I would slip and fall on my ass in front of the receptionist. Mom signed us in at the visitors' log while I viewed the place. A cozy waiting area with a gas fireplace was to the right. Straight ahead against the wall was a beautiful steel sculpture of a nun leaning over a boy in a wheelchair.

The receptionist buzzed us in, and we took the elevator to the second floor. The doors opened to a nurse walking by, pushing a girl in a wheelchair. The girl had a long face, and her thick tongue stuck out with a strand of drool dangling from the tip. The nurse whispered something to her and the girl grinned widely, displaying a mouthful of crooked teeth.

We walked down a hallway lined with more wheelchairs. A boy with a large head concave on one side moaned as we walked by. Another was spitting up globs of greenish mucus. A girl with crossed eyes screeched with joy when we passed as if we were there to visit her. I felt like I was in a twisted carnival fun house.

Dad said McAuley housed kids who needed the most help, the ones who needed twenty-four-hour care and weren't physically capable of doing anything on their own. Hannah's room was at the end of the hall. In the middle of the floor were two boys in wheelchairs—one with an oversized head, the other with a tube coming out of his throat. And then there was Hannah, perfect little Hannah, sitting in her stroller, wearing denim overalls over a pink shirt with blue balloons on it. Her curly, shoulder-length hair was pulled into ponytails. Her head slumped forward, and a strand of drool slipped from her mouth. Mom wiped it from her chin.

I unsnapped the belt from Hannah's stroller and hoisted her up. Her dead weight made her feel much heavier than most babies her age. Her hair smelled of baby shampoo. Her eyes, which were usually cast down toward the floor, opened wide and made contact with mine. I kissed her on the tip of her nose, and she smiled.

Why is she here? I wanted to ask. *She doesn't have a weird-shaped head or crooked eyes or twisted limbs like the others.* She looked like any normal baby. Wasn't there a better place for her to be?

I swallowed back tears during the ride home. "You made a huge mistake," I said.

Dad lowered the radio's volume, and Mom turned around in her seat. "What?"

"Hannah doesn't belong there. She's not a retard like those other kids."

Mom sighed and turned back toward the front. "Don't say 'retard,' Caroline."

Dad peered at me in the rearview mirror. "She's where she needs to be."

"Why can't we take care of her?"

"Our home isn't equipped for her needs," Dad said. "She's

allergic to everything, and she needs a live-in nurse. We can't afford that."

I thought back to that afternoon when I was babysitting Hannah, that fateful day she'd turned blue. What could I have done differently? Should I have called my parents first? Maybe Mom would've known what to do right away, and Hannah wouldn't have had to be rushed to the hospital. Maybe if I'd tried harder with CPR. Or maybe we had something in the house that I should've given to her to prevent her from turning blue. Should I have not put her to bed and instead let her fall asleep in her swing so I could've kept an eye on her?

When Mom and Dad rushed into the hospital that day, they hadn't noticed me sitting in the waiting room. But that was understandable. They needed to be with Hannah, and I had known they would come out to me once she was stable—once the color came back to her face and the doctor confirmed she was going to be okay.

I'd waited for them to thank me, pull me into a hug, and tell me how brave I was. I wanted them to tell me they understood how traumatic it must have been for me.

I waited, but they never came out.

Chapter 15

JILLIAN

Whenever I was stressed or needed some alone time, I jumped in our car and went for long rides around town. Ferndale, Illinois, where I was born and raised, had almost 50,000 residents, spanned seventeen square miles, and sat right along Lake Michigan. Ferndale was usually described as affluent, but I considered its residents to be middle class and upper-middle class. I loved that Ferndale still had a town: a central location with a post office, library, city hall, fire department, and police department, surrounded by neighborhoods and postwar subdivisions. Only one strip mall existed along the expressway. We lived in the modest middle-class neighborhood of Deer Prairie. The subdivision entrance didn't have any fancy signs, just rows of split-levels that were obviously developed by the same builder.

Nate and I bought our house when Caroline was a year old, and over the years we'd succeeded in making it a home, giving it a lived-in look and keeping the curb appeal up to date. It wasn't a fancy home, but it was our home.

Several days after Hannah moved into Misericordia, I decided to go for a drive to clear my head. I drove down Willow Road, which took me through town, past City Hall, coffee shops, and overpriced boutiques. I drove through the neighborhood of my childhood home on a side of town called Briarwood and spotted my house, which still had the same grey siding and a picture window as the focal point. Kate's childhood home, a small Cape Cod where her parents still lived, was three blocks away. I slowed down as I passed her old house, recognizing the same '70s-style floor lamp standing in the window that Kate and I used to sit next to for hours, talking or flipping through teen magazines. On any other day, I would've stopped in to say hello to her parents, but I needed to get home to make dinner.

As I headed toward home my curiosity piqued, and I steered the car to the other side of town, where the upper-middle class lived. I'd always admired a subdivision called Oak Vista on the southeast side of town where the homes were ample but not ridiculously huge. Built about thirty years ago, the colonials, Tudors, and Cape Cods had stood the test of time, maintaining their curb appeal while still fulfilling the needs of today's lifestyles. I'd always wanted to live in Oak Vista, if Nate and I ever made enough money for a mortgage twice the amount of our current one and triple the real estate taxes.

I turned down a street called Timber Ridge and came to a stop about halfway down the road, in front of a comfortable colonial that belonged to Dr. Jeffrey Stewart. It was the kind of home I'd seen in ReMax commercials: pale yellow with black shutters, a front porch, and a three-car garage. It sat back from the road and was surrounded by old oaks and leafy elms. The vibrant-green lawn was manicured like a golf course, and the driveway was paved with bricks. A swing hung from the front porch, surrounded by flowerpots filled with begonias and hydrangeas.

I had driven by the Stewarts' house several times since Hannah's birth. But this was the first time I'd actually parked and shut off the engine.

I stared at their posh home and wondered what kind of problems they had. Were they worried about their children? Did they pray every night that their child wouldn't have to suffer? Were they as close as they ever were as a couple, or were they drawing further apart? Maybe they were deep in debt built up by fancy cars and extravagant vacations. Maybe his wife was cheating on him.

One can only hope.

Since Hannah had moved out, I'd grown more curious about the life of Dr. Stewart—correction: *Mr.* Stewart. Calling him a doctor was an insult to real doctors. Finding pieces of the puzzle by observing his home from afar, I wanted to learn more about his life, hoping for a sign that he was somehow suffering, too. Here he was, living large, comfortable, and carefree, while my family was falling apart little by little each day.

I dug inside my purse and pulled out a fresh pack of Winstons I'd impulsively purchased at the gas station when I filled up the car. I unwrapped the plastic and opened the box. I breathed in the pungent smell of tobacco as I pulled out a stick and lit it, inhaling the sweet and tangy smoke into my lungs. I leaned back and shut my eyes, savoring the effect of the nicotine.

I took another drag and looked back at the colonial across the street. I imagined walking up to the front door and ringing the bell, then seeing the expression on Mr. Stewart's face when he answered the door. I would tell him there's a special place in Hell for people like him. I would tell him I was a firm believer in karma and that he would get what was coming to him soon enough. I would ask him why. Why did he leave me in the hospital, unattended for so long while my baby swallowed meconium? Why, during my first postpartum appointment, did he not even remember who the hell I was? Were all his patients as insignificant to him as I was?

I wanted to throw a rock through his cozy bay window. I wanted to take a baseball bat to Mr. Stewart's obnoxiously pimped-up Mercedes Benz that was sitting in the driveway. I rubbed my hand across my forehead. I didn't know who I was anymore. I used to be content, confident, and peaceful. But I was unraveling into a tangled mess of despair, vengefulness, and anger.

I started at the sound of the garage door opening, and Mr. Stewart walked out of the garage with a young boy of about thirteen or fourteen, whom I assumed was his son. They were walking bicycles down the driveway when the boy noticed me sitting in the car. I turned away and rummaged in my purse, pretending to search for something, hiding my face from their view.

"Shit." I sank in my seat and kept my head down until they walked down the street in the opposite direction. I adjusted the rearview mirror and watched them get smaller as they rode away. I took a final drag on the cigarette and tossed the butt out the window, fantasizing about it landing on their front porch and burning down their house.

I started the engine and headed home, back to our modest mid-century split-level across town. As I pulled in the driveway, my cell phone rang. It was Mark Leventhal.

STANDING NEXT TO EACH OTHER, Mark Leventhal and John Marquart were polar opposites. Leventhal, standing over six feet tall, was trim, dapper, and olive skinned, contrasting drastically to Marquart's shorter stature, portly build, and ruddy complexion. Yet together, they made a great team. After being in business together for thirteen years, they'd built a healthy and reputable law firm along with their partners. As Nate and I sat in a small conference room at Leventhal, Dole, Marquart & Simon, I silently prayed that this powerful team would help us.

Leventhal took a seat across the table from me and scanned the notes he'd scribbled on the yellow legal pad in front of him. He loosened his tie as he flipped through the pages. John Marquart walked in, carrying a stack of file folders, and sat at the head of the table. Nate reached for my hand.

"We've reviewed all the records we received from the hospitals," Leventhal said, "as well as the neurologist, pediatrician, and your obstetrician, Dr. Stewart. We also had an independent consultant review all the documents and provide his point of view on the matter." Leventhal looked up at me. "At this point, we feel that we definitely have a case."

I exhaled what felt like months of built-up tension from my lungs. "Thank you," I managed to whisper. I turned to Nate. He smiled and squeezed my hand.

"What happens next?" Nate asked.

"Well, we'd like to get the case tried in Cook County, as opposed to Lake County," Leventhal said. "We feel the juries are friendlier in Cook County."

"Can it be tried in Cook County?" I asked.

Marquart nodded. "Even though Hannah was born in Lake County, she was treated at Children's Memorial Hospital, which is in Cook."

"The lawyers for the defendant will fight to keep it in Lake," Leventhal said, "but we will fight just as hard. After we secure the location, we'll start the depositions. You'll be one of the first deposed, Jillian."

"When will the depositions be?" I asked.

"Well, the venue motions may take some time," Marquart said. "Could be several months. Then we we'll have more research to do to prepare for the depos. It could be a couple of years before we begin."

"Years?" Nate asked.

Marquart nodded.

"If we win," I said, leaning forward in my seat, "what happens to Dr. Stewart?"

"Nothing." Leventhal put down his pen and leaned back in his chair. "This case is about money. It's about providing for Hannah's future and making sure she has what she needs."

"So Dr. Stewart won't get fired or anything?" Nate asked.

Leventhal shook his head. "There are very few cases of discipline in instances like this. Civil litigation is the only recourse."

In the car driving home, Nate and I were silent. A conflicting cocktail of hope and frustration mixed inside me. I wasn't sure what kind of outcome I'd expected. Of course, I wanted Hannah to be taken care of. We had no idea at that point what kind of future she was going to have, and if we won the case, we wouldn't have to worry about finances. But at the same time, Dr. Stewart would still be practicing, potentially causing harm to others. Was that justice?

Without a word, Nate turned on his right turn signal, got off at the Petersen Avenue exit, and drove us to Misericordia. We still didn't speak as we entered McAuley and rode the elevator to the second floor. Hannah was in her room, sitting in her chair, gazing down at her lap. As we walked in, she lifted her head and laughed, as if she were certain everything would be all right.

PART II

2007

Chapter 16

JILLIAN

I pulled into the garage and put the car in park. For a moment, I sat staring straight ahead, focusing on the half-empty paint cans and dirty flowerpots on the shelf. I was exhausted and wanted nothing more than to climb into bed and sleep away the rest of the day, but I had no energy to move. I pulled out a cigarette and held it between my lips. My hands trembled as I brought the lighter to the tip. The first inhale didn't seem to relax me as it usually did. I glanced around the garage, realizing how easy it would be to push the garage door button strapped to the sun visor while the car was still idling. All I had to do was lift a finger. It would be so simple. I closed my eyes and replayed some of the grueling day in my mind, trying to find any mistakes that I may have made.

"Mrs. Moore, did you take care of yourself the entire term of your pregnancy?" the lawyer in the hideous turquoise suit had asked as she sat across from me, staring me down.

I shifted in my seat and clasped my hands in my lap. "Of course."

"No smoking?"

"No."

"Did you drink any alcoholic beverages? Even a sip?"

"No."

"Did you exercise?"

"I did some prenatal yoga, but not consistently." Did that really matter? I glanced at my lawyer, Mark Leventhal, who was writing something on the legal pad.

"Mrs. Moore," the lawyer in the navy pinstripe suit said, "can you think of anything that would have harmed the fetus?"

The fetus. I had known that word would come up. Leventhal had told me it was how the opposing lawyers would refer to Hannah. They would never use her real name if they didn't have to. That would humanize her and make Dr. Stewart appear even worse than he already did.

I looked away, pretending to consider the question the lawyer had asked me. Of course there was nothing to consider. *Isn't it obvious what happened?* But Leventhal had warned me they needed to cover absolutely all the bases before the trial would begin. "No," I said.

"Mrs. Moore, do you have a good marriage?"

I rubbed my forehead. *What the hell does that have to do with it?* I turned to Leventhal, who gave me a slight nod of encouragement. "Do not let them get to you," he had told me.

"Yes, very good." If I were strapped to a polygraph, the pointer would be scribbling out of control. Really, how much in love are you still supposed to be after eighteen years of marriage? How good is our marriage if he's not even here sitting beside me while I'm being interrogated?

"Your other daughter was"—another lawyer flipped through her legal pad—"almost thirteen years old when you got pregnant again. Is that correct?"

"Yes."

"Why did you wait so many years to have another child?"

I stayed calm. "The pregnancy wasn't planned."

"Did you really want the child?"

The question came out with a suggestive tone, and I hardened inside. I took a deep breath and composed myself before answering. "At first, it came as a surprise, but there was no doubt in my mind that I wanted to keep my baby."

"Didn't you think thirty-seven was too old to be having another child?"

"To some people, it might seem old. But my mother was the same age when she had me. So it didn't concern me." I looked straight into the lawyer's eyes. "And besides, shouldn't the fact that I was thirty-seven mean that I should've gotten better care from the hospital staff instead of being ignored?" *Take that, bastards.*

The lawyer held up her hand to stop me from saying anything else. Too late. It was already out there. "How was the birth of your first daughter?"

"She was two weeks late. So Dr. Stewart was well aware that my pregnancies tended to go late."

"So you went into labor with your second child early Friday morning, May the tenth, correct?"

"Yes."

"Then what happened?"

"I waited until the contractions were five minutes apart, then I called Dr. Stewart, and he told me to go to the hospital. After they admitted me, the labor pains stopped. I was four centimeters dilated. By that time, I had a feeling something was wrong. I asked for a Cesarean, but they told me to relax, that it was too early to start thinking about a C-section."

I glanced at Leventhal. Another nod. *Well done.*

The lawyers scribbled on their pads. I watched them closely. What do they have to gain from all this? A partnership in the law firm? Don't they have a conscience? Dr. Stewart's insurance company would cover the settlement if we won. He wouldn't lose his license to practice. Leventhal told me we didn't have any power to make that happen, which infuriated me. How could someone like that be allowed to practice? Didn't his patients have a right to know the danger they could be in?

"When did Dr. Stewart arrive?" A third lawyer, a man in his late twenties, spoke up for the first time.

"He came in around nine to break my water. After that, I didn't see him again for several hours."

"How many hours exactly?"

"He came back around three p.m. So six hours."

"What did he do when he came back at three p.m.?"

"He checked the monitor, reviewed my chart, then said we needed to do a C-section. I told him I had been asking for one for hours."

"When Dr. Stewart broke your water in the morning, did he say if anything was wrong?"

"No."

"He didn't inform you there was any meconium in the fluid?"

"Not at that time, no."

"After the baby was born, what happened?"

"She wasn't breathing. They took her away. I didn't know what was happening. It wasn't until about an hour later that they came in—"

"Who's 'they'?"

"Dr. Stewart and the nurse. They came in to tell me she was having difficulty breathing because of meconium aspiration and that they were rushing her down to Children's Memorial."

"Why was she transferred to Children's Memorial?"

"Ferndale Hospital did not have the proper equipment to keep her alive."

"What time was she transferred to Children's?"

"We had to wait for the transport team from Children's. They didn't come until a few hours later."

"How many hours?"

"She was born at 3:30, and Children's came at 7:30."

"Why did it take so long?"

"Like I said, they had to wait for a doctor and nurse to be available to come and get her."

It went on for four hours. The lawyers kept lobbing questions at me about that horrible day at the hospital, my pregnancy, my health, and my relationships. I felt as if I were answering the same questions over and over. By the time we finally wrapped up, my head was in a fog. I had wanted nothing more than to drive straight home and take a nap.

"That went very well," Leventhal said. "You did a great job not letting them intimidate you."

I closed my eyes and pinched the bridge of my nose. "What's next?"

"We'll see if they have more questions. If not, a trial date will be set."

I rubbed my burning eyes. I couldn't imagine what the trial would be like.

"Go home and get some rest," Leventhal said, resting a hand on my shoulder. "I think things went in our favor today."

So why, as I sat in the idling car in the garage, did I feel as if it would be much easier to end it all?

The door to the house opened, and Nate came out, making me realize it must already be after six o'clock since he was home from work. He came up to the driver's side and opened the door. "How did it go?"

I pulled myself out of the car and shrugged. "Fine."

"What did Leventhal say?"

"That I did well."

We went inside the house. A frozen pizza was cooking in the oven.

"I made dinner," Nate said.

"Thanks." I dropped my purse and keys on the counter. "Where's Caroline?"

"She's not home yet. She went to a soccer game with her friends. Pizza will be ready in ten minutes."

"I'm not hungry," I said. "I need to go lay down for a while."

As I climbed the stairs, I thought of Hannah's life at Misericordia so far. In the past three years, we'd come close to losing her twice. Or so the doctors said.

The first time was when she'd had pneumonia at nine months old. We'd rushed her to the hospital after she'd started coughing up greenish-yellow phlegm and her breaths became short gasps. After three days on oxygen, the doctor on staff sat Nate and I down and told us to prepare for the worst.

"Babies born with complications like Hannah"—he paused, carefully picking out the words—"don't usually live past the age of six."

That was the first time any doctor had given us a prognosis of Hannah's future. Even Dr. Greenwald, the neurosurgeon, hadn't given me this news the day he'd told us Hannah would never get better.

The next few days, we walked around in a trance as Hannah held on. Preparing for what we thought was the inevitable felt like a bad dream. We discussed pallbearer options, and I settled on an outfit for Hannah to be buried in. We broke the news to Caroline, who put on a brave face in front of us, but later sobbed in her bedroom when she thought no one could hear. Nate mentioned that he wanted the wake to be brief, rather than spending hours a few feet away from his young daughter lying in a casket as friends and acquaintances filed by to pay their condolences.

A priest stopped by to read her the last rites. We took turns sitting vigil by her bedside each night. As the days and nights inched by, Hannah's lungs began to clear, the phlegm cough-ups were less frequent, and she was able to switch back to her special formula without vomiting. On the third day, the doctors released her with a shrug of bewilderment. We brought her back to Misericordia with her life expectancy hidden away in the backs of our minds, for the time being.

Shortly after Hannah entered Misericordia, when she was a little over a year old, she got the flu. Her temperature spiked up to 104. She vomited her formula as soon as it entered her stomach, so she took Pedialyte intravenously to keep from dehydrating. Again, the doctor on staff told us Hannah probably would only live another week or two. But this time, a strange calm came over me. While I was tormented that she wouldn't be around much longer, I was at peace knowing she wouldn't have to suffer anymore. I bought a black dress at Macy's. The following day, her fever broke, and once again, she recovered.

In our bedroom, I pulled the shades down to block the sunset and took two ibuprofen before climbing into bed and curling into the fetal position. As I relaxed, I recounted Hannah's numerous tests and various medications.

When she was around fifteen months old, she had a nasogastric tube inserted for her feedings to prevent her from vomiting. Since then, she'd lived with a tube up her nose and was fed formula from a plastic bag hung on an IV pole instead of from a bottle. She spent most of her day in bed or sitting in her custom-built wheelchair, unable to communicate what she was feeling, tell someone if she had an itch, or tell anyone if an eyelash had fallen into her eye. As she got older, she didn't always cry when she wasn't feeling good, making it more challenging for us to know when something was wrong.

We were fortunate enough to be able to afford the annual tuition at Misericordia, and our insurance covered her hospital stays. But what if she needed surgery? How many other hospital stays will she have? Will our insurance cover it all? If we won the lawsuit, the settlement would be our financial cushion. If we didn't win, we would have an even more challenging future ahead of us.

My head swam with details from the afternoon of depositions mixed with Hannah's medical episodes throughout her short life as I dozed off into a deep sleep. I didn't wake until the next morning.

Chapter 17

CAROLINE

The pot was more potent than usual. "Where did you get this stuff?" I asked.

"Valerie," Courtney said. "I always get my shit from Valerie."

I held the joint between my lips and took another drag. The pungent flavor instantly brought a wave of calm over me. *Here's to a great junior year of high school.* We stood outside the main entrance to the school, around the corner and down a grassy lawn where smokers went to light up. School administrators had banned smoking within ten feet of the building as a lame attempt to get students to curb their dirty habit, so we couldn't use the smoking area that used to be outside the cafeteria. That only encouraged us to move to the more secluded location by the dumpsters. Occasionally, a janitor would spot us while he unloaded trash, but he usually pretended not to see us.

The summer had lasted into early September for the start of my third year of high school. The blazing sun forced me to move to a spot under a tree for some shade. Courtney opted to stay in the sun, turning her face upward, in hopes of getting some color in the remaining moments of our summer break. I took another pull from the joint before handing it back to her. I didn't want to be too stoned during first period. New year, new habit.

The first time I got high was freshman year when Courtney bought a joint from her cousin Valerie, and we spent the evening in her basement passing it back and forth. I inhaled slowly, like Valerie told me to, then held it in for a few seconds before exhaling. But as Courtney and Val grew increasingly high, I didn't feel a thing. Courtney told me I was doing it wrong. But, really, how can you *inhale* wrong? Valerie told me it takes a few tries before you feel the effects. By the end of the first semester, Courtney and I were smoking several times a week, thanks to Val and her reliable dealer. I think my parents noticed. They're not totally clueless about the signs of someone who's stoned. But they never said anything, not directly to me anyway. Pot kept the peace in our home, so they looked the other way. They had bigger things to worry about anyway. The lawsuit against Hannah's doctor was finally starting, and it preoccupied my parents enough to not pay attention when I walked in the door with dilated pupils.

As I handed the joint back to Courtney, I made the decision to cut back. Unlike Courtney, who occasionally snorted coke, I wasn't interested in moving up to the hard stuff. I guess I was getting over being stoned all the time. Of course, I still liked smoking once in a while, just not every other day. It's too expensive anyway.

Sometimes, when I was stoned, I thought of Hannah and imagined the kind of girl she would be if she had been normal. At three years old she would've been talking, running around, and using the potty. I would have taught her how to sing the alphabet song and how to count to ten. Maybe she would have a hard time saying my name, pronouncing it *Cay-line*. Maybe she'd have a nickname for me, like Cece.

I didn't visit Hannah as often as I should have. I couldn't handle going down there every Sunday with my parents. First of all, I hated waking up so early. When I asked my parents if we could go later, like around noon, they said that was too late and would throw off their Sunday schedule. *What the fuck?* They never did anything on Sundays. And second, going to Misericordia and hanging out with all those sick kids was depressing—and boring. The family room had a TV but no cable, so only two local channels with bad reception came in. There wasn't a lot to watch on network television on Sunday morning anyway. Hannah would sit, staring into space, while Mom sang church songs to her and Dad played with the rabbit ears on the TV. This is what went on for two hours.

Courtney put out the joint and tucked it into her purse right as the first bell rang. She straightened her golden ponytail. "Did you do your biology homework? Can I see it at lunch? I want to make sure my answers are right."

"What makes you think mine are right?" I asked, spotting Brody walking toward us.

"They're always right," she scoffed. "See you later. Hey, Bro," she said to Brody as she walked away. He hated being called Bro.

"I thought I'd find you out here," he said as he leaned in to me. His lips tasted like coffee.

He stepped back, and I got a good look at his gorgeous face. The sight of him still made my heart rate triple, even after dating for two months.

"Getting high before first period?" He grabbed my hand, and we walked toward the entrance.

"No," I said. "I mean, just a little."

He reached down, grabbed my butt, and pulled me into another kiss. Brody didn't like getting high for some reason. When I first met him at Travis Hoffman's house, he was the only one who wasn't smoking.

At first, I barely noticed Brody Stewart among the five or six other guys who were there along with me and Courtney, hanging out in the basement, drinking beers stolen from the fridge. Brody was subtly good looking: wavy brown hair, hazel eyes, and a medium build. His quiet and humble nature got lost among his group of crass and obnoxious friends. But as the night went on, and we consumed more beers, his personality came out as he offered retorts to Travis's smart-ass comments.

We noticed each other. He paid attention to me that night, more than I was used to from guys. I think we were both on our third beer when he awkwardly asked me out and I awkwardly agreed, scribbling my number on a piece of rolling paper.

The next morning, sober and regretful, I confided in Courtney that I wasn't expecting him to call.

"Why not?" she'd said. "Travis told me that Brody thinks you're hot."

"Really?" I was not used to being described as hot. While I was awkward looking in junior high, I was just then, in my third year of high school, beginning to bloom. I noticed it when I looked in the mirror every morning, pulling the hair straightener through my frizzy locks. My eyes were a light hazel that was enhanced when I lined them with moss-green eyeliner. I learned to live with my long nose that hooked at the tip. And I was fortunate to have never had to worry about my weight.

Courtney, on the other hand, wasn't what I would describe as beautiful. She had a simple look, with shoulder-length honey-blond hair that she usually pulled back into a ponytail. Her eyes were a dull grey and they were set far apart on her face, so I used to call her "blowfish" when we were little. Her asset was her personality and her ample boobs, which she referred to as "the sisters."

"I don't know why you can't see what other people see," Courtney told me. "You're gorgeous. How can you not know that?"

I smiled at the compliment but I still didn't believe. I refused to get my hopes up about Brody ever calling me.

So the next afternoon, I almost choked on my Coke when Dad came into my room and said, "Some guy named Body or Brady is on the phone?"

Brody picked me up the next night. I introduced him to my parents, and Dad gave him a firm handshake. Mom asked him about being on the soccer team. He took me to my favorite Mexican restaurant, where we noshed on chicken quesadillas and guacamole. Afterward, we went for ice cream and strolled around town. He made me laugh a lot on our first date, which was something I hadn't realized was important to me until then. I hadn't had that much fun in a long time. When we pulled in to my driveway at the end of the night, we awkwardly searched for the right closing words to prolong the moment. As he slowly leaned in, my doubt kicked in. *Should I back away? Turn my cheek?* A thousand thoughts ran through my head as I froze and let his lips meet mine.

After our first date, Brody and I spent a lot of time together, letting our relationship grow organically. I was learning how to be a girlfriend, since this was my first real relationship. I was learning to understand that the flutter in my stomach, my tense shoulders, and the feeling deep down inside that he may never call again were all signs that I really liked him and was afraid of losing him. And when he did call, and when we went out or hung out with our friends, it meant our relationship was progressing in the right direction. I learned that my insecurity would nudge me once in a while into second-guessing our whole relationship. I thought of the old saying, "If it's too good to be true, it probably is."

For the past two months, I'd done my best to enjoy my time with Brody, while tucked away in my soul, I was waiting for the bomb to drop. But with each passing day, I let my guard down little by little, letting him see into me and learn who I really was without scaring him off.

The second bell rang, and Brody reached for my hand as we walked to first period. We were officially late for class.

"You coming to the game after school?" he asked when we stopped in front of Room 212, where I had U.S. History.

"Yeah." I smiled, thinking of Brody's adorable tight butt as he kicked the soccer ball across the field.

He leaned in for another kiss. "See you at lunch."

I watched him walk away and wondered the same thing I always did. *What does he see in me?*

~

ONE DAY OVER THE SUMMER, about a week before I met Brody, Courtney and I were sitting in my room, reading the latest issue of *Cosmopolitan,* when we came across an article on the top ten tips to enhance your orgasms. Courtney sat on my bed, her legs crossed, and read each of them aloud, taking mental notes for "next time."

"Next time?" I asked. As far as I knew, she was still a virgin like me.

"Next time I masturbate," she said.

"You masturbate?" I whispered, in case one of my parents was walking by my room.

"Yeah. Don't you?"

I hesitated.

"You never masturbated?"

"Why is that a surprise?"

"Well, why haven't you?" She pushed a strand of hair behind her ear as she turned to face me.

"I don't know. I guess I never had a reason to."

"You don't need a reason. Do you know how to do it?"

Suddenly, I felt a little uncomfortable. "Courtney, I don't know..."

"Hey, it's no big deal," she said. "Don't you want to experience that feeling?"

"Of course. I always thought I'd experience it with a guy."

"You will. But until then, why wait?" She handed me the magazine. "Read this. And just try it. You can't really do it wrong."

The page was open to a photo of a young woman in her bra and panties, lying on a bed, a flushed hue on her cheeks. Masturbation had never entered my mind as something I could do. I suppose my Catholic upbringing made me feel ashamed. Courtney must have overcome the shame. She was raised Catholic, too.

"What does it feel like?" I asked.

Courtney looked away, her mouth turning up in a wry smile. "It's like... your body gets all hot, you know? And your nipples start to tingle. And there's this build-up inside of you. And then you... explode."

I raised my eyebrows.

"You have to experience it to really understand," she said.

That night, after reading the article and with the lights turned off, I lay still in my bed. I slowly lowered my hand down my smooth skin, past the navel piercing I'd gotten last spring, down between my legs to "my velvet underground," as the article called it. It felt warm, and my pubic hair was coarse, but somewhat soft. I touched myself with my middle finger, feeling a smooth and damp surface between the lips. I rubbed the area. I flicked. I stroked.

After ten minutes, I was bored and felt nothing. No hot sensation. No tingling nipples. No explosion that Courtney had bragged about. *Guess she was mistaken. I can do it wrong.* Shame rushed over me, and I pulled my hand away.

Brody and I hadn't slept together yet. After I started dating him, Courtney gave me tips on giving good head, and that was as far as we'd gotten. He hadn't even gone down on me. He'd lowered his head under my skirt a few times, but I'd pulled him back up, pretending I wanted to kiss instead. I didn't know what my hang-up was. I wasn't even sure why we hadn't had sex yet. Guess I was still waiting to see if he would really stick around.

WE ACTUALLY MADE it to the game on time for kickoff, which was unusual since Courtney usually spent twenty minutes primping in the bathroom beforehand. I shifted in my seat on the bleachers, trying to get the blood flow back into my left butt cheek as I watched Brody standing in the hot sun on the sidelines, wiping the sweat from his brow.

Courtney nudged me and motioned toward Brody, "Do you think he'll ask you to homecoming?"

The smile I didn't realize was plastered on my face began to fade. "I don't know."

"I'm sure he will," she said. "He's into you. Why are you having a hard time believing that?"

"What makes you think I am?"

"Because I know you."

Brody was on the field, kicking the ball he had just stolen. He made it halfway across the field before the other team got it back from him. I loved focusing on his ass while he played.

"You know," Courtney continued, "It's been three years since Hannah was born. Don't you think it's time to stop blaming yourself for what happened?"

I stared at her. "What are you talking about?"

"Don't you think you deserve to be happy?"

"What does Hannah have to do with it?"

She rolled her eyes. "You blame yourself for what happened to Hannah, for some stupid reason. And you're always down on yourself all the time. I'm sorry." Her voice softened. "I'm just so sick of seeing you like this. Get therapy if you need it, but what the fuck? Let yourself be happy. Stop being such a downer on yourself."

"Seeing me like what?" I asked. "How am I a downer?"

"You're not, in general. You're just mopey all the time. Like there's always a dark cloud hanging over you. You were never this sad when we were little. I think it started after Hannah was born. And I see Brody bringing you out of that."

I'd always felt that dark cloud hovering over me, but I never bothered to deal with it. I never consciously blamed myself for what had happened to Hannah. I was young, insecure, and lonely. I thought the world hated me. I thought God didn't love me anymore and was punishing me by making my friends better than me, making all the boys ignore me, making all the cool kids look down on me, and by making my baby sister brain damaged.

After winning the soccer game, Brody took me out for a burger. I watched him over a plate of fries as he replayed which steps in the game he could've played better. Even while being hard on himself, he still had a positive disposition. Once in a while, he stopped and smiled at me or made a lame joke and winked. He dipped a fry in the ketchup and fed it to me. Then he asked me to homecoming.

Later that night, as I sat on my bed, the afterglow still emanating from my skin. I replayed the night in my mind, remembering the way Brody had leaned into me when he talked during dinner, how he always looked at me a beat longer than normal and with a grin on his face, and the gentle kiss he'd given me when he dropped me off at home.

I lay down in bed, pulled the covers to my chin, and thought about the kiss, but I took it a step further in my imagination. I pictured his hands running down my back and me grabbing his pelvis and pulling it closer. He brushes his fingers through my hair as he slips his tongue inside my mouth. I squeeze the back of his neck as he leaves a trail of kisses down my neck. I wrap my leg around his waist as his hand slips up my thigh.

I felt a warm feeling between my legs. And this time, when I slid my hand down there, it felt warm and wet instead of rough and dry like it had before. This time, as I repeated the tips from the article, as I pictured Brody going down on me and imagined my finger as his tongue, my body heated up, my nipples tingled, and the explosion happened.

And I knew I wasn't doing it wrong anymore.

Chapter 18

JILLIAN

Saturday was the first time we had seen the sun in ten days. After several days of downpours, I felt hopeful on a day that was going to be sunny and seventy-five.

Nate's side of the bed was empty. He'd gotten up early to go for a run. Caroline was still sleeping, no doubt. She usually didn't rise out of bed until noon on the weekends. I stretched my arms out in front of me and made a mental note not to waste the day worrying about anything, especially the lawsuit. On a day this beautiful, I wanted to clear my mind, relax, and enjoy it, whatever I decided to do. I wouldn't be able to accomplish that with my mind on Mr. Stewart.

I walked down to the kitchen. The pot of coffee Nate had made earlier was still half full. I poured a cup and sat at the kitchen table facing the window that looked out on our backyard, at the sandbox that we'd built for Caroline all those years ago. One weekend morning, about four years ago, Nate and Caroline went out in the backyard, pulled out the weeds around the edges of the sandbox, dug out all the old sand, and refilled it with fresh sand in preparation for the new baby. I'd sat right there at the kitchen table, watching them and laughing. "You know it's going to be a couple of years until the baby's old enough to play in it,"

I'd called through the open window. Nate built a plywood cover and placed it over the sandbox. I don't think the cover was ever taken off after that day.

I jumped up from the table and went through the cabinets and fridge to see if we needed any groceries. But they were well stocked. I called Kate to see if she wanted to get together, but the call went to voice mail. The house was pretty clean. I remembered the cell phone bill that had to be paid that day. So that was something to do. I could run into town to pay it, then stop off at the coffee shop and relax with book.

Back when I was working full time, before Hannah was born, I'd always envied people at the coffee shops during a weekday, browsing the Internet or leisurely reading books, not having to rush to the office for a full day of meetings and conference calls. After Hannah moved to Misericordia, I went back to work on a contract basis and earned an hourly wage working on projects that lasted for several weeks or months. I actually enjoyed working freelance. I had more control over my hours. I could take off at a moment's notice if Hannah got sick. And when I wasn't working a project, I had enough downtime to be one of those people in the coffee shops. However, with steady work projects coming in over the last couple of years, I hadn't had much time off from work.

I threw the latest *Newsweek* and a novel that I'd started reading months ago into my bag. I drove to the Verizon store, paid the bill, and walked down the street to the Starbucks on the corner. After ordering a latte, I was lucky to find a table outside in the sun.

I spent a few minutes enjoying the moment. People strolled by, heading to lunch appointments or running errands. My neighbor Karen Colson was on her way to the dentist. She stopped to chat for a moment and asked about Hannah. After she left, I pulled out the book and tried to lose myself in the plot, but the bright sun distracted me. I turned my face up to it every few minutes and let it shine on my cheeks. It made me think of

Hannah and how she felt when we took her out for walks in the sun. Leventhal seemed genuinely pleased with the outcome of the depositions the other day, and he was the expert. I really couldn't have done anything differently to prevent Hannah from...

I stopped, shook the thought from my head, and refocused on the book, and soon, I was lost again, lost enough to not hear someone addressing me.

"Excuse me." The voice registered the second time it spoke. I shielded the bright sun with my hand to see a man standing before me. It took a moment to pull myself away from the family drama I was reading about and come back to reality, here at the Starbucks on this beautiful day. And I found myself looking straight at Mr. Stewart.

I barged through the back door, hoping someone would be home. I needed to talk to Nate, Caroline—*anyone*. I needed to yell or punch the wall. But the house was empty. I called Kate and got her voice mail again. I paced the floor in the family room. The conversation replayed in my head like a cruel joke.

He hadn't changed much since the last time I'd seen him. His hairline had receded a little more, and his face had aged, but I still recognized him. I still saw the man behind the surgical mask telling me my baby was not breathing.

I remembered a time when I really liked Dr. Stewart. He was my ob-gyn for fifteen years before Hannah was born. He had delivered Caroline and had been there for me through all the miscarriages. He knew how hard we had worked to have another baby. He knew when we had decided to give up and shower our only child with all our love. He knew my shock and surprise when he'd told me I was pregnant again. I would never understand what had made such a seemingly decent and trustworthy person betray me in the worst way possible.

"I'm sorry to bother you," he'd said. He held a coffee cup in his hand, and a rolled up *Chicago Tribune* was wedged under his arm.

I stared at him for a moment, absorbing the fact that he was even speaking to me. My mind raced. *What the hell could he want?* I glanced around at the people who were blissfully unaware of the significance of our meeting as they sat reading their books, typing on their laptops, and sipping their coffees.

"I know this is awkward." He fidgeted with the sleeve on his cup.

I opened my mouth to speak but couldn't say a word.

"I have something I want to say to you. May I sit down?"

"No!" I managed to blurt out. "Is this about the lawsuit? You're not supposed to be talking to me."

"No, no. It's not about that." He spoke in a low voice as he continued to tug at the cup sleeve. "I don't mean to make you uncomfortable. I saw you sitting here, and I have something I need to say to you. So I thought now was a good time."

"Well, what is it?"

His eyes shifted from me to the floor, then back up, and met my gaze. "I understand your hatred toward me."

He paused for a response. When I didn't have one, he went on. "I wanted to say," he spoke slowly, "that I'm sorry if I caused you and your family any pain."

My mouth hung open. Neither of us said anything for a few moments. A girl was chatting on her cell phone nearby. A guy was texting on his phone. Life went on outside of this surreal interaction.

Stewart paused again, as if he had more to say. His face was drawn and sad. His tired eyes sagged. "Have a nice day," he simply said. And he turned and left.

NATE CAME home about a half hour later, and I told him what had happened. He sat on the couch, staring at the floor with his elbows resting on his knees as he listened. When I finished, he shook his head. "If I'd been there, I would have punched the motherfucker in the face."

"It doesn't make any sense," I said. "Why would he tell me this now?"

"Doesn't matter." Nate got up and grabbed his cell phone. "He admitted liability. I'm calling Leventhal."

"He didn't admit liability," I corrected. "All he said was that he was sorry *if* he caused us any pain."

"Still, Leventhal should know about this. Stewart isn't even supposed to be talking to us."

As Nate made the call, I went outside in the backyard. The beautiful day had taken on a different meaning. I used to be the type of person who was able to bite back. I was on the debate team throughout high school. I could zing out a comeback without a thought. But this conversation with Dr. Stewart had thrown me off. I was not prepared to rebut. I'd never imagined I would ever run into him in public, even though we lived in the same town. I walked over to the sandbox and pulled off the plywood cover. As I pulled off my sandals and stepped into the cold, damp sand, I rehashed our conversation over and over again in my mind.

Why? Why would he apologize to me now? Why not three years ago when he pulled Hannah out of me? Why not when I went to the follow-up appointment where he completely forgot who I even was? Why now, after all the doctors' appointments and hospital visits and Misericordia?

If only I could rewind the afternoon and start the scene over. "Don't apologize to me," I would've said. "Hannah's the one whose life you ruined. So I suggest you drive down to the home for disabled children where she's spending the rest of her life strapped to a wheelchair and tell her how sorry you are."

That would've been the appropriate response—the right retort to slap him across the face with. Maybe I would get the chance to say it to his face if I ran into him again. I would be prepared next time. *I'll know exactly what to say.*

~

HANNAH LOVED THE SUN. We took her out for walks around the Misericordia campus whenever the weather was nice so she could turn her head up toward the sky and let the warm sunlight shine down on her face. She didn't seem to mind that it made her squint. Sometimes, I tried putting sunglasses on her, but she would whine and squirm until I took them off. One time, during a walk on a December afternoon, it started snowing. The large flakes floated out of the sky and landed on Hannah's face, on the tip of her nose, her eyelashes. I think a snowflake even fell into her open mouth. She started giggling. It was the first time she'd felt snow on her face.

Abbie Fishman and I took Hannah and Jacob for walks regularly on the weekends. When our husbands didn't come, it was especially nice. As we waited for Abbie and Jacob outside in the courtyard, Hannah faced the sky and laughed at the feel of the heat on her skin. Abbie arrived ten minutes later, pushing Jacob in his wheelchair and carrying a bag of freshly baked cookies from her bakery.

"I gave you a variety." She handed me the bag so she could line up Jacob's chair next to Hannah's. Jacob turned to Hannah and cooed. "I hope you like them."

"Are you kidding?" I grabbed the bag and stuck my nose in for a deep inhale. I pulled out a chocolate chip cookie and bit into it. The gooey chips smudged melted chocolate on my lips. "How are they still warm?"

"I have one of those insulated carriers in the car."

"Genius." I shoved the rest of the cookie into my mouth. "You want one?"

"Please." She held up a hand. "They're all I eat every day."

"Jacob looks good," I said, wiping my mouth with a napkin. "How's he been doing?"

"Okay," Abbie said. Jacob flapped his hands and released a drawn-out, sort of animalistic groan that probably would've sounded disturbing to someone not used to hearing it on a regular basis. To people like Abbie and me, it was a sign that our child is in a talkative mood.

I had called Abbie a few weeks after meeting her on Hannah's first day at Misericordia. She knew how it felt to leave her child behind and let someone else raise him. The first few nights after Hannah was admitted, I woke up in the middle of the night, certain I heard her crying. One night, I even got up from bed and rushed to her crib, only to find it empty. I was about to pull Hannah out of Misericordia and bring her home for good when I called Abbie instead.

"I remember the first month or so after Jacob moved out," she'd said to me. "I slept on the floor in his room. It stilled smelled like him, and I just wanted to be around that. My husband, Jeff, was patient at first, but then he was really annoyed. He told me to either come back to our bedroom or move all my stuff into Jacob's room."

Jacob was three and a half when he moved into Misericordia. He was on the waiting list for only six months, which was very fortunate. We were lucky, too, for only having to wait four months for a place for Hannah. Some people waited for years before a bed opened up. I thought again of the parents of the child who used to sleep in Hannah's bed.

Unlike Hannah, Jacob was not born with cerebral palsy. His story is a terrible twist of fate. He was playing in the family room while Abbie prepared dinner in the kitchen, only one room away. Jacob reached into his toy box for something, and the lid came down on his head, cutting off the oxygen. When Abbie found him, he'd already been unconscious for a couple of minutes.

"One minute, I could hear him playing. The next minute, it

was quiet. I thought he found a book or something. I still blame myself."

"I thought the newer toy boxes were safe."

She raised her eyebrows. "So did we."

Abbie and Jeff also went through a lawsuit. They sued the toy company and won an undisclosed settlement. Even after living through Jacob's accident, Abbie was a strong person. Comparing her tragedy to mine was difficult. She had memories of Jacob when he'd been a healthy little boy, and she'd watched his personality bloom as he toddled around the house and babbled baby gibberish. That was all taken away from her in one crucial moment. I'd only known Hannah one way. I wondered which was worse.

Abbie persevered. She opened her own bakery after making cookies for her older son, Matthew's, fifth birthday party. She'd searched everywhere for a cookie cutter in the shape of Buzz Lightyear, but couldn't find one. So she traced the image of Buzz on a piece of tissue paper, then traced it onto cardboard as a template. She got carried away with the decorating, paying close attention to detail, making the cookies appear professionally made. Everyone raved about them and started placing orders with her after the party.

I envied Abbie. At times, I thought about leaving the advertising business behind and going into something fun. But what? I didn't know how to do anything but manage promising advertising campaigns.

I pulled out a peanut butter cookie in the shape of a tulip and bit into it, mumbling about not wanting to go back to work tomorrow.

Abbie brushed away a leaf that had fallen from a nearby tree on to Jacob's shoulder. "One of these days, when you don't have a freelance project, come into the bakery with me. It'll be a nice change for you."

"The only cookies I know how to bake are from a refrigerated roll."

"I'll teach you. It's a great distraction." Jacob started coughing, and she got up and patted his chest, soothing him until he settled down. "If you could do anything you wanted, and money wasn't an option, what would you do?"

Hannah smiled at the sun. Her mouth opened, and she let out a satisfied groan. "I guess I'd volunteer here so I could be with Hannah more often."

"You really think that's a good idea?"

"Why not?"

"I don't know if you could get on with your life if you were here on a regular basis."

"What do you mean get on with my life? She's my daughter. I'm supposed to be with her on a regular basis."

Abbie held up a hand. "I understand what you're saying. You know that. I just mean that if you were here every day or every other day, you'd become obsessed with every little thing going on with Hannah. I know because it almost happened to me. In the beginning, I'd call Misericordia twice a day, every day, checking up on Jacob. Did he have a fever? How was his breathing? Did he poop today? This was before I started the business, so I'd drive down and see him two or three times a week, sometimes more. And sometimes, his color looked off, so I thought he wasn't getting any oxygen. Sometimes, I'd think his breathing was more labored than it should be. Or he looked uncomfortable, so I'd shift his position in his bed. Claire, thank God, was so patient with me. For several weeks, this went on. Then one day, she pulled me aside and gently told me to back off."

I raised my eyebrows. "Back off?"

"She told me I would drive myself crazy and drive my husband away if I kept this up. Jacob was in good hands with professionals. You have to know when to let go. You can't be around them twenty-four/seven. You can't keep an eye on every-thing they do." Her voice trailed off, and she grew quiet.

I knew what she was trying to tell me. But she sounded as if she were talking about someone whose child had died. Yet

Hannah was sitting right in front of me. I reached over and gently pulled her head up, which had dropped forward. I got up and adjusted her wheelchair so her head would fall back in the head-rest and she could face the sun.

Hannah was still alive, and I was still her mother.

I CAME home to find Caroline in her room, wearing the midnight-blue halter dress she'd worn to my cousin's wedding the summer before. She was standing in front of the full-length mirror, turning each way to check out the dress.

"What are you doing, honey?"

She briefly made eye contact with me in the mirror. "Brody asked me to the homecoming dance."

"Really? That's wonderful."

"I thought I'd wear this dress instead of spending money on a new one."

"Don't be ridiculous. Let's buy you a new one. I think you wore that one twice already before."

"No, I think I only wore it once. To Samantha's wedding."

"And you wore it to Tom and Christie's wedding, too." I sat on her bed.

"Oh, yeah," she said. "I guess it would be nice to wear a new dress." And then she looked at herself in the mirror and smiled.

I hadn't seen her smile in so long. After Hannah was born, our lives were consumed with Hannah's needs. Even after she moved to Misericordia, we were always interrupted by phone calls from Claire, telling us Hannah had been having seizures that day and they had increased the dosage of Phenobarbital, or she was having a severe asthma attack and had been put on oxygen, or she was running a high fever. Once, they had to rush her to the hospital because she wasn't breathing and the oxygen hadn't helped. We depended so much on Caroline to understand.

Every night, before I went to bed, I called Misericordia to see how Hannah was doing. I sensed that the staff was annoyed by my persistence. Even Nate questioned why I had to call every single night.

I recalled Abbie's words that afternoon. Hannah wasn't mine anymore. She was the responsibility of the staff at Misericordia. They changed her diapers, fed her, administered her meds, talked to her, held her, and rocked her to sleep. She didn't need me anymore. That phone call every night let me hold on to that last piece, the only opportunity I had to be her mother.

I watched my oldest daughter standing in front of the mirror, looking at her reflection with so much hope in her eyes.

That afternoon, I took Caroline to the mall, where she tried on dozens of dresses at four different stores, until finally, we both fell in love with a strapless pale-pink tulle dress. Caroline looked like an angel in it. The color brought out the pink undertones of her luminous skin. We picked out a pair of strappy silver sandals, and I bought her a deep-rose lipstick and blush from the cosmetics counter. It had been a long time since I'd spent quality time with Caroline. She told me more about Brody. Her face lit up as she told me how he was quiet at first, but funny when he opened up. He'd been on the soccer team for three years and didn't have an arrogant bone in his body. Her eyes smiled as she described him and the dance she was so looking forward to.

If only I could have been there to see her go.

Chapter 19

CAROLINE

Courtney and I spent the afternoon before the dance at Salon Millicent, a local salon that had been pampering bored Ferndale housewives since the 1950s. The last time I was at Millicent's was with Mom when I was thirteen, shortly after Hannah was born, for a mother/daughter day of indulgence. It was a way for her to reconnect with her other daughter, the one who didn't need as much attention. I had chosen a bright-pink polish that made my fingertips look as if they could glow in the dark.

The receptionist checked us in and led us to the pedicure stations, where we settled into comfy massage chairs. The knobs kneaded out the tension in my back as my feet soaked in a hot whirlpool tub.

Courtney took a sip of lemon water and let out a satisfied sigh. "Tonight's going to be so much more fun than last year's dance."

"What was wrong with homecoming last year?" I asked. My pedicurist lifted my right foot out of the tub and sloughed off the dead skin with a pumice stone.

"The Oppenheim twins? Please. They were dorks," Courtney said with a wave of her hand.

The year before, Benji and Todd Oppenheim had asked us at the same time. They'd come right up to us in the cafeteria, and Courtney had said yes for both of us. Later, we talked about who was going with whom, since that hadn't been discussed. I wanted to go with Benji. She wanted Todd. But somehow, when we arrived at the dance, it ended up the other way around.

This year, Courtney was going with Brody's friend Travis. She'd given him head in the backseat of his car after his team won their first soccer game. At first, they kept it casual, but it eventually developed into a full-blown relationship wrought with the inevitable drama the two of them were so good at making.

I had been to high school dances before, but this was the first time I was going with someone I really liked. I was especially excited to have Dad take pictures of us in the living room while mom gushed about how pretty I looked in the dress we bought together.

The manicurist painted my toenails a deep burgundy and my fingernails a shade lighter. After getting our hands and feet polished, we waddled over to the hair department, wearing bright yellow disposable flip-flops with tissue woven between our toes. I was due for a trim, but when I sat in the salon chair, I decided I wanted a change. Two hours later, I walked out of Salon Millicent with a layered shoulder-length bob with honey highlights.

I strutted up our driveway as if I were on a runway, my shiny hair bouncing and swinging like in the shampoo commercials. As I headed toward the front door, the garage grumbled open. My parents were rushing into the car.

"Where are you going?" I called out.

They turned to me, both seeming surprised to see me. Mom looked me over, as if she were trying to recognize me. "Misericordia called. Hannah's sick, and they're rushing her to the hospital."

"Is she going to be okay?"

"I'm sure she'll be fine, Care-Bear," Dad said.

"Do you want me to come, too?"

"No, don't be silly." Mom came over to me and kissed me on the cheek, squeezing me tight. "Go to the dance and have a wonderful time tonight. I know how much you were looking forward to it. I love your hair," she added.

"We'll call you later and let you know how she is," Dad said.

Mom called out to me to take lots of pictures as they loaded into the car, and the engine started. I stepped aside as they pulled out of the driveway, Mom turned down to her cell phone and Dad waving lamely as he maneuvered the car out of the driveway. I watched as the car disappeared down the street.

The house was still when I walked in and made my way upstairs to the bathroom. I drew a bath and sprinkled some lilac-scented bath flakes under the rushing water. I sat on the edge of the tub and pinned up my newly styled hair then covered it with a shower cap. The mountain of bubbles grew, its peak reaching the top of the faucet. I shut off the water and stepped into the hot bath, lowering myself underneath the blanket of bubbles until it reached my chin. I closed my eyes and inhaled the lilac scent, hoping the heat that enveloped me would alleviate the pain pressing on my chest.

I tried not to think about Hannah being rushed to the hospital, gazing at the unfamiliar faces trying to keep her alive. Instead, I imagined Brody in a suit, standing in our doorway, holding a corsage. I pictured him slipping the flowers onto my wrist as my parents took pictures. Only it wasn't going to happen that way. The image of Brody morphed into Hannah.

The night ahead didn't seem so exciting anymore. Everything felt trivial—the new dress, my highlighted hair, slow dancing in Brody's arms. What was the point of it all?

My cell phone rang from the other room. I sank deeper in the tub and closed my eyes until it stopped. I needed to get to a place where I could still enjoy myself at the dance without punishing myself. After fifteen minutes, I got out of the tub, wrapped myself in a terrycloth robe, and went to my room to find my cell. The little envelope flashed on the screen, and I hoped it was a message from Mom or Dad, telling me not to worry and to have a great time, reassuring me that I deserved it. But it was Courtney reminding me to bring my camera because hers was broken. I deleted the message and threw the phone on my bed. For several minutes, I sat at the edge of my bed in my bathrobe. It was only four o'clock. I had plenty of time to call Brody and cancel. He would understand. But then what would I do? Stay home and worry, waiting for my parents to come back? They might not be home for a while; they might even stay at the hospital all night.

I rested my face in my hands. If I went to the dance, I would feel as though I were disappointing my parents. If I skipped the dance, I would disappoint Brody and Courtney. I had no way of getting down to the hospital, and I wasn't even sure which hospital she was at.

I sat on my bed and stewed for an hour, weighing the pros and cons.

Finally, I stood up, unpinned my hair, and slipped into the dress. I strapped on the silver sandals with two-inch heels, and my freshly polished toenails shined like rubies. I dumped the contents of the small shopping bag onto my bed, removing each new cosmetic from its black box. I dipped a brush into the eye shadow, tapped off the excess, just as the saleswoman had taught me, and swept the dark silvery-grey color across my lids. I applied the black gel eyeliner in perfectly straight lines above my lashes. I brushed on mascara and swept the nude lipstick over my lips. I skipped the blush that Mom had insisted on buying me.

After I was done, I stood in front of the full-length mirror like I had done many times before. But this time, I didn't see the awkward body, the frizzy unmanageable hair, or the bland face. My skin glowed from the spray-on tan. My hair was smooth and polished. The fresh makeup made my hazel eyes pop. I smiled at my image in the mirror.

Brody arrived at seven o'clock sharp. I double-checked to make sure I had everything I needed in my tiny evening purse—

license, lipstick, compact, camera, cash—then went downstairs to answer the door.

He was standing on the stoop, holding a corsage in a clear plastic container, just as I had imagined, except my parents weren't standing behind me to greet him. He wore a navy-blue suit with a white shirt and burgundy tie. He'd left his hair in all its tousled glory, mixing his dapper style with his laid-back personality. I invited him in, for what, I wasn't sure. No one was home to fuss over us.

"Do you want something to drink before we go?" I asked.

"A glass of water would be great," he said.

I motioned for him to have a seat on the couch as I went to the kitchen and poured us each a glass of water. When I returned carrying two glasses of water and the boutonnière I'd bought earlier that day, Brody was sitting on the loveseat, his elbows resting on his knees, looking at a family picture from last Thanksgiving at Misericordia. Dad and Mom were smiling widely. My lips were closed and only slightly turned up at the corners. The three of us were standing around Hannah in her chair. Claire, who'd offered to take the photo for us, managed to get Hannah to open her eyes by snapping her fingers above her head and calling her name. Hannah stared past Claire, her big brown eyes focused on something in the distance, giving her that lost look she always had, as if she were continually searching for answers.

I handed Brody a glass.

"Where are your parents?" he asked.

"They had to leave." I smoothed the skirt of my dress. "My sister's in the hospital."

His eyes widened. "Is she all right?"

"She had trouble breathing. It happens every once in a while. Her lungs are weak."

"Oh." He put the glass down on the coffee table. "Are you still up for going to the dance? Because if not, I totally understand."

"No, no." I held out my hands to show my completed look. "I'm all set to go. My parents are going to call me later to give me an update. They insisted that I have a good time tonight." I hoped I sounded convincing.

Brody stood up and popped open the plastic container. He took out a bouquet of red and white roses fastened to an elastic band and slipped it on my wrist. Then I pinned the boutonnière of white roses to his lapel. We laughed at the silliness of it all, standing alone in the living room, no over-enthusiastic parents endlessly snapping photographs. I took a long whiff of the corsage on my wrist, inhaling the tingly sweet scent. Then I sneezed.

THE HOMECOMING COMMITTEE had overdone it, as usual. The cafeteria where the dance was held exploded with helium-filled balloons in the school colors of red and gold, with ribbons hanging down and matching streamers zigzagging from one corner to the next. I imagined giddy teenaged girls decorating the place, chatting excitedly about their dresses and their cute dates. Brody and I stood in the entrance of the cafeteria, scanning the crowds until we spotted Courtney and Travis over by the drink table.

Courtney greeted me with a hug and compliments. She wore a midnight-blue halter dress with a beaded bodice. Her hair was pulled back in a loose bun with tendrils framing her face, exposing shimmering shoulders. Travis wore a hunter-green jacket over a white shirt and a black tie. He greeted Brody with a handshake and a slap on the shoulder. We stood around the table, drinking already stale pop served in plastic Solo cups, and commented on what people were wearing and the couples on the dance floor. My mind occasionally wandered to Hannah, but each time, I quickly shook her from my mind. We mingled with our classmates. We danced when the DJ played great songs by the Black-Eyed Peas and Beyoncé. Courtney and I snapped random pictures that would undoubtedly end up on Facebook.

When the DJ slowed things down with a cheesy Celine Dion song, we decided to head outside to cool off and have a smoke.

The chilled air was a welcome to our bodies, which radiated heat. Travis pulled out a pack of Winstons and passed it around. We leaned against the wall, smoking, enjoying the silence, and savoring the quiet break from the thump-thump of the music. Brody held his cigarette in front of him, studying it. He took one drag then dropped it on the ground to crush it with his shoe. He wasn't much of a smoker because he played soccer. I thought of Hannah again, and I realized my parents hadn't called from the hospital to let me know how she was. It had to be almost nine o'clock, so they'd been there for hours. I pulled out my cell and dialed Mom. The phone rang six times before she picked up. I stepped away for some privacy.

"Oh, hi, sweetie. We were just going to call you," she said. "How's the dance?"

"Fine," I dug the toe of my sandal into the gravel. "How's Hannah?"

"She's doing a little better. They gave her a treatment, and they have her on oxygen. I'm going to stay here tonight. Dad's coming home."

"Okay." The encouraging words were supposed to make me feel better. "What hospital is she at?"

"Rush Presbyterian," she said. "Are you having a nice time?"

"Yeah." I noticed Brody watching me. "Yeah, the DJ is playing really cool music, everyone looks nice..."

"Well, Dad said he won't wait up for you, so have fun."

After hanging up, I stood for a moment staring out at the half-empty parking lot. The straps from my new shoes were digging into my ankles, and the cigarette had given me a headache.

Brody came up behind me and rested his hands on my shoulders. "How's Hannah?"

"She's doing better."

"Good to hear."

"Yeah," I said tentatively.

"Are you okay?"

I brushed it off with a light laugh. "It's fine, really." We walked back toward Courtney and Travis, who by then were smoking a joint. Courtney took a long pull and held it out to me. I shook my head.

"You don't want any?" She sounded surprised.

"No, not tonight." Usually, a little pot eased the conflicts on my mind. That night should've been perfect for a little weed. But I wasn't in the mood. Courtney held out the joint to Brody, who also refused.

Courtney and Travis walked toward a crowd mingling by the front entrance. I scanned for a place to sit and decided that the curb was clean enough.

"Hold on," Brody took off his jacket and laid it on the curb.

"Thanks." I motioned for him to sit next to me.

We sat quietly for a few moments, watching the others mingle, hearing the bass of the music that the DJ had sped up again. Over by a row of classroom windows, Giselle Flores was hunched over, puking, as Jett Krusinski, her patient date, held her hair back. There must have been a pre-party somewhere. *She's going to feel like shit tomorrow*, I thought. *I wonder how Hannah's going to feel tomorrow.*

"What are you thinking about?" Brody wrapped an arm around me.

"Nothing." I rested my head on his shoulder, content with just sitting with him, watching everyone else's night progress.

He turned to me. "Why don't we skip Akemi. We can go visit your sister instead?"

I'd been wanting to go to the trendy sushi restaurant in the heart of downtown Chicago since it had opened a few years ago. I shook my head. "No, that's okay. I'll be fine."

"What hospital is she staying at?"

"Rush Presbyterian. It's all the way on the west side."

He thought for a moment, then pulled out his cell phone and dialed a number. "I have a reservation for ten o'clock for two. Can we move that to eleven? Great, thanks." He snapped the phone shut. "Done."

"Brody..."

"We'll stop by the hospital. It's not far from the restaurant. You can say hi to your sister, then we'll go to dinner."

The compassion in his voice brought tears to my eyes. He had never met Hannah, and I was a little hesitant about taking him to see her. I wasn't sure if I was ready for him to meet her or if he was ready to meet her. Seeing kids like Hannah can be uncomfortable to some people. And this was supposed to be a fun night for both of us. It wasn't supposed to include him driving me to a hospital. I dropped my head and sobbed as Brody rested his hand on my back. I reached into my purse for a tissue and dabbed at the tears on my cheeks.

"I'm sorry," Brody said. "I thought maybe if you got to see your sister, you'd be able to have a better time."

I wiped my nose. "I'm sorry, too, that I'm such a shitty date."

"No, that's not what I meant." For a moment, he seemed frustrated. "I can see how unhappy you are. You probably wanted your parents to be home for you tonight. And now your sister's sick..."

"Thanks for understanding."

He looked at me with a smile. "So, how about a road trip to Rush Presbyterian? Sounds like fun?"

I laughed as he stood up and held out his hand to help me up from the curb.

WE ARRIVED at the hospital and went straight up to Room 515. Brody said he'd wait in the waiting area. "Take your time," he said.

The door was open a crack. I pushed it open a little more for a peek inside the dark room before entering. Mom was sitting on a cot covered with a sheet and a blanket, watching a show on the TV that hung from the ceiling. I startled her when I walked in.

"Caroline, what are you doing here?" she whispered.

"I wanted to see Hannah."

"You didn't have to leave your date for that, honey." She got up and pulled me into a hug.

"I didn't. He drove me down."

"He's here?"

I nodded. "He's waiting outside." I leaned over Hannah, who was sound asleep, and gave her a light kiss on the cheek. The straps of the oxygen mask left red indentations across her face. I tried repositioning the mask to make it more comfortable, but it didn't seem to make a difference.

"You look beautiful," Mom said, speaking a little louder.

"Thanks," I said.

"You just missed Dad. He left about twenty minutes ago." She cleared some magazines and her purse off a chair for me to sit.

Hannah took a deep breath and made clicking noises with her tongue, then stretched her arms and opened her eyes. The oxygen mask shifted against her face. She gazed up at the ceiling and smiled. It amazed me that she always had something to smile about. She lay in her bed every day, blissfully ignorant of the cards that she'd been dealt. She accepted her fate. Maybe we could all learn something from her.

"Did you have a nice time at the dance?" Mom asked.

I nodded.

"You smell like smoke. How many cigarettes did you have?"

"Just one." Mom knew I had picked up the habit. She tried lecturing me on the health hazards of tobacco, but she quickly gave up, focusing her attention on more pressing issues in her life.

"What about pot?" She eyed me.

I shook my head. I straightened my skirt then fidgeted with the ring on my index finger.

"I'm sorry I wasn't there tonight when he came to pick you up. I had the camera ready and everything."

I remembered seeing Dad's digital camera sitting on the kitchen table, but I hadn't given it a second thought. It didn't even dawn on me that it was there to capture my homecoming moments.

"What did the doctors say?" I asked.

Mom inhaled deeply as she looked down at Hannah. "It's pneumonia."

I pulled up a chair next to her bed, leaned in close, and rested my hand on hers. It was so peaceful in the room listening to the tiny noises coming from Hannah. A faint sigh. A gurgle from her stomach. We sat in silence for about half an hour, then Mom told me I shouldn't let Brody wait too long and to go have a nice dinner. She gave me a long hug, then stood back, resting her hands on my shoulders. "Your hair looks really nice. When did you decide to get highlights?"

"I've been thinking about it for a while," I said with a shrug.

I gave Hannah a few kisses on her forehead. She opened her eyes and giggled.

Chapter 20

JILLIAN

The day of Caroline's homecoming dance, I indulged. For breakfast, I made French toast with challah bread. For lunch, I had a gourmet sub sandwich. By two in the afternoon, all the gluten had brought on a terrible headache. I wanted to be rested and pain free when Caroline got home so that I could help her get ready for the dance, so I took two ibuprofen and lay down with the satin lavender-scented eye pillow over my eyes to take a brief nap. Just as I was dozing off, the telephone jolted me awake. I ignored it, expecting Nathan to answer it. He finally did, after the fourth ring, and a minute later, he was standing in the doorway. "Hannah's sick. They're taking her to the hospital."

I bolted up, the eye pillow tumbling to my lap. *Hospital? It's that bad already?* We were out the door in minutes, passing Caroline on the way. I quickly apologized for leaving her on homecoming.

Here we go again, I thought as we raced to Rush Presbyterian. After an X-ray in the ER showed Hannah's lungs were almost completely full, the doctors admitted her. They set up a cot in her room so one of us could stay with her.

"She may have an infection, and her body may not be strong enough to fight it," the doctor told us.

We went through the usual motions. Trading nights sleeping on a cot. Calling the nurse when Hannah needed another albuterol treatment. Watching her temperature rise and fall. The entire time, the words of that other doctor rang in my head: *Babies born with complications like Hannah don't usually live past the age of six.*

This time, was it really the end?

By Tuesday, her breathing had improved, her lungs had cleared, and her fever had broken, so she was released from the hospital. Nate went back to work. I rode in the ambulance that transported her back to Misericordia and got her settled back into her routine. Claire greeted us from down the hall as I pushed Hannah in her wheelchair.

"Well, look who's back!" she called out, her deep voice echoing off the hardwood floors. She was seated in front of Jacob, feeding him pureed food with a baby spoon. "We missed you, Miss Hannah. You need to stop scaring us like this."

I wheeled Hannah up to where they were sitting by the nurse's station and sighed. "I don't know how much more we can take, Hannah-Banana," I said.

"Jacob and Juan have missed you," Claire said. "If she's ready for lunch, her formula's set up in her room."

I wheeled her into her room and put her into bed, resting her on her right side, the side she seemed to tolerate more. Claire came in and hooked up the IV to her nasogastric tube, and before long, the bland formula snaked through the tube, up her nose, and into her stomach like a lifeline. Hannah never had to taste it. She rarely tasted anything. Once in a while, we gave her a taste of a lollipop. We'd rub the candy on her tongue and watched as she tasted the foreign tangy sweetness, her eyes opening wide in wonder at the rare treat. Once, Caroline stuck the whole sucker in Hannah's mouth, and Hannah clamped down on it for dear life. We had to coax her into singing so she would open her mouth and we could pull it out.

As I tucked Hannah into bed, I thought about her latest near-death prognosis. Unlike the other times, I seemed to have held it together through this one. I didn't panic or cry. Nate and I didn't discuss her funeral. Caroline didn't ask if Hannah was going to die. The process of preparing for Hannah's death had become routine for us. What are we supposed to do when the doctors tell us Hannah is going to die? They had been wrong before—many times. But we still had to go through the motions in case they were right this time.

A mother is supposed to cry when she's told her daughter is going to die. She's supposed to coil up into a spiral of grief, misery, and anger. That was how I'd reacted the other times Hannah was gravely ill. I didn't know if I had any energy left in me to cry anymore.

I pulled the covers up to Hannah's shoulders. Her arms bent upward at the elbow, so her hands stuck out from under the blanket. I thought about what life would be like if she died. Would it go back to the way it was before she was born? Would my marriage improve? Would Caroline go back to the spirited girl she used to be? I shook the thoughts from my head. Hannah turned to me as though she were reading my mind.

"None of this is your fault," I whispered to her.

KATE POURED me another vodka and orange juice and handed me the glass. I drank half in three gulps.

"You need to stop beating yourself up over this," Kate said. "You've been through this so many times. You're on autopilot."

I responded with words I'd never thought I would hear myself say. "Maybe I'm ready."

"For what? For Hannah to die?"

I nodded.

"You'll never be ready. You're just preparing yourself for the worst. There's only so much a mother can take." She grabbed the vodka bottle and refilled my glass. "I think you need to go back to work. You need something to fill your days."

"There aren't any freelance jobs available," I said. "I checked."

"What about permanent?"

"I don't want to go back to work permanently. Nate's making a little more money now, so we'll do fine. Plus I want to have the flexibility for Hannah."

"Well, how about volunteering? Somewhere. It doesn't have to be Misericordia. Or I think you should consider working for Abbie."

"Making cookies?"

"Sure. It would be a great creative outlet for you."

I shrugged. I didn't want to think about working or volunteering. I didn't want to plan for the future. I didn't even want to think about what to make for dinner that night. I took another gulp of my cocktail.

"You're a great mother," Kate said. "Everyone knows how important Hannah is to you."

She reached over and touched my arm. And then the tears finally came.

Chapter 21

CAROLINE

I hadn't been to the Stop N Golf since Angela Rodriguez's ninth birthday party when I made a hole in one at the Sears Tower course. On a whim, Brody and I decided to go one Saturday night. We rented our clubs and Easter-egg-colored golf balls and made our way to the first putt.

"I think it's fair to warn you," Brody said with a mocking expression on his adorable face, "I've taken lessons."

"Mini golf lessons? How big of a dork were you as a child?"

"You don't know the half of it." He held out a hand and stood aside. "Ladies first."

I placed a yellow ball on the tee and knelt to review my aim. Once I figured out the proper angle to hit the ball, I positioned myself and swung the club. The ball shot down the tarp toward the clown's giant mouth, hitting him in the lip and bouncing off to the side.

"So close," Brody said. "Step aside and watch how it's done." He placed his green ball on the tee, lined up his club, and tapped the ball with light force. It rolled down the course, into the clown's mouth, and out the back bridge, then came to rest about four inches from the hole. Brody crossed his left foot over his right, leaned on his club, and grinned.

"No hole in one?" I asked.

"Hey, don't feel bad about your weak shot. I'll give you a do-over."

I fetched my ball and set it on the tee. This time, not bothering to line up my shot, I simply tapped it, trying to mimic Brody's move, and the ball sailed down the runway, into the clown's hungry mouth, out through the bridge, and into the hole.

Brody's mouth dropped open. He walked over to the hole where his lonely green ball sat and peered inside.

"And not a single lesson," I said.

We finished playing two rounds of mini golf around ten thirty at night. It was too late for a movie, and we'd eaten hot dogs and pretzels at the concession stand, so we weren't hungry. We were sitting in Brody's parked car watching the cars speed by on Route 27 when he announced he had an idea where to go.

We drove down a remote stretch of Route 27, through Banebury, a village that was still being developed. Acres of farmland that seemed miles away from the big city were now being turned into cookie-cutter subdivisions with oversized homes on tiny plots of land. My mother had once called Banebury a strange town because it didn't have a downtown area, just a bunch of strip malls with chain restaurants and multiplexes along the highway.

Brody turned down a one-lane gravel road lined with tall elms on either side. He drove slowly down the dark road. The headlights illuminated nothing but a gravel lane with patches of weeds sprouting through here and there.

"Where are we?" I asked. The night was mild, so I rolled down the window and listened to the wind blowing through the trees and tires crunching on gravel.

We approached a large iron gate at the foot of the drive. "Good, it's still open," Brody said.

He eased through the gates and parked the car. As I got out of the car, I looked around for a recognizable object. I couldn't see two feet in front of my face.

"Where the hell are we?" I asked again.

"'Hell' is not a good word to say here." He grabbed my hand. The gravel beneath our feet turned into grass as we walked.

As my eyes adjusted, rows of headstones appeared in front of us. "We're in a graveyard?"

"Not just any graveyard. One of the oldest graveyards in Illinois."

"I never even knew this was here."

"It's set far back from the highway." He led me through the rows of headstones. "I like to come here sometimes."

"By yourself?"

"Yeah."

"In the middle of the night?"

"During the day. You should see some of the headstones. Some of them have creepy old pictures on them."

I pulled the pashmina around my shoulders. A soft wind rustled through the leaves. The clouds shifted, and the bright moon came into view, giving me a clearer view of our surroundings.

Brody sat down on the grass and crossed his legs. He motioned for me to sit next to him. I wrapped the pashmina around both of us. "What do you do when you come here by yourself?"

"Think."

"Can't you do that at home?"

He laughed. "It's because it's so quiet and deserted here. These people have been dead for so long, they probably don't have any more living relatives to come visit them. It's so far off the street. It's like being in another world."

I listened but couldn't hear the highway traffic. The cemetery was like our own secret hideaway.

"It's weird. I know," Brody said. "I've been coming here for a couple of years now. It's like a peaceful getaway for me."

As strange as it was, I understood why he found the place peaceful and private.

I wondered how many other girls Brody had brought there.

We sat quietly, enjoying the silence. I lay back on the cool lawn, and Brody did the same. We gazed up at the stars, and I searched for the Big Dipper, like I always did. It reminded me of a hot meal cooking on the stove when Mom used to make dinner—before Hannah.

I heard a car in the distance, inching closer, gradually breaking through the peace. Several doors opened and closed, and laughter interrupted the tranquility. The chuckling got closer, and three teenagers dressed in head-to-toe black materialized from the darkness. They looked momentarily shocked to see us, and a girl jumped back a little at the sight of us.

"Oh," she said. "Hey."

"Hey," Brody said. I waved.

"Didn't know anyone else knew about this place," one of the guys said. He had his fists shoved into the pockets of his leather jacket. His dark hair fell over his right eye like a curtain.

"Thought it was my little secret," Brody said. "Guess not."

The girl wore torn fishnet stockings and combat boots under a denim miniskirt. She nudged the guy next to her. "I think we're interrupting," she said.

"No," I said. "We're just... hanging."

The third guy pulled a baggie from his coat pocket. "Hey, you guys want some weed? Being high and sitting in this place—it's a whole new experience."

It sounded like a great idea to me. I hadn't gotten high in a while. Courtney had even asked me if I was on the wagon.

Brody shook his head. "I'm okay." He turned to me. "You can if you want."

I decided being the only one stoned on a date wasn't a good idea. "No thanks."

The guy shrugged. "Have a good one."

They stumbled into the darkness, and the girl's cackle diminished as they walked farther away.

"So, how come you never smoked pot?" I asked.

He shrugged. "Just never got into drugs. Never had the desire."

I lay back down, "Well, it's not for everyone."

"You really could've smoked if you wanted. I wouldn't have cared."

"I haven't smoked in a while," I said. "Maybe a month or two."

He lay back down. Since I could no longer hear the three Goth kids, I wondered how big the cemetery was.

"My dad was a drug addict," he said. His eyes were closed, his arm thrown over his forehead. He said it so nonchalantly that I supposed it wasn't much different than me telling people about Hannah. It didn't bother me any more. She was a part of our life.

"When?" I asked.

"A few years ago, it was really bad."

"What kind of drugs?"

"Not sure. Coke, I think. My parents kept me and my brother out of it as much as they could. He spent a lot of time away from home. He didn't talk much. Looked like shit all the time. He fought with my mom. Pretty much ignored me and my little brother. Then he went away for a while, about a month. Mom said he was taking a break. But I knew he was gone because of his problem, and I wasn't sure if he was coming back. I thought for sure they'd get a divorce. Didn't bother asking Mom because I knew she wouldn't tell me anything."

It reminded me of when Hannah was born. Everyone tried to keep as much from me as they could, not wanting to burden me with worry.

"Then he came back," Brody continued. "Things were a little awkward for a while, but they eventually went back to normal. He seems to be doing okay now. He doesn't like talking about it. So I don't ask."

"What does he do?" I brought my arms up and rested my head in my hands.

"He's an ob-gyn."

"Do you get along with him?"

"Sometimes." He opened his eyes. "I'm a little closer to my mom. But they're both freaks."

I remembered a time when Mom and I were close—before Hannah. Everything changed, all because of Hannah.

"Hey," Brody turned to me. "I want to meet your sister someday."

"You would? Why?"

He shrugged. "She's a huge part of your life. It's like a turning point. My dad's addiction was a turning point for me. Life changes after something bad like that happens."

I still wasn't sure taking him to Misericordia was such a good idea. Courtney came with us one Sunday to visit Hannah. The small children with deformed heads and twisted limbs had shocked her into an awkward silence. She played a little with Hannah, attempting to participate by shaking a rattle in her face and making baby noises, but for the most part, she stood out of the way, feeling noticeably uncomfortable. When we left, she was in tears.

"I don't know, Brody," I said.

"Why not?" He sat up.

"It's hard for some people to see kids like that."

"Like what?"

"Like *that*." I waved a hand for emphasis. "There's this one boy that lives down the hall from Hannah. He was born totally normal until his mother's boyfriend threw him down the stairs when he was three. And Jacob, Hannah's roommate? He was perfectly healthy until the lid on his toy box came down on his head and suffocated him. Now they're living in an institution." I flinched at the word "institution." The staff at Misericordia always advised us not to use that word. Misericordia isn't an institution, like a mental institution, but "a home for people with disabilities." They called it "people first" language. They taught visitors to say, "people with disabilities" instead of "disabled people."

Brody was quiet. He started picking at the dirt on his

sneakers.

I thought about the boys I'd mentioned and what it must have been like for their parents. "You know, as shitty as it was for us with Hannah, I think that when you have a normal child that becomes disabled, in some ways... it may be harder to deal with. One day, your child is walking and talking and playing, and the next day, he's a vegetable."

I wondered what my parents would say if they'd heard me say that. If they thought of it themselves. It's not that we didn't suffer as much as the other families did. But my family had only known Hannah one way: as a severely disabled girl. We never got to see her how she might have been, how she was supposed to be.

I'm not really sure which is worse.

I imagined Brody meeting Hannah for the first time. Would he be visibly uncomfortable like Courtney? Would he wipe the drool from Hannah's chin? Not too many sixteen-year-old guys would drive their girlfriend to see her sister in the hospital during the homecoming dance. Brody was different. His thoughtful nature came out unexpectedly at different times. He filled the void that Courtney and my parents couldn't.

I leaned in and kissed him. The moon disappeared behind the clouds, and we were in the dark again. Brody trailed kisses down my neck as we lay back down on the cool grass. His hand slid up my shirt, and he cupped it over my breast. As I unbuttoned his jeans, I wondered if we were moving too quickly. But I heard Courtney in the back of my mind. *What are you waiting for?* Here I was with a guy who was exactly what I needed in my life. He was the missing piece of my soul. I smiled, thinking how just a few months ago I was learning to masturbate, and now, Brody's dick was inside me.

I wondered if losing my virginity in a cemetery was a mortal sin. But as Brody looked into my eyes, gently thrusting inside me, his breath on my lips, I decided it didn't matter. We were sharing a beautiful thing.

I just hoped it wasn't a Catholic cemetery.

Chapter 22

JILLIAN

Jacob's Crumbles was located in a storefront shop in downtown Lake Bluff. An inviting bay window with a yellow striped awning encouraged passersby to peek inside and watch as Abbie and her staff made the latest batch of creations. A fan installed in the transom above the door blew out the enticing scent of fresh-baked cookies. Inside, the pale-yellow walls were covered with pink, red, and green polka dots the size of silver dollars. Old-fashioned ice cream parlor tables and chairs lined the wall for customers who couldn't wait to eat their goodies at home. The countertop displayed trays of edible artwork: teddy bears, kittens in wicker baskets, rose bouquets tied with ribbon, pink ballet slippers, robots, dinosaurs, and all the latest cartoon characters like SpongeBob SquarePants and Dora the Explorer. My favorite section was the trays full of cookies for the ladies: stilettos, a lipstick case, purses, hats, cell phones, sunglasses, and martini glasses.

Abbie handed me a cookie shaped like a cappuccino cup. "Try this."

I bit into it. "Is it coffee flavored?"

"No. That's what I was thinking. Should the frosting be coffee flavored?" She jotted something down in a notebook on the counter. "Not sure how that'll taste."

The Saturday morning sun was starting to peek over the rooftops. Abbie had invited me to her store to help her bake before she opened up. I believed it was all part of her come-work-for-me plan. She knew I couldn't afford to quit my contract work but said she wanted to show me the process just for fun. She'd taught me how to make the batter for her chocolate sugar cookies. The secret recipe was hidden in a premixed batter that was dumped into a commercial-grade mixer. We added a dozen eggs, a pound of butter, and half a cup of vanilla extract before switching on the engine. I watched the large mixing attachment spin the ingredients together, mesmerized by how they folded into a gooey dough that I wanted to plunge my hands into. While the dough mixed, Abbie pulled out sheets of dough that were already rolled out and ready for cutting and handed me a cookie cutter.

"What is it?" I eyed the rectangular shape with rounded edges.

"It'll be an iPhone," she said. "We've also used that shape to create envelopes for Valentine's Day and Louis Vuitton wallets."

She grabbed another iPhone-shaped cutter, and together, we pressed out shapes from the dough and placed them on Silpat-covered cookie sheets. After filling three trays with two dozen cookies, Abbie shoved them into a large oven. "Now they bake for twenty minutes, and we let them cool for an hour before frosting."

"What do we do while they're cooling?"

Abbie pulled out another two trays of the cappuccino cookies. "We can finish frosting these. I'll give you some of the damaged ones to practice on."

She demonstrated with a piping bag filled with white sugar frosting. She traced the entire cookie, then she switched to pastel-pink icing and covered almost the entire cookie, saving the top edge for the mocha-colored frosting. She handed me some cookies with broken handles and irreparable cracks. With a shaky hand, I piped the white frosting around the edge, creating a broken line that I tried to repair, but it ended up looking jagged. I practiced on some waxed paper, tracing long, thin lines of frosting in circles until I got the hang of it. Then I moved on to a cookie and managed to draw a smooth line around the perimeter. Next I flooded the area with the pink frosting then frosted the top with the mocha icing. For an added touch, I dotted the handle with light-blue polka dots.

"How's that?" I displayed my artwork.

"Hey," Abbie wiped her hands on a towel. "That's great. See? I knew you had the knack for this."

The sugary scent of the warm iPhone cookies in the oven wafted through the room, and we were in the groove of frosting the cappuccino cookies. When I got to a place where I was comfortable enough to frost and chat at the same time, I brought up my last visit with Hannah, three weeks ago, the day she was released from the hospital and I'd taken her back to Misericordia.

"I can't put my finger on it. It's like I'm done." I spread my hands out for effect. "But I don't really know what that means."

Abbie pulled out the iPhone cookies and slid them into the cooling trays. "You're distancing yourself from her because you don't want to feel the pain of losing her. I do the same thing every time Jacob gets sick."

"But why would I want to distance myself from her when she needs me most? I'm her mother."

"It's a defense mechanism," she said. "It's perfectly normal. And her needs are already being met."

It was a harsh statement only parents like Abbie and I could get away with saying out loud. We weren't responsible for our children. The staff at Misericordia was.

I shook my head. "It's not right."

"You need to cut yourself some slack," she said. "You've had to prepare for her death, what, five or six times? And she's only three years old. A person can only take so much."

I flooded six cookies with a mint-green frosting, watching as the icing ran to the white piping around the border, trapped like water in a dam. I felt a pang in my chest. I wanted to go see Hannah that very minute, pull her to me, and ask her for forgiveness and assure her that I didn't want her to die. Losing her would feel like the end for me. I dropped the piping bag and sighed.

"Why don't you take this time to spend some quality time with your other daughter?" Abbie asked.

"What do you mean? I spend quality time with Caroline."

"When was the last time?" She was now copying my idea and adding polka dots to the cups.

"We went shopping for her homecoming dress."

Abbie nodded. "Because she needed a new dress to wear. And how long ago was that? A month?"

"About." I squeezed some frosting onto my finger and licked it off. "We had a nice time that day."

"So why not take her downtown for lunch or shopping along Michigan Avenue? If you're going to take this time to allow yourself some space from Hannah, at least use the time to build your relationship with your other daughter."

Caroline had changed so much since she'd started dating that guy, Brody. On one hand, I worried that she was relying solely on her relationship with him for happiness. Before him, she was sullen and lost. Her pot use was getting heavier. She often came home from school with bloodshot eyes and dilated pupils. But she seemed more content because of Brody. She didn't pick fights with me as much. I couldn't remember the last time I'd seen her stoned. She smiled more often, usually when she was on the phone with him. I hated giving Brody all the credit for her new outlook. How would she handle it if he dumped her? This was her first real boyfriend, and I knew how sensitive she was.

"I haven't been downtown in a long time," I said. "Not since Hannah was..."

Abbie put a hand on my shoulder. "I think you both need some quality time together."

"That is, if Caroline would want to spend some quality time with me."

"What sixteen-year-old girl is going to turn down a trip to the city for shopping and eating out?"

"When it means spending the afternoon with her mother."

"You underestimate her. She wants your attention. She wants to spend time with you."

"How do you know that?"

"Because I went through the same thing with Matthew."

Abbie's older son, Matthew, was nine years old, four years older than Jacob. Abbie told me how his teacher had called a special parent/teacher conference with her and Jeff. Matthew was acting out in class, biting and slapping his classmates. At first, Abbie and Jeff defended their son, believing the behavior was typical for a boy his age. But then the teacher asked if Matthew was getting enough attention at home. Apparently, she knew all about Jacob and what had happened to him.

"It never dawned on me that Matthew was being neglected. It's hard when you have kids with special needs," she said. "You're so focused on them, and you assume that everyone else in your family will understand. But they're kids. They don't understand. They shouldn't have to."

When I got home that afternoon, Caroline was in the kitchen, leaning against the counter and eating a bowl of Froot Loops. "Hey," she said.

"Hi." I dropped my purse and keys on the table. "How was school?"

"Fine."

I opened the fridge and scanned the contents, trying to figure out what to make for dinner. I needed to go grocery shopping.

"So I was thinking," I pulled out a plastic container and pulled back the lid. Leftover sloppy joe meat. I sniffed. It still smelled good enough to finish for supper. "I haven't seen much of you lately. You've been busy with school and Brody. I was thinking we could go downtown one Saturday. Spend some time together."

Caroline looked up from the bowl and blinked. "And do what?"

"I don't know." I popped the container in the microwave and set it to two minutes. "Go shopping at Water Tower? Maybe go to a museum?"

Caroline shoved another spoonful of cereal into her mouth, then placed the bowl and spoon in the sink. The spoon made a loud clink when it hit the stainless steel. "When?"

"How about tomorrow?"

Caroline hesitated. She cocked her head to the right and peered up toward the ceiling. "I can't tomorrow. How about next Saturday?"

"Sure. What are you doing tomorrow?"

"Going to Brody's."

"Again?"

"Yeah," she sneered. "Why?"

"It's fine," I said. "Will you be home for dinner?"

"I doubt it," she said.

She disappeared upstairs. The microwave dinged, and I removed the sloppy joe meat for dinner.

Chapter 23

CAROLINE

The smell of Immaculate Conception Church always brought me back to my childhood, back when I was young enough that my parents would let me lie down in the pew and nap instead of listening to mass. Back then, going to church had meant that afterward we were going to have our traditional Sunday brunch with blueberry pancakes, scrambled eggs, sausage, and bacon. My mom would carry me on her hip as she went up for Communion, and I would open my mouth like a little bird, hoping the priest would place a cracker in my mouth, too. Being Catholic had meant something to me then.

I don't know what compelled me to go to confession Saturday morning. I hadn't gone since the fourth grade when the priest yelled at me for eating Chicken McNuggets on a Friday during Lent. When I first walked in, elderly women fingering their rosary beads dotted the sea of pews, probably begging forgiveness for something harmless like taking the Lord's name in vain. I sat in an empty pew toward the back, looking around at the architectural details that I'd spent hours of my childhood staring at. Like the way the light fixtures on the ceiling resembled an exclamation point. And how I used to think the organ player sat hidden in a secret room behind the giant wall mural. The red vinyl kneelers, now cracked with age, reminded me of the color of Kate's lipstick. I thought about why I never went to church anymore. And what I was doing there that morning.

The last few months, I'd felt a sense of happiness that I hadn't felt in years, relief that started deep inside my heart and spread through my veins. I'd had this contentment since Brody and I began dating, and I didn't want to jinx it.

I didn't regret having sex with Brody. Sharing that with him was beautiful and intimate. But I knew God was watching over me, and sometimes, I wanted to make sure I didn't piss him off. As I got up from the pew and walked to the confessional, I wondered if I was going to get the same priest who had yelled at me for eating the McNuggets.

The confessional door closed behind me with a large bang that bounced off the cathedral ceiling. Inside the tiny dark room were a small screened window and a kneeler. Behind the screen was the slightly obscured face of a young priest with a long nose and a touch of stubble on his chin.

"Good morning," he said.

I knelt, made the sign of the cross, and recited the confessional opening. "Bless me, Father, for I have sinned. It's been... uh... I don't know... four years since my last confession."

"That's a long time," the priest said. "What's on your mind?"

I took a deep breath. *This is a bad idea. What did I think I was going to get out of this? Forgiveness? Absolution? I'm going to be damned to hell.* My parents raised me the best they could in the church, but as I got older, and especially after the Chicken McNuggets incident, I started having doubts. But there I was, sitting opposite a priest, ready to spill it. Maybe I just needed some one to talk to.

"I haven't been getting along with my parents," I said.

"That's understandable. We can't always agree with our parents." His voice was soft and soothing, very different from Father McNuggets.

"They don't seem to understand me." I started picking at the loose skin around my thumbnail.

"They won't always be able to."

"I have a new boyfriend," I blurted, "and he makes me happy. I haven't felt this happy in a long time."

"That's good. What about him makes you so happy?"

I wasn't expecting him to ask me any questions. What did that have to do with confession my sins? I thought for a moment. "He makes me feel good about myself."

"And what else?"

"He makes me feel important. He cares about what I have to say."

"Sounds like he really respects you."

Respect. That was it. He respected me more than anyone else in my life did. More than my parents. More than Courtney. "Yes," I said, "and he loves me. We love each other."

"Love is a strong bond between two people."

"So I slept with him."

The priest skipped a beat. "Oh."

"In a cemetery."

Another beat. "Hmm."

And I'm not sure I'm sorry for it.

"Do you plan on sleeping with him again?"

I bit my lip. If I said no I would be lying. If I said yes, he would damn me to hell right then and there. "I don't know."

"It's understandable to have the desire to share that kind of love with your boyfriend. But you must remember that sex is a sacred thing between a man and woman who have taken the vow of marriage."

"Uh-huh."

"You must try to channel those desires into other passions outside of sex."

"Like what?"

He seemed surprised by the question. "Well, other activities that you can do together as a couple. An activity that can still show your love for each other without having intercourse."

Blow jobs popped into my head, but I don't think that's what he meant.

"Remember that Jesus died for our sins, and when we have these indiscretions, we know how to atone for them. Say three Hail Marys and two Our Fathers."

As I exited the confessional, an old woman wearing a black scarf on her head glared at me as if she'd heard the whole thing. I knew at that point that saying a bunch of prayers wasn't going to change anything. I wasn't going to ask for forgiveness for loving my boyfriend. Lots of teenagers had sex. That didn't make them bad.

I gazed up at the grand altar with the crucifix hanging above, peering down at me, like my conscience. I used to feel intimidated by that crucifix, even though it was supposed to be our God dying on a cross. His face was long and anguished. His eyes were open slightly, as if he were letting us know he wasn't quite dead yet and was still with us, watching over us. How can he really judge me for showing love to the most important guy in my life right now? This is a guy who brought me out of darkness. Who gave me hope as I looked toward the future. Brody makes me want to be a better person. How can that be wrong?

I turned to leave. As I passed the old woman, she glared at me with an expression of disdain, knowing that I was skipping out on saying the penance I'd been assigned. *Kneel and beg God for forgiveness, young lady!* her eyes said.

I smiled and winked at her, then walked out of the church.

I LOVED WATCHING Brody's orgasm face. Right before he climaxed, he rested his damp forehead on the pillow, gave me another thrust or two then lifted his head to the sky as if thanking God. His face never contorted like Courtney says Travis's does or like the hairy actors in the porn we were watching the other day at Zeke's. Instead, his mouth opened slightly, the corners turning up in a subtle grin. His eyes closed, and his expression turned the most tranquil I'd ever seen it, as if he were in another world and another body for a moment.

I slapped my hand over his mouth after he let out a loud groan. "My parents are home," I reminded him.

We were upstairs in my room on a Saturday afternoon. Mom usually didn't like it when we were in my room with the door closed, but we did it anyway. Sometimes, she butted in and knocked on the door, then opened it a crack and stuck her head in. "You know this door is supposed to be open, Caroline," she would nag, and we would leave it open for a few minutes until she went back downstairs, then close it again. This time, I'd shoved my faded yellow wingback chair against the door to buy us a little time if she came knocking.

Brody rolled off me and sighed. "Sorry. But it's your fault."

I turned on my side to meet his face and smiled. Our relationship was going on four months, and we seemed to click in every way possible: physically, mentally, and emotionally. Inside, I was bursting with excitement at the thought of how much things had changed for me. Everything had seemed so bleak not long after Hannah was born, as if I would never experience happiness again.

Brody yawned and scratched his forearm.

I had become a woman. I was no longer an awkward girl trying to find her way. Even my parents noticed the change. They'd gotten used to seeing Brody at my side. When I ran out the door, telling them that I was studying at Brody's, they didn't argue. Even though I never really got any studying done when I was with him, my parents didn't care. My grades held steady. I stopped smoking pot. Maybe that's what my parents liked the most—the positive impact he had on my life.

Since my parents approved of Brody, it was the right time for him to meet Hannah.

~

THE FOLLOWING SATURDAY, Courtney gave me a ride to Brody's house, a comfortable colonial on the other side of town from us. I loved hanging out at Brody's house. We didn't live in a shack or anything. Our house was a decent but boring split-level. But Brody's house was like a luxurious resort, with an indoor pool and a Jacuzzi. His basement was equipped with a fifty-two-inch flat screen and a full bar. Its contents were locked in a cabinet, but Brody had the key. His bedroom was clear across the house from his parents, and he had his own en suite bathroom. He hid bottles of beer behind cans of Coke in the small fridge plugged in next to his desk. And his parents didn't care if we were in his room with the door closed.

I jumped out of Courtney's car and rang the bell at the Stewarts.

"Good morning, Caroline," Mrs. Stewart greeted me. She was dressed in a light-green button-down blouse and dark denim jeans. Her blond hair was pulled back in a high ponytail, and her face was bare. I was used to seeing her in full makeup. She waved me into the foyer. "You're here early for a Saturday. What do you and my son have planned today?"

"Just going for a ride," I said, unsure if Brody had told her we were going down to Chicago to see Hannah. I doubted she would care, though. I wasn't even sure she knew about Hannah.

Brody came down the stairs, fingering the bills in his wallet, which he then stuffed in his back pocket. We ate bagels and lox that was set up on the kitchen island and gulped down French roast before leaving in his mom's navy BMW.

I was supposed to go downtown with my mother for our mother/daughter outing, but I'd blown her off with an excuse that Brody had a family emergency and needed me. I think she bought it.

We drove to Misericordia in forty minutes. I signed us in at the front desk of McAuley, and we took the elevator to the second floor. Brody commented on how nice the place was as we walked down the hallway. It wasn't what I had expected when I'd first visited. Instead of cold, sterile, and bland like a hospital, McAuley was warm, inviting, and tastefully decorated.

Claire looked up from the dresser, where she was putting clothes away, when we walked in. "Caroline! What a surprise to see you. Are your parents here, too?"

"No, just me and my boyfriend." I introduced Brody to Claire. "How's Hannah today?"

"She's a little angel, like always. But this morning, she made a big poop." Claire went back to putting clothes away. "It got all over her clothes, the sheets, the floor. We had to give her a bath and mop up the floor. Jacob cried. He doesn't like the smell."

Hannah was lying on her side in her bed, gazing down, blinking as her eyes shifted back and forth. Her eyes often appeared to be closed when she was really looking down at nothing in particular. I never knew why.

"Hi, pumpkin." I reached through the crib bars and pushed the curls away from her face. "This is my friend, Brody. He came to meet you."

I unlatched the side of the crib and pulled it down. Brody came and stood beside me. He stared at Hannah for a moment—her atrophied muscles, her blank stare, and her twisted hands. Then he leaned down to her. "Pleased to meet you, Hannah." He kissed her right hand like a gentleman greeting a Victorian lady.

Claire suggested that we take Hannah for a walk, so I picked her up and placed her in her wheelchair. The chair tilted back to prevent her from slumping forward, and the seat curved around her body and legs to hold her in place. The chair came with an attachable tray, although Hannah never really needed it since she didn't write or eat on her own. We strapped her in with the multiple seat belts that hung from the chair, then we said goodbye to Claire.

We walked down the hall toward the atrium. A mural of the sky at dusk, including a shooting star and a full moon, was painted on the ceiling. Hannah cooed and smiled as we came to a stop next to the piano. A few other residents were in the room with a couple of caretakers watching over them: Chris, a recent graduate from DePaul, and Shawn, a volunteer with mild autism who can guess what day of the week you were born. They were with David, a resident with cerebral palsy and Tourette's.

"Bullshit!" David screamed.

"David," Chris said, "you know if you swear you don't get to watch *Grease* after dinner."

"Bitch!" he spat.

Shawn approached us when we walked in, and I introduced him to Brody. "When's your birthday?" He pointed at Brody.

"July eighteenth," Brody said.

"What year?"

"Nineteen-ninety-one."

Shawn paused for a second, still pointing, and gazing up at the ceiling as he calculated. "You were born on a Thursday." Then he turned to me. "And you were born—wait, don't tell me—November eleventh, nineteen-ninety-one, on a Monday."

"Wow," Brody said. "That's really cool."

A boy named Mark, another resident on Hannah's floor, steered his motorized wheelchair over to us.

"Hi, Mark," I said. "How's it going?"

"Fine." He held a wrinkled Best Buy catalogue in his hand.

"This is my friend, Brody," I said.

"Hi, Mark," Brody held out his hand, and Mark shook it. "What've you got there? Are you shopping for a new TV?"

"Yes." Mark pointed to a picture of a laptop.

"Do you want to get a new laptop, too?" Brody asked.

"Yes."

"Do you want to write a story on the laptop?"

Mark nodded.

"What do you want to write about?"

Mark pointed to Chris and smiled. Chris laughed. "You want to write about me, buddy? Thanks."

Mark moved on, steering his wheelchair down the hall. "Bye," he called out.

After hanging out in the atrium for a few minutes, we took the elevator down to the hydrotherapy room. I showed Brody the high-tech equipment, including large whirlpools. I pointed out the track that was installed on the ceiling that easily transported the resident from a wheelchair to the pool without having to lift them. Brody asked a lot of questions about the therapy program, but I didn't have a lot of answers.

An hour later, we took Hannah back to her room, right on time for her lunch. We watched as Claire hooked the NG-tube to the bag of formula hung on an IV pole. She adjusted the drip to the right pace so it didn't back up in the tube, and the formula wound its way up Hannah's nose, down her throat, and into her stomach. Hannah sighed with contentment as her belly filled. We bid her *buon appetito*, and I kissed her goodbye.

During the ride home, Brody said very little about his experience visiting Misericordia, except that it was a beautiful place and that Hannah seemed happy living there.

"Makes you think," he said, "how kids like Hannah can be so happy all the time, and how people like us take things for granted."

The following Monday in school, Brody surprised me by asking if we could visit Hannah again the next Saturday. I'd thought he wanted to meet her once, get to know her a little, and to understand a little more about her illness and how she impacted our lives. I wasn't expecting him to want to visit her again so soon.

The following Saturday, at seven in the morning, the sun was barely over the rooftops, and Brody pulled into our driveway.

"Fuck, Brody," I said as I got into the car, carrying a travel mug of coffee. "Why are we going so damn early?"

"I don't want to hit traffic."

"There's no traffic on Saturday morning." I fastened my seat belt.

When we arrived, Hannah was in the multipurpose room with all the other residents. *Toy Story 2* was playing on the DVD player, and each resident was seated in his or her wheelchair, facing the TV. Most of them stared blankly at the walls. Mark was listening to music on his iPod. Jacob dozed in his chair. Hannah sat toward the back, her head slumped down, and a long string of saliva hung down from her mouth. She laughed as I wiped the drool with a bib. Brody suggested we take her for a walk again. We went down to the family room on the first floor. The simple room had grey carpeting, ugly sofas, and a TV with no cable. As I lay the blanket on the floor, Brody lifted Hannah out of her chair and laid her on the blanket. I watched as he talked to her about soccer and his classes at school. Hannah peered up at him from the blanket.

"So I ended up dropping European History," Brody said. "I didn't feel like it was important for me to know about King Henry's reign, you know?"

Hannah smiled as if she understood. Then she jerked forward, curled in a fetal position, and started coughing violently.

Brody turned white. "Should I get someone?"

"It's okay." I knelt on the blanket, picked up Hannah, sat her in my lap, and lifted her arms above her head. Her tummy contracted as she hacked up a blob of greenish mucus. I caught it in the bib and wiped her chin. I thought Brody would be disgusted, but instead, he reached out and took the dirty bib then handed me a clean one that we'd brought along.

"Something went down the wrong way," I said.

Hannah leaned back against my shoulder. Her chest was congested, rising and falling with each labored breath. We took her back upstairs, where Claire could give her a nebulizer treatment. We stood back as she strapped a mask to Hannah's face.

"How long does she have to stay on it?" Brody asked.

"Usually, her daily dose is five minutes every five hours. Depends on how bad her attack is," Claire said. She turned on the oxygen machine, and a cloud of medicated steam filled the mask. Hannah took deep breaths.

Brody asked Claire more specific questions, mostly about Hannah's day-to-day life, like what she ate and what she did when she went downstairs for day training. When he went to use the bathroom, Claire leaned into me. "He's a nice guy. Hope you plan on keeping him."

"I do." I smiled, hoping he was planning the same thing.

Chapter 24

JILLIAN

I spotted a chip on the nail of my right index finger. *Damn nail polish. Salon brand, my ass.* I dug through the small manicure basket I shared with Caroline and pulled out the burgundy OPI nail polish. I shook the bottle then unscrewed the cap. I lightly coated the brush with polish then dotted it on the chip. The ridge wasn't as noticeable. And we were only spending the day downtown, not going to a charity ball.

As it turned out, "next Saturday" didn't work for Caroline. Neither did the Saturday after that. For a couple of weeks, she came up with an excuse that she was busy doing something with Brody. Finally, one Saturday in early November, she was free. I suspected it was because Brody had other plans, but I was going to take it.

I woke up that morning, feeling better than I had in a long time. A day out together was exactly what Caroline and I needed. Besides the time we went shopping for a homecoming dress, we hadn't really seen much of each other. I was ashamed to realize that I had spent more time with Hannah at Misericordia than I had with Caroline, who lived under the same roof that I did. I wanted Caroline to know that I was sorry for neglecting her. I planned on telling her so that day. Maybe during lunch or while we were getting pedicures.

Nate came into the family room. He stood watching me painting my fingernail, and then looked around the room as if he were trying to find something to amuse him. "Where's Caroline?"

"She said she had to go somewhere, but will be right back."

"What kind of errand?"

"I didn't ask."

Nate was still watching me.

"What?" I said, blowing on my index finger.

"Nothing."

I wondered if he wanted to come with us and thought about him tagging along as we walked through Water Tower Place, Nordstrom's , and Bloomingdale's. Usually, his idea of fun was having the house to himself so he could watch old sitcoms all day. But when was the last time the three of us were together?

"Do you want to come with us?" I asked, dropping the nail polish bottle back in the basket.

Nate hesitated. "Nah, you girls go and have your day together. I'll stay here and..."

"And put the Christmas lights out? It's a perfect day to do it before the temperature drops."

Nate made a face and drooped his shoulders.

"Or you can put the plastic up on the porch screens before it snows."

"I guess."

We stood quietly, awkwardly.

"Or," I said, "you can come with your wife and daughter to the city."

"Better than putting up Christmas lights."

"I think it would be good for us to go as a family," I told him. "It's been a long time. We've been focused on Hannah for so long."

"Yeah." He sat down next to me.

I reached over and touched his arm lightly. The act of intimacy between us felt foreign. Maybe Nate and I could use a day alone together, too. We gazed at each other and smiled. The unsaid words between us transmitted through our eye contact.

The back door swung open and Caroline walked into the kitchen, her cell phone to her ear, laughing hysterically.

"No, Courtney, that's not what I meant. Get your mind out of the gutter." She noticed us sitting on the couch in the family room and told Courtney she would call her back. "Is something wrong? Is it Hannah?"

"No, nothing's wrong," I said.

"Why are you guys sitting there with the TV off, holding hands? You're freaking me out."

I stood up and walked to the kitchen. "Dad's coming with us. I know we talked about having a mother/daughter day, but I thought it would be great if the three of us went together. We can have pizza at Gino's East. Maybe go to Navy Pier?"

Caroline looked from me to Nate, then down at her shoes. "Oh."

"Hey, Care-Bear," Nate said. "If you really wanted this time alone with Mom, I understand. We could do it another time."

"No," she said. "Maybe you two need some time alone. I don't mind."

"What do you mean?" I asked.

"I mean, you and Dad. Why don't you two go? When was the last time you had a date?"

"Don't be silly," I said. "We want to do this together. We had this planned for weeks."

"I know, but I wouldn't mind if you wanted some couple time."

I focused on her. *She's bailing on us. On me.* "Caroline, do you not want to go?" I asked. "What is it this time? Another family emergency with Brody?"

"No," she said. "He called and wants me to help him study for his science test, and —"

"Study? Since when do you study on a Saturday afternoon?"

"He's got a test on Monday."

"Science isn't even your best subject. I doubt you'd be any help."

Caroline rolled her eyes.

"You saw Brody last night," I went on. "You see him every day in school. Not to mention every Saturday."

"Jillian," Nate said.

"Nate, please." I turned back to Caroline. "I was really looking forward to this, and I think it's important for us to spend some family time together."

"Family time?" Caroline laughed. "When was the last time we had family time? When I was, like, seven?" Her cell phone beeped, and she turned away from me to read a text and punch in a response.

Usually, I would've understood her wanting to dump us for Brody. What teenage girl wouldn't rather spend her Saturday with her boyfriend than her parents? But for some reason, on the day that was supposed to be our day, the thought of her brushing me off for that boy was like a slap in the face. "We're going," I said. "We're leaving in ten minutes."

Caroline sneered at me. "Great. Can't wait for a day of fun with the Moore family." She went back to texting.

The tension in the car ride was palpable. I tried to make conversation, asking Caroline about Brody and school. Her answers were terse. When Nate exited onto the Ohio Street ramp, I turned to her. "Do me a favor, Caroline. At least pretend like you're having a good time. It's only a few hours out of your busy life."

Nate parked in a garage on Erie Street by Northwestern Memorial, and we walked to Michigan Avenue, where Christmas lights already hung in the trees lining the median. The sidewalks were packed with people who had the same idea we did: spend a mild Saturday in November downtown.

We went to the Cheesecake Factory for lunch. Caroline spent the half-hour wait with her nose to her phone, texting. I waited until she snapped the phone shut, then reached out and grabbed it from her.

"What the hell?" Her face twisted in annoyance.

"You've been on it all morning," I said, dropping the phone into my purse.

"I'm waiting for a call."

"That's what voice mail is for," I said. "You can have it back after lunch."

Caroline folded her arms and mumbled something under her breath that I didn't care to hear. She turned to her dad, hoping he would side with her.

Nate pulled her into his arms. "Hey, Care-Bear, remember when you were little, and we went to Cheesecake Factory at Old Orchard? And you asked us if you could have cheesecake for lunch and dessert?"

"No." She pushed away from him after a brief embrace.

"Sure you do. I think it was your birthday."

"No," I said. "She had gotten a gold star on her report about the Great Chicago Fire."

"Oh, yeah. Great memory, Jilly." He turned back to Caroline. "You worked so hard on that report. So we decided, probably against our better judgment, to let you eat cheesecake for lunch. I think you ordered the Oreo cheesecake."

The corners of her mouth turned up in a reluctant smile. "It was the Snickers cheesecake."

"Snickers? Oh. Well, maybe I ordered the Oreo."

"You did," Caroline said, "for dessert. And I had the pumpkin pie cheesecake for dessert. And I think we brought home a whole mixed berry cheesecake."

"What kind of cheesecake do you want today?" Nate asked.

She made a face. "I don't know, Dad. It's too fattening."

The pager went off in my hand, indicating that our table was ready, and the hostess led us through the large dining room packed with tourists and suburbanites to a cozy corner booth just big enough for the three of us. We said nothing as we perused the menus, as though we didn't want to jinx the newfound peace by continuing the conversation. Then Nate closed his menu. "I'm getting the Reuben."

"Your cholesterol is too high," I said. "You should get something lighter. How about the turkey club?"

"I've been good lately," he said. "I've had salads for lunch every day this week. One Reuben isn't going to hurt me."

"You know how much cholesterol is in one Reuben," I said.

"Jesus, Mom," Caroline snapped, "let him get the fucking Reuben."

Another awkward silence followed. The waitress arrived and took our orders. After she left, no one said a word for a couple of minutes. Then Nate spoke.

"So, Care-bear, how's Brody?"

"He's fine," Caroline said.

Nate held out his hands. "What does he like to do?"

"Play soccer."

"That's cool. Is he any good?"

She shrugged. "He's okay, I guess."

"What else does he like?"

Caroline sighed and took a sip of water. "I don't know. Listening to music? Going to the movies? Typical teenage stuff."

Nate took the hint and stopped asking mundane questions. The waitress brought our drinks, and Caroline took a sip of her Diet Coke.

"We've been going down to visit Hannah on Saturdays," she said.

Nate raised his eyebrows. "You and Brody?"

"Yeah."

"You've been visiting Hannah?" I asked. "I didn't know that. Why didn't you tell us?"

"I don't know. I didn't think of it." She twisted the straw wrapper around her finger, pulling it tight until the tip of her finger turned a deep red. "Anyway, he likes Misericordia. What the caretakers do. The therapists." As she spoke, her clenched facial muscles loosened.

"That's wonderful," I said. "You know, you and Brody can come with us on Sundays, too, if you want."

"Maybe," she replied, which was code for, "No frickin' way."

The waitress brought our orders. Nate dug into his Reuben, and Caroline shoveled forkfuls of Cobb salad into her mouth. I was suddenly not hungry for my turkey club and only took a few forced bites.

After lunch, we headed to Water Tower Place. I'd given Caroline her phone back after lunch, as promised, so she trailed behind us, her head down at the keyboard. I asked her if she wanted to stop at Express.

"Fine," she said. So we merged with a continuous stream of people taking the escalators and traveled up to the fifth floor of the shopping mall. The halls were decked with red poinsettias and fake Christmas trees.

At Express, I tried to coax Caroline out of her texting stupor by pulling out cute dresses and tops for her to try on. She disappeared into the dressing room a few times to try on some outfits, and if anything, I came away with a few ideas for Christmas gifts. Nate sat patiently on a sofa right outside the dressing rooms that was probably put there for the sole purpose of giving men a place to wait. I took a seat next to him, and we provided commentary on each outfit Caroline had on when she came out of the dressing room. I thought about the girl she had been a few years before, shortly after Hannah was born: the sullen and withdrawn girl who'd had no one to turn to during a crucial point in her life and the daughter I had neglected to notice because I was too preoccupied with my other daughter.

But as I watched her turn in front of the three-way mirror, ignoring our compliments, I saw the person she had become. When she'd first started high school, I had hoped that a new school with new friends would be a good change for her and draw her out of her shell. But she had become more withdrawn once she started smoking marijuana. When I confronted her about it, she denied everything. I tried reaching out to her, but she pushed me further away. She was already gone. She'd already moved on from needing me, leaving me to deal with Hannah and not worry about her, insisting that she didn't need me anymore and could take care of herself. Nate had advised me to leave her alone. "She'll come to us when she needs to," he'd said. So I let her be. But I always kept one eye on her.

It occurred to me as I sat in Express that even though she continued to act as though she was doing us a favor by spending the day with us, she was happier and more confident than I had ever seen her. I guess I had to give some credit to the new man in her life.

Chapter 25

CAROLINE

Visiting Hannah on Saturdays became a regular activity for Brody and me. Each time we went, he spent some time talking with Claire and the other CNAs and therapists. He asked questions about the therapies, how things worked, and who did what. At that point, he knew more about Misericordia than I did. He was even becoming good friends with Chris, anotherC CNA.

Once, I saw Brody talking to Chris and Eugenia, the Director of Services.

"What was that all about?" I asked when Brody walked back over to where I was sitting with Hannah.

"I was talking to her about volunteering. She told me to come in next Saturday for an interview."

"Here?"

"Yeah." He smiled. "Isn't it great? I can work with kids like Hannah."

It all made sense, looking back on the last few weeks. Brody always stopped to say "Hi" to each kid as we walked down the hall. He struck up conversations with the administrators. He was getting to know the staff more than I was.

"Really?" I said. "What made you decide this?"

"Something I've been thinking about for a while now. Coming here made me see it more clearly. I'm thinking about becoming a therapist. Not sure what kind yet, but I'd love to find a way to work with these kids. Maybe as a physical therapist, or massage therapist, or maybe a CNA like Claire."

Hannah's head slumped forward, so Brody gently pulled it up and adjusted her seat so she could lean back.

"I've already talked to my guidance counselor about colleges that have therapy programs," he said. "University of Illinois has a good one."

I envied his ambition. Unlike him, I had no direction. I had no clue what I wanted to do with my life. I was almost seventeen. How was I supposed to know what I wanted to do for the rest of my life? I knew people who had graduated college and still wondered what they should do next. Courtney wanted to be a teacher. I think Travis had said something about going to law school and then running for office.

But me? I couldn't work with kids with disabilities. The thought of changing their diapers disturbed me. When Claire changed Hannah's diaper, Dad and I usually left the room while Mom stayed behind to help. I didn't want to see Hannah lying there like a slug while Claire wiped her ass. And it would only get worse as she got older and started sprouting pubes.

I pictured Brody at Misericordia a couple days a week, playing with the residents, taking them for walks, talking with them about their day. He would probably see Hannah more than I would. He might even run into my parents on Sundays. Thinking of him becoming that close to a place that was a big part of my family felt strange. But it felt as though he was officially becoming part of our family, too.

Hannah's leg started to spasm. The heel of her loafer tapped against the footrest of her wheelchair, making her knee tremble as though she were nervous. Brody reached out, wrapped both hands around her calf, and gently squeezed until her leg relaxed. I'd seen Claire and my mother do the same thing.

"How did you know to do that?" I asked him.

He just looked at me and shrugged.

Chapter 26

JILLIAN

I filled two travel mugs with coffee. "Nate," I called up the stairs. "Are you almost ready? I don't want to hit traffic."

I heard steps coming down the stairs, but I could tell they weren't from Nate's heavy gait. Caroline walked in, fully dressed in tight jeans and a heather-grey T-shirt. Her hair was pulled back in a ponytail, and her face was freshly done in minimal makeup. She went to the cabinet, pulled out another travel mug, and filled it with coffee.

"Where are you going so early on a Sunday?" I asked.

Caroline added three tablespoons of sugar and about a quarter cup of cream to her coffee. "With you to see Hannah."

"Oh." I screwed the tops on the mugs. Lately, Caroline hadn't been joining us on Sundays to see Hannah since she'd been going on Saturdays with Brody. "Didn't you and Brody visit Hannah yesterday?"

"No." She pulled a protein bar from the pantry and unwrapped it. "He's going to be there today. He's volunteering there now." She took a bite and munched on the granola and almonds.

"Brody is volunteering at Misericordia? Since when?"

"Since last week."

"What kind of work will he be doing?"

"Um…" She took another bite. "Visiting with the kids. Playing with them. Whatever they need him to do."

"What made him decide to do this?"

"He wants to be a therapist." She crumpled the protein bar wrapper and threw it in the trash. It bounced off the side and landed on the floor in front of the garbage can. She ignored it.

Nate came into the kitchen. "Coffee ready? Hey, Care-Bear." He kissed her on the top of her head.

"Caroline's coming with us today," I said. "Brody started volunteering there last week."

"Really," Nate said. "Is he volunteering today?"

"Of course. That's why she's coming, Nate." I handed him his travel mug.

"That's not the only reason I'm coming," Caroline said as we filed into the garage. "I want to see my sister."

I doubted very much that she would have gone with us had Brody not been volunteering, but I wasn't about to start an argument.

We arrived at Misericordia just as Hannah was finishing the last few drops of her breakfast. Claire had dressed her in a pink terrycloth sweat suit, and Hannah's hair was still damp from her morning bath. Dark braids hung down on each side of her face.

"Hannah," I sang, trying to stimulate her so that she would open her eyes. "It's Mamma."

"Hannah-Banana," Nate said. "You look so pretty today."

Hannah stretched and yawned, so unimpressed that we were visiting.

Caroline reached out and touched Hannah's arm. "Hey, baby girl."

With that touch, Hannah lifted her chin, and her eyes opened wide. Her dark brown irises looked like cocoa in the sunlight coming through the window. I leaned down and gave her kisses on her cheek, her nose, and her mouth. She giggled.

"Hiya, Mr. and Mrs. M." Claire came in and unhooked the

feeding tube. "Our girl is doin' fine this morning. She woke up early and started singing. Woke up Jacob and Juan, and they were not happy."

Singing was yet another characteristic of a person with cerebral palsy. Hannah, in her own way of communicating, would take a deep breath, open her mouth wide, and belt out a drawn-out moan. One time, when Hannah was about twenty months old, we brought her home for Easter weekend and took her to church dressed in a sunny pastel dress and a frilly bonnet, just like all the other toddlers. Opting to leave the wheelchair at home, I held Hannah during the service. We blended with the other families celebrating the holiday together. Hannah fell asleep shortly after mass began, resting her head on my shoulder. Then the choir started singing a hymn. Hannah stirred. She opened her eyes, listening to the organ notes bouncing off the cathedral ceiling. She smiled, opened her mouth wide, and hollered along with the choir, actually in tune with the music. Regardless, people turned to stare at us. Caroline slumped in her seat. Nate told me to stick a pacifier in her mouth. She continued singing even after the choir finished, like a soloist. The priest resumed speaking, but Hannah's voice overpowered him. I tried to get her to take her pacifier, but she kept spitting it out as she continued to bellow her own personal tune. We ended up leaving church halfway through the service. That was the last time we ever took Hannah to church.

After Claire unhooked the feeding tube, we wheeled Hannah to the family room on the first floor. On our way to the elevator, we met Brody at the nurses' station.

He greeted us and kissed Hannah on her forehead. He wore a lanyard around his neck with a pass that identified him as a volunteer. Caroline immediately gravitated toward him like a magnet and pulled him into a hug. I asked him how he liked volunteering.

"I love it." His face lit up as he spoke, and he reached out and tousled Hannah's hair. She grinned up at him. "Hannah was the first person I hung out with."

"What else have you done?" I asked.

"I took Samantha for a walk, then we sat and listened to Scott play the piano. And I played cards with Mark. He beat me three times at Go Fish."

"It's wonderful that you're doing this," I said. "Caroline, how come you haven't thought about volunteering here?"

She responded with a sigh and rolled her eyes.

Chapter 27

CAROLINE

I took each step slowly as I held two plastic cups filled to the rim with beer in each hand. I weaved through the throng of people who had already gathered in Zeke's basement. My buzz was already at its peak: the moment where I'd had enough alcohol to reach that level of euphoria but was still coherent enough to have a great time. To keep the buzz level, I needed to keep drinking but slowly enough to avoid going over the edge into a drunken stupor that would ruin the whole night.

Second semester had begun. The holiday season in the Moore household had come and gone without a ton of drama. In fact, my mother and I had gotten along better than we had in months. I thought it was because she'd gotten to know Brody and knew how important he was to me. She often asked how Brody was doing and if he still liked volunteering at Misericordia. She'd even invited him over for dinner a couple of times. I didn't really care what she thought, though. I would have stayed with Brody even if she didn't like him. But having her on my side made it a lot easier. I didn't have the urge to push her buttons as much, and she gave me my space when it came to Brody. Dad was content with the newfound peace at home.

I gripped the cups tighter as I walked behind a guy who was

talking with a group of football players. He jutted out his elbow right as I passed, knocking into me and causing the beer to splash onto my jeans.

"Sorry," he said casually, then went back to talking. *Fucker*.

I spotted Brody over by Travis's iPad, scrolling through the endless selection of songs on iTunes.

Brody. My gorgeous boyfriend of six months. I beamed at that thought as I handed him a cup. He waved it away.

"No thanks, babe. I don't want to be hung over tomorrow."

He had been volunteering at Misericordia for a few months and hadn't stopped talking about it. He called me after returning from shifts to tell me all about the residents he'd worked with, who was sick, and, of course, how Hannah was doing. He saw her more often than I did.

"Zeke's music selection is all over the place. He should've made a party playlist," he said.

Courtney came up to us, took the extra beer out of my hand, and gulped it down. "It's too loud in here. Wanna go outside?"

"Go ahead," Brody said, fumbling with his own iPod and trying to hook it up to the stereo. "I gotta figure this out."

Courtney grabbed my hand and weaved us through the crowd to the back door. Outside, concrete steps led us upstairs to the backyard, which was dotted with small groups of smokers. We joined Jane Duray and her group. They were passing around a joint.

"Are you still on the wagon?" Courtney asked me before taking a long drag of the joint Jane handed her.

"Don't you smoke anymore, Caroline?" Jane asked.

"I haven't in a while."

Paula Mirando took a few drags and passed it to Julia Johannes. "Why the hell not?"

I shot a look at Courtney before she could make a snide remark about Brody. "No reason."

"I can't imagine living without weed," Julia said. "Dealing with my mother sober is not possible."

Dealing with my parents was probably the main reason why I smoked so much. But since we'd been getting along and because of Brody, I hadn't had the urge to light up.

But that night, I did.

Maybe it was the alcohol. Maybe I was in the mood. I reached for the joint, and Julia handed it to me. *Just a small drag. Brody won't notice, let alone care.* I took another pull. The medicinal effects of the weed were soon mingling with the alcohol in my veins.

By nine o'clock, the party was packed with people from our high school as well as students from nearby towns. Every time I turned, a friend or acquaintance stopped to chat with me. The euphoric cocktail of pot and beer overtook me and was more powerful than the simple buzz I'd been trying to maintain. Brody had managed to get his iPod hooked up to the stereo, and a Black Eyed Peas song was blaring from the speakers. Someone dimmed the lights, and Zeke's basement became a nightclub. The scene became surreal as I gulped down more beer. Courtney grabbed my arm and pulled me into the center of the floor. We danced wildly as the bass thumped deep in our chests. Charla Lucchesi, the senior class president and homecoming queen, joined us. Nearby, a guy we called Stoner Stu was swaying as if Bob Dylan were singing instead of will.i.am. For a while, I lived in a universe with no true boundaries and no measurement of popularity.

Brody and Zeke made their way to the dance floor, and the room became a pulsing enclave outside of space and time. Everyone pumped, twisted, and gyrated in the middle of the floor while I downed another beer to quench my thirst. Lady Gaga belted out a song about being on the edge of glory while Courtney danced on the coffee table.

My heart raced and the room spun. "I need to sit down," I told no one in particular. I wandered over to the couch and crashed on it, leaning my head back and closing my eyes. Cool air from the ceiling fan right above me felt good on my sweaty face. I let the sounds of the room envelop me for a few minutes while I waited for my heart beat to slow down. I wished Brody were next to me, pushing the hair from my face and letting me rest my head on his shoulder. I opened my eyes a crack. A blur of people rushed past me. I closed my eyes again. The floating images in the back of my eyelids were more soothing than the visuals on the other side. I took a deep breath, willing my heart rate to slow down. The music stopped. I welcomed the silence and took another deep breath. *Brody? Where's Brody?* I suddenly had the urge to tell him I loved him. The lights came back on, turning the back of my eyelids a bright grey. I grimaced, throwing my arm over my eyes. Darkness overtook me again. People ran past me, leaving a gust of wind in their wake. A mix of words hung in the air.

"Go…"

"Oh fuck!"

"…grab my purse…"

"…back door…"

"Shit!"

I tried to open my eyes again, but my lids felt like stone.

"Get her," someone said.

A shadow fell over me, and someone tugged my arm. "Get up. C'mon!"

"Stop." I yanked my arm away.

"Caroline, get up!"

I opened my eyes a crack and squinted against the florescent lights. Brody was standing over me, his hand hooked under my arm as he tried to pull me up off the couch.

"Don't," I whined.

"The cops are here." He put his arm around my waist and pulled me to him. "We have to get out of here. Walk with me."

I opened my eyes wider. The crowd was smaller. Courtney stood next to me, holding on to my other arm.

"How much did she have?" Brody asked.

I didn't hear an answer. *Left foot, right foot, left foot.* Two cops appeared at the bottom of the stairs.

"Who lives here?" one of them asked. He was a big dude with a ridiculous mustache that made me giggle.

"Uh," Brody stammered. "I dunno."

"Yeah, that's what we thought," he said. "You're all coming down to the station. Maybe that'll refresh your memory."

Chapter 28

JILLIAN

"Jillian," Nate shook me out of my sleep. "Jillian, wake up."

I opened my eyes and searched his face for any familiar signs that Misericordia had called. "Is it Hannah?"

"No," he said. "It's Caroline. She's at the police station."

I sat up. "What? Is she okay?"

"She was at a party. Drunk. Cops busted it."

I slumped against the pillow. "Great. Just what we need." I climbed out of bed and reached for the sweater and jeans I had thrown on the back of the chair.

We made our way downstairs and out to the garage.

"It's not like we didn't drink when we were her age," he said.

"I didn't drink that much in high school. Not as much as her. She's turning into my father."

"You're overreacting. She doesn't have a drinking problem. She's just a teenager."

We drove to the police station in silence. We gave our daughter's name to the person at the front desk and sat in the waiting area while she was being released.

"Why are you always defending her?" I spoke softly. "She said she was going to the movies with Brody, so she lied."

"I'm not always defending her." Nate rubbed sleep out of the corner of his eye and wiped it on his jeans. "She's never done anything that we didn't do."

"Speak for yourself." I dug through my purse for a piece of gum and found a smashed piece of Trident in the side pocket. The wrapper stuck to the gum's gooey surface as I peeled it off. "We just paid two hundred bucks to get our daughter out of jail. How do you think we should react when she comes out? Run up and hug her?"

"Stop being ridiculous." Nate leaned his head against the wall. "She's always been a good kid. She stayed out of trouble. Her grades are always good. We never had to worry about her. Even before Hannah was born, she was a model child that everyone dreamed of having. She knows we have a lot to deal with because of Hannah, so she tries to stay out of our way. She slipped up this one time. It's not like she was shooting up heroin."

I folded my arms and stared straight ahead. She wasn't shooting up, but I did remember a time when Caroline often stumbled through the door after school or after a night out with friends, her eyes glassed over, her pupils darkening her hazel eyes. Nate had seen it, too. For a while, I'd worried she had a problem with drugs more than alcohol. Then she started dating Brody, and she came home stoned less and less frequently. I guess Nathan was right. This was a slip-up, albeit a big one since she'd gotten arrested.

The Ferndale Police Department was quiet at that time of night. In an affluent northern suburban town like Ferndale, not much ever went on. The party bust was probably the excitement of their night.

"Remember in college when I had to carry you out of that Delta party?" Nathan had his eyes closed, his head still resting against the wall.

I cracked a reluctant smile. How could I forget? I'd vomited all night and woken up the next day with broken blood vessels on the tip of my nose that didn't go away for three days. Makeup wouldn't even cover it up.

"We'd just started dating, didn't we?" he asked.

"It was not long after. You said I was a priss, so I wanted to prove you wrong."

"So you got smashed and spent the night puking. Yeah, you sure showed me."

"It worked, didn't it?"

He laughed. "After that, I was hooked."

A side door opened, and Caroline walked out with a cop trailing behind. Her hair was pulled back in a low, disheveled ponytail. Loose tendrils framed her face. Her eye makeup was smudged. She glanced at us with anticipation then quickly ducked her head. Nate and I stood as she approached.

"How are you, sweetie?" Nate asked.

Our sixteen-year-old daughter had just been arrested for underage intoxication, and he was calling her sweetie. I stood with a stone expression as Nate hugged Caroline.

"Tired," she said.

"We'll talk about it when we get home," I said.

"Can't we talk about it tomorrow? I want to go to bed."

"We can talk about it tonight." I picked up my purse from the bench. "Let's go."

Caroline looked over my shoulder, and I turned to see Brody standing up at the front desk with his parents. They headed to the door at the same time as we did, and we all stopped at the entrance. His mother was petite and dressed in a pale-green jogging suit. She clutched her Louis Vuitton to her side, as if a thug in the station would snatch it from her. And then I noticed Brody's father. Everything went in slow motion as his features registered in my mind.

Once again, Dr. Jeffrey Stewart stood before me.

I DRAGGED Caroline out of the station by her arm, into the parking lot.

"You knew, didn't you?" I asked. "You knew all this time?"

"Knew what?" She twisted her arm free. "What is wrong with you?"

I looked into her eyes, unable to read whether she was being honest. Lately, it had been hard to tell.

Nate unlocked the car and motioned for us to get inside. The drive home was like a bad dream. I was sleep deprived and reeling with annoyance at having to pick up my daughter at the police station. And, the most twisted outcome possible had come true. I was at a loss for words as Nate drove through the sleeping town. My head spun. I replayed the last several months in my head. This felt like an awful joke or a conspiracy to drive me over the edge.

"Will someone please tell me what the fuck is going on?" Caroline said from the backseat.

"Watch your mouth," Nate said lamely, but we were way beyond the issue of swearing.

"Is this because we were drinking?" she asked. "Like you guys never drank when you were in high school. Hypocrites."

Nate stared straight ahead as he drove, gripping the steering wheel.

"How could you embarrass me like that?" she continued. "This wasn't Brody's fault. It's not like he forced me to drink and smoke."

I jerked around. "Oh, you were smoking pot, too? I thought you were past that."

"I just took a few drags." She crossed her arms and stared out the window.

I was beginning to believe that she honestly thought I was angry about the drugs and alcohol.

Nate punched the button on the garage opener, and the door yawned opened as we pulled into the driveway.

Caroline headed straight for the stairs as soon as we walked in.

"Where are you going, Caroline?" I asked. "We're not done discussing this."

She sighed dramatically, slumping her shoulders under the weight of annoyance, and sat down at the kitchen table. "Just ground me and get it over with so I can go upstairs. My head is still spinning."

I rested my hands on the table and bent down so my face met hers. "I'm going to ask you this one more time, Caroline, and I want you to look me in the eyes and tell me the truth." I bore my eyes into hers, not missing the speck of amber floating in the hazel iris of her left eye, just like her baby sister's. "Did you know that Brody's father was Dr. Stewart?"

She sneered. "Of course I knew his dad was a doctor."

I shook my head. "No. That's not what I'm talking about."

She raised her eyebrows at me, waiting for an explanation. I quickly skimmed over the last few years in my mind. Having Hannah. Caroline suffering through puberty alone. Nate pulling further away from me. Things were about to get so much worse.

An hour ago, I'd been worried Caroline had a drinking problem like my dad's. That would've been easier to cope with than this. Behind me, the refrigerator door opened and closed, then I heard a top pop. Nate leaned against the counter with his arms crossed, swigging from a bottle of Bud Lite and waiting for me to explain.

I sat down next to her. "Listen to me. Did you know that Brody's father was the doctor that delivered Hannah?"

Her eyes narrowed as she focused on me. She didn't break eye contact for a minute before turning and staring out into the backyard. The yard was overcast with blue as night was inching toward dawn. A squirrel carrying a nut bigger than its head scurried across the patio and up the magnolia tree. Caroline watched its journey to the top of the tree, where it held tightly to its treasure. She mumbled something as a tear slipped from the corner of her eye.

"Can I go to my room now?" she asked.

~

I PULLED the photo album from the top shelf of my closet and accidentally inhaled the cloud of dust that plumed from its cover, making me sneeze. I blew my nose as I sat on my bed. Then I flipped through the pages, watching my early teen years go by in faded photos, until I spotted the picture I was searching for. Jesse Hamilton. My first big crush. I remembered the flutter in my chest when he first spoke to me during freshman advisory class in high school. I spent three hours getting ready for our first date, and we went to see *The Breakfast Club*. My head spun after he first kissed me while we waited in line for popcorn. We dated for a year. God, I loved him. Then he tore my heart to shreds when he dumped me for Amy Bergdorf. I pined for him for most of sophomore year before finally moving on. But I never forgot the searing pain in the center of my chest.

I thought of Caroline, locked in her room since the night before, feeling that same devastating ache in her heart.

Did she really not know?

I wanted to believe my daughter, but how could she not realize who Dr. Stewart was? She'd heard us mention his name over the years in conversations about Hannah and the lawsuit. Why didn't she put two and two together? The thought of her and Brody together... She'd gone to his house—to Dr. Stewart's house. She'd met him, probably talked to him about school and where she wanted to go to college. Had she slept with Brody? What if she had gotten pregnant? I shook the image from my mind, realizing how much worse this could've been had it continued. Caroline had been so content since she'd started dating Brody. At that moment, she was sitting in her room, feeling the same agony I had when Jesse broke up with me.

I slammed the photo album shut.

This was a completely different situation. He was Dr. Stewart's *son*—his flesh and blood. No matter how great a boyfriend he was to my daughter, he still had his father's despicable genes. I could never look past that.

What were the chances of this happening? They lived in the same town, but in another grade school district. That was why they didn't meet until high school.

And homecoming. I'd spent all that time with Caroline, shopping for a dress, makeup, and shoes. I'd made such an effort to make it a special day for us—all so she could go to the dance with *him*. If Hannah hadn't gotten sick, we would've been home to take pictures. But we still wouldn't have found out who his father was that day. No one would've been able to put the pieces together, not unless we'd sat him down for a talk before they left and asked him where he lived and what his parents did. And what would we have done if we had known that night? Forbid that she go to the dance? Throw Brody out of our house? It would have been a disaster, but at least we would've stopped their relationship from going any further.

And then he drove her to the hospital to see Hannah that night. He'd waited out in the hallway while Caroline visited with her sister. And...

I froze, gripping the photo album.

Misericordia. Hannah. She and Brody had been visiting Hannah. And Brody volunteered there. My head spun. I sat back down on the bed and covered my face with my hands. *What if we run into him when we're visiting Hannah? I'll have to talk to the administration about keeping him away from her. Maybe I can have him fired. It would be inappropriate for him to work there anyway. It had to be a conflict of interest.*

I sat on the bed, rubbing my temples as the thought of informing Caroline that I'd had her boyfriend fired brought on yet another headache.

THE NEXT AFTERNOON, Nate and I came back from our Sunday

visit with Hannah to find Caroline still holed up in her bedroom.

"Let it pass. She'll come down when she's ready," Nate said.

I wanted to strangle him. Instead, I climbed the stairs toward her room, steeling myself for battle. For the entire ride to Misericordia and on the way back, I continued replaying the events of the last few months to Nate. Our tangled lives were playing out like the plot of a sappy *Lifetime* movie.

I put my ear to the door of Caroline's room, listening for a sign of life. I heard nothing but silence. I knocked. "Caroline?"

She wasn't going to respond.

I opened the door and peeked inside, half expecting it to be empty with an open window and a note on the pillow.

The shades were drawn, and the room was stuffy. I noticed a lump under the covers. It moved. "Get out."

"It's after noon. Are you planning on getting up?" I stepped over textbooks and piles of dirty clothes and sat on the edge of her bed.

"No. Get out." Her voice was hoarse and congested.

"I believe you," I said. "That you didn't know who Brody's dad was."

Silence.

"It's all just an awful coincidence," I added.

She didn't say anything for so long that I wondered if she had even heard me. Then she sat up. "So I can still see Brody?"

I blinked. "Well, no, of course not. That's not what I'm saying. I just wanted you..."

"Whatever. Get out."

"Honey, it's wrong. You and him together. It can't happen. Don't you understand that?"

"Don't you trust me?"

"It has nothing to do with trust. We're in the middle of a lawsuit against his father, remember? He almost killed your sister. She is the way she is because of him. Everything we've gone through over the years is all his fault. Why would you even want to be with his son?"

"Because I love him." She sniffed.

"You're only sixteen," I told her, disregarding the same feelings I'd had for Jesse at fourteen. "You'll meet someone else."

"Oh, that's great, Mom. Thanks!" She jumped out of bed and reached for her jeans on the floor. "Again, I'm being punished because of Hannah. What about me? Doesn't what I feel matter anymore?"

I noticed Nate's shadow outside in the hall.

I took a deep breath before talking. "I know how difficult everything with Hannah has been on you."

"Why do Brody and I have to be punished for it?" She wiped her nose. "We didn't do anything wrong."

"No one's punishing you, Care-Bear." Nate walked in. "Look at it from our point of view."

"Hannah was the one that was punished, Caroline. Not you," I said.

She pulled open a drawer and dug through for a sweater. "It's always about Hannah. Everything is always about her. Never me. Never anyone else. Just her."

"Stop it—"

"Everything always revolves around her."

"How can you say that? What kind of life do you think she's living compared to yours?"

She pulled on a green sweater over the T-shirt she'd worn to bed. "Why does her life have to interfere with mine?" Her eyes filled with tears.

"Believe me. I wish it didn't have to be this way."

"Yeah, well, I wish Hannah was never born. Life would be a lot—"

My hand shot out and slapped her across the face. It happened so quickly that I even stunned myself. We all stood in silence.

Caroline's expression hardened. Her eyes darkened. "I hate you," she spat.

~

I REACHED in the medicine cabinet for the ibuprofen, but the bottle only had one capsule left. *Figures.* I threw the bottle in the sink and choked back the tears. Caroline had run out of the house after I'd hit her, leaving a wave of swear words in her wake. Nate had reached for me, but I'd pushed him aside and dashed for our bedroom to find solitude, perhaps burrow under my covers for the next several days.

I looked down at my hand, which was still red and throbbing. I'd never hit Caroline before. I'd never even spanked her. She was pulling away from me, further and further, and I had no idea how to bring her back to reality.

Nate walked into the bathroom holding a glass of water and two aspirin he must have gotten from the kitchen. He dropped the two tablets into my hand. I gulped them down in one swallow and muttered a weak thank you.

Maybe I was expecting too much from her. Maybe she was too young to really understand the situation. I knew where she was coming from. She and Brody had nothing to do with any of it.

I walked to the bed as I thought of baby Hannah and everything she'd been forced to sacrifice and of the life she had to live. She was trapped in a battered body, constantly being poked, masked, tubed, and tested. I thought of the life she could've lived. Caroline and Brody took theirs for granted, but Hannah had surrendered her entire life. For that, they could sacrifice their teenage love. It wasn't a lot to ask.

I wiped my cheek with the back of my stinging hand as Nate helped me into bed. As I lay with my satin eye pillow over my eyes and the sheets pulled over my head, I heard Nate punching his voicemail code into his cell phone.

"Hi, Nate and Jillian. It's Mark Leventhal," the voice said through the speakerphone. "Please give me a call at your earliest convenience. There's been a development in the case."

Chapter 29

CAROLINE

Monday morning was going to come sooner or later. It was unavoidable. What made it somehow more bearable was that I wasn't waking up in my own bed.

Courtney stood over me, shaking my body out of sleep. "C'mon. You're going to school. That was the deal."

After my mother slapped me the day before, I had packed a bag and headed straight for Courtney's without telling anyone where I was going. I'd had no idea what I was going to do once I got there. The only thing I was sure of was that I needed to get out of that house and away from my parents. When I got to Courtney's, her mother had insisted on calling my parents to let them know where I was. I would've preferred to make them worry. Courtney's mom spoke to my dad and talked him into letting me spend the night, as long as she promised I would go to school the next day.

I'd thrown a haphazard mix of mismatched clothes into my backpack, so Courtney let me borrow one of her outfits. I pulled my dirty hair into a low ponytail and topped it off with a grey newsboy cap. I painted a light layer of foundation on my face to make it look like I gave a shit and swiped a light-pink lip balm on my mouth.

I'd spent the last twenty-four hours reeling over the injustice of my parents keeping me from the one person who meant anything to me. I was stunned by the cruel irony of how he was connected to the tragedy that was the turning point of my young life. On the way to school something dawned on me.

What had Brody's parents told him? After the scene my mom made in the police station Saturday night, I was sure Brody had heard a mouthful when he got home, too. Did his parents remember everything that had happened when Hannah was born almost four years before? Did they tell him about the lawsuit? Maybe he'd taken their side and hated me. My mind was swimming with scenarios of Brody confronting me in the hallway in front of our classmates. Suddenly, I wanted to turn around and go back home. Courtney talked me off the ledge as we pulled into the student parking lot, reminding me that I hadn't done anything wrong.

It's the scandal of the year, I thought as we made our way into the school. Everyone knew. People were staring at me. Courtney tried to keep my mind occupied by telling me about her latest tiff with Travis. But this only made me think of Brody, since he was Travis's best friend. *What does Travis think? What advice did he give Brody?*

Stop. Focus. Get through this day as if nothing has changed. Hold your chin up like little orphan Annie. I started humming the chorus to "Tomorrow."

"Just avoid him," Courtney advised me. That was easy enough. I knew his schedule by heart. I blew off English, faked cramps, and spent the period napping in the nurse's office. During lunch, instead of sitting at the table in the back of the cafeteria with my friends and Brody, I holed up in one of the cubicles at the library, munching on Fritos I had snuck in. I stared at my opened French textbook, trying to concentrate on conjugating the word *conduire*, not focusing on what was probably the topic of conversation in the cafeteria.

The words on the page blurred as my mind wandered back to

last week and how great everything had been. The worst thing I had to deal with at that time was my annoying mother. But even she approved of my relationship with Brody and was starting to leave us alone. Last week, Brody and I walked to class holding hands. We ate lunch together. We studied together. We visited Hannah together. Last week, we'd planned on having a fun Saturday night at Zeke's party. If only we hadn't gone. Our relationship wouldn't have ended. We could've been blissfully ignorant for a little while longer.

Someone placed a wrapped egg salad sandwich right under my nose, waking me from my daydream.

"Thought you'd be hungry," Brody said in an attempt at a casual tone.

"I have Fritos," was all I could say.

It had only been two days, but I already felt like I was looking at a friend from long ago. His dark curls were mussed and tucked into a Cubs hat. He still had sleep in his eyes. I spotted the mole on his neck that I used to kiss.

"What are you doing in here?" he asked.

"I have a quiz to study for."

"Since when do you study for French?" He turned a chair around to straddle it.

"I have to get my grade up." I turned back to my book and took a deep breath to slow down my heartbeat.

He quietly unwrapped the sandwich and handed me half. I took it.

"You weren't in English. Thought maybe you were home sick," he said.

"Nurse's office. Cramps."

"Didn't you have your period last week?"

I picked a piece of chopped egg from the sandwich and popped it into my mouth.

"So," he said. "I bet no one saw this one coming."

I turned away as the tears stung the back of my eyes. "Sure blew me away."

He picked at the crust on the bread. "I'm sorry. I don't know if that helps at this point. But I'm sorry for whatever my dad did to your sister."

"I'm sorry, too."

"For what?"

I shrugged. For dragging you into my family problems. For having to see you in pain. For my parents punishing you for something you didn't do. "Everything," I said and took another bite of the sandwich. I forced myself to swallow, feeling the back of my throat constrict.

"What did your parents tell you?" I asked.

"They wouldn't tell me much. Go figure."

I remembered him telling me that his parents had kept him in the dark with the details about his dad's drug problem. My parents did the same thing after Hannah was born. I guess parents think they're doing what's best by keeping the truth from their kids.

"My dad told me to stay away from you," he continued. "When I asked what happened, he's like, 'It's not any of your concern.'" He mimicked his dad's deeper voice. "Asshole."

Brody stared straight ahead. I took another bite of the sandwich, not because I was hungry, but more to show Brody I appreciated his sharing it with me.

"I asked what he did to your mom, to your sister. He wouldn't go into any detail. Just said there was a mistake and that these things happen. Can you believe that? He actually said that. We were yelling at each other. Got kinda ugly." He wrapped up the rest of his sandwich and chucked it into the garbage. "Fucking bastard. I knew I hated him for something."

I didn't want him to hate his father. But why not? Why shouldn't he hate him? Mom hated him. Dad probably did, too. I wasn't sure if I hated him. Up until that point, I hadn't given it much thought. The few times I'd met Dr. Stewart, he was always so kind and funny, always interested in me and what was going on in my life. He never asked me about my family. If he had, I'm sure I would've told him about Hannah. Then he would've put the pieces together and discovered who I was. He would've forced us to break up before my parents found out.

I should've hated Dr. Stewart. I should've wanted to scream when I pictured his face and peel his face off if I ran into him in town. I should've had a deep-seated anger for the man boiling inside of me.

But I didn't. And I didn't want to be responsible for Brody hating his dad, either.

Brody sighed and stood up. "Well, I'll let you get back to not studying French."

He turned to leave. I searched for ways to make him stay.

"Brody," I said as my throat swelled. "These last six months have been so great. But I don't think we should..." I couldn't find the words to finish my sentence. Or maybe I didn't want to find them, just leave them to hang for interpretation.

Brody reached over and wiped the tear from my cheek, then he whispered goodbye.

Chapter 30

JILLIAN

I scratched at the crusted stain on my skirt as we waited in Leventhal's office Monday morning. He wouldn't go into details over the phone the day before. So we'd spent the last eighteen hours waiting anxiously, running possible outcomes through our minds and wondering if his news was going to make things worse than they already were or just a little bit better.

The door swung open, and Leventhal and Marquart walked in.

"Sorry to keep you waiting." Leventhal nodded at each of us. "Jillian. Nate. Good to see you both." He unbuttoned his suit jacket and sat down behind his desk.

I tried to read their expressions as I reached for Nate's hand. Maybe the defense had found something in our backgrounds to use against us. My mind raced through my past for something I'd done wrong that they could use as ammo. If we didn't win this case, paying for Hannah's care was going to be challenging. I wasn't sure our insurance would be enough to cover all her needs if she needed hospital care. I squeezed Nate's hand.

"They made a settlement offer," Leventhal said.

Nate and I both leaned forward.

"A settlement?" I asked.

"They agreed to pay an estate to Hannah in the amount of $9.9 million," he said, "and an additional $1.7 million to you and your family for the disruption this has caused."

I blinked. "You mean it's over?"

"Well, if you agree to the offer, then yes, it's over."

"And then there'd be no trial?"

"They didn't want to take the case to court because they found Dr. Stewart to be negligent," Marquart said. "We feel this is an appropriate amount, and it's our recommendation that you take it. Of course, in the end, it has to be your decision."

With that amount of money, Hannah would be taken care of for the rest of her life. And with the $1.7 million they awarded us, we could pay for Caroline to go to college wherever she wanted. We could pay off our mortgage and our credit card bills. Maybe take a nice vacation.

I turned to Nate. "What do you think?"

"You feel this is a good offer?" Nate asked Leventhal.

"Absolutely," he said. "We had an economics expert review the case and determine an appropriate amount to provide adequate care for Hannah based on her life expectancy."

I stiffened at that phrase that was a cruel part of our reality. We didn't know for sure how long Hannah was going to live, but the doctors' collective opinion hung over our lives like a dark cloud: *six years.*

"In the event of Hannah's death," Leventhal continued, "the remainder of her estate will be awarded to you."

I thought back to Dr. Stewart's strange apology at Starbucks a couple of weeks ago, probably around the time Leventhal and Marquart were negotiating the settlement. Had Stewart known then that it was over?

Nate turned to me, his smiling eyes clouding over the sorrow that he kept buried within him. I looked at him for a few moments and saw him through the years, from the time we'd met up until that moment, and everything we'd been through. He nodded so slightly that I almost didn't notice it.

"Okay," I said to Leventhal and Marquart. "Let's finally end this."

~

AFTER DROPPING Nate off at his office downtown, I immediately pulled out a cigarette and lit up. Driving home alone was exactly what I wanted. I needed the time to process the mess of thoughts spinning in my mind.

I was more than grateful that we had the means to take care of our daughters and ourselves. I was thankful that I wasn't going to have to endure a painful trial, where I was sure to be crucified on the stand by Stewart's lawyers. So why was I feeling so conflicted?

I took a long pull from the cigarette as I took our usual exit off the Edens Expressway, but instead of going west to our neighborhood, I found myself steering the car east. I didn't know what I was going to find. I knew the answers wouldn't be there, but I had the compulsion to drive by and see if there was a sign of anything. Defeat? Anger? Despair?

The colonial looked as immaculate as always. I didn't know what I was hoping to see. Maybe patches of dead grass or chipping paint on the columns.

How were their lives going to change? Hannah would be taken care of, but, really, how did this affect Stewart's life? He would still get to practice. He still had patients. His insurance would cover the cost of the settlement, but his life would remain the same in that posh colonial on the affluent side of town. There wasn't anything we could do about that.

The front door opened, and the monster himself walked out, wearing khaki pants with gym shoes and a Northwestern polo shirt. He immediately spotted me, did a double take, then locked eyes with mine. I didn't break my stare. I wasn't trespassing or breaking any law, so there was nothing he could do. At first, I thought he was going to ignore me. He walked to the mailbox at the end of his brick-paved, oil-stain-free driveway and pulled out the day's delivery. He leafed through the envelopes then looked over his shoulder at me. He tucked the mail under his arm and started walking toward me. His expression was calm, like he was approaching a friendly neighbor for a chat.

What could he possibly have to say to me? Something about the settlement? That it was exorbitant? As I watched him get closer and his facial features came into focus, I was taken back to that dreadful afternoon. I recalled the nurse dabbing at his sweaty forehead as he stood over my open stomach, a look of anguish reflected in his bloodshot eyes as he pulled a limp baby out of my womb.

He was just a few feet away when I took one last drag of the cigarette and flicked it at him before driving off. It missed his face by mere inches.

Chapter 31

CAROLINE

The one bright side about not being with Brody anymore was that I could smoke weed again. Misery and marijuana seemed to go hand in hand. Pot was my old friend, my true love. I was comfortable with it in my life.

Courtney came into my room a few days after Brody and I split up and handed me a baggie and some rolling papers, like she'd known all along that weed and I would become reacquainted. I smoked it gradually, over a few days, until the familiarity of it came back. My parents noticed. The conflict was visible in my mother's face. *Marijuana or that wicked doctor's son?* she seemed to ask. *Which is the lesser of two evils?*

The only thing I had motivation to do after the breakup was smoke weed. If I had to live in this empty world, I might as well be under the influence. Courtney and I spent a lot of time holed up in her basement or sitting under the slide in the park after dark and getting baked. Pot gave me an appetite. It gave me humor. It was the only way I could laugh.

Sometimes, I smoked in my room late at night after everyone had gone to bed. I would pull up a chair, crack the window, and let my mind delve deep into darkness. I wondered about all the other people in the world who had shitty lives like mine. Some had to be even shittier.

Somewhere, at that very moment, a teenager was probably attempting suicide and would succeed. Somewhere, some poor misguided bride was being left at the altar. Somewhere, a mother was sitting at the deathbed of her child. Somewhere, a family was struggling to make ends meet. Somewhere, a child was being physically abused by his stepfather. These dark scenarios swirled around my baked head. And I thought about them over and over to remind myself that things could be much worse than they were. Sometimes it worked, and I would feel a moment of hope—until I sobered up.

"Jordan Cartman wants to ask you out," Courtney told me one mild February night under the slide. "He said he was waiting for you and Brody to break up so he can take you out for dinner."

I frowned. Jordan Cartman was pudgy and had hairy arms.

"I'm not ready." I leaned back against the leg of the slide.

"When will you ever be ready? It's not about being ready. It's about proving to yourself and, more importantly, to Brody that you moved on."

My life was becoming miserably comfortable. I rarely went out. I stayed in my room with my earbuds in, staring at the ceiling, only eating when I was stoned. Misery was becoming my only ally. But Courtney was right. I needed to at least try to move forward. Or at least pretend to. *Fake it 'til you make it.* So when Jordan finally got around to asking me out, I said yes.

See? Brody who?

Courtney was in my room, lying on my bed, as I got ready for the date. I dug in my closet, purposely pulling clothes that weren't too suggestive, like a black turtleneck and a sweater set to wear with jeans. Courtney shook her head. "Don't try too hard to look like you don't care. Are you guys going to Polly Bonner's party?"

"Yeah. Wish you were going, too."

"I would if I didn't promise my cousin I'd babysit her bitchy daughter. I better fucking get paid for this." She sat up and shook her head vehemently at the red V-neck sweater and wool skirt I had pulled out of the closet. "Do you think Brody's going to be there?"

"I don't know. I hope not," I lied. "Did Travis say anything?"

"I don't know. I'm not talking to him."

My heart sank a little at the thought of my last link to Brody being broken. "You're fighting? About what this time?"

"He's been so busy with soccer and his friends. It's like he doesn't really care about me anymore. He says I'm being dramatic. So I called him an asshole and hung up on him. I've been ignoring his texts." She checked her cell phone for any new texts from her desperate lover.

I settled on a pale-yellow, scoop-neck baby-doll top and wore it over skinny jeans with black ballet flats. I flat-ironed my hair and applied minimal makeup. Courtney nodded at my finished look and gave me a hug before she left. "Remember. It's not a marriage proposal."

I tried beating my mother to the door as soon as I heard the doorbell ring, but I lost. Jordan had already greeted her and was standing in the foyer by the time I made it downstairs. His moppy hair hung down past his chin. He wore faded blue jeans and a striped button-down that looked like it had never seen an iron.

"Where are you going tonight?" Mom asked.

"Polly Bonner's party," I said. "Her parents are out of town. So she's having some friends over."

Mom held my gaze. "I don't know if that's a good idea. Remember the last party you went to? You got hauled into the police station." She turned to Jordan. "Why don't you go see a movie instead?"

Jordan shrugged, but I spoke up. "No," I pulled on a light coat. "I won't drink anything. And it's only a few people."

"Caroline, I really would rather you didn't go to any party."

My muscles stiffened in response to her shrill voice. Jordan fidgeted and mumbled about waiting in the car.

"Why do you have to embarrass me in front of him?" I said after he left.

"You could get in trouble again. You're already on probation from the last time."

I had gone to court the week before for the incident at Zeke's party. I pleaded guilty, and the judge yelled at me as if he could scare me into sobriety. I stood there as he barked my sentence of probation for six months and a five-hundred-dollar fine.

I stood in the foyer as my mother nagged. This was going nowhere, and I knew it would never end in my favor. "Fine." I held up my hands. "We'll go see a damn movie. Happy?"

"Why does everything have to be a contest with you?" she yelled as I slammed the door.

Jordan was changing the channels on the radio in his car. He turned the down volume when he saw me coming. "Hey, I don't mind seeing a movie. That new Adam Sandler movie is supposed to be really good."

"Fuck her," I said, fastening my seat belt. "We're going to Polly's."

Jordan looked at me, then shrugged and pulled a bowl out of his glove compartment. "Wanna hit before we go?"

POLLY BONNER LIVED IN HAVENWOOD, the one gated community in Ferndale. Her father was a surgeon, and her mother was in pharmaceutical sales. Together, they made an income big enough to live in a McMansion that was usually the location of parties whenever they were on vacation, which was often. The house had a swimming pool inside and another outside, with a tunnel connecting them. She had a Jacuzzi on the deck and a sauna in the basement, just off the recreation room that was equipped with a fully stocked bar and an eighty-inch flat screen. As far as we knew, the sauna was only used for one thing at Polly's parties. And it wasn't to take a steam.

I sat on the couch, drinking stale beer and half listening to Polly blab about her new boyfriend who went to Illinois State. Polly and I had become friends in French class that year, and she knew that Brody and I had recently broken up. I wasn't sure if she knew why, and I wasn't about to share the details.

My peripheral vision was on alert. Every time a mid-sized guy with dark hair walked in the room, I turned to see if it was Brody. It was a new habit. At a store or the mall, I would instinctively turn whenever a guy with roughly the same physical appearance as Brody walked by. I'd decided to go to church with Courtney and her family—I had no idea why; maybe for amusement?— even there, I jerked my head toward the entrance when a dark-haired guy walked in. That was ridiculous since Brody was Methodist.

"He's coming," Polly said.

"What?" I asked. "Who?"

"Who? Brody. He'll be here. He's coming with Travis and Zeke. Melanie told me. She has geometry with Zeke."

"I don't care if he's coming."

"Bullshit," she waved her hand. "You don't have to pretend with me. I can't believe you guys broke up. You seemed so happy together. What happened?"

I hesitated. If I said "conflict of interest," it would draw more questions. "We grew apart."

"That happens. Sucks." She took a sip of beer. "Anyway, Jordan's cool, too. You like him?"

"Yeah," I lied. "He's a nice guy."

Polly smirked. "Yeah, right. Well, I'm going to see who's in the sauna. I think I saw Malcolm Holzer go in there with Trina

Kapowski." She shrugged with a questioning expression. "If I see you-know-who, I'll let you know."

"Not necessary," I called as she walked away.

I spotted Jordan by the bar with a few of his friends. When I walked up to them, I realized they were talking about baseball. It was too late to turn around.

"Hey, Caroline, you like the Cubs, right?" he said, "Please, tell me you're not a Sox fan."

Jordan rambled on about last season's lineup, a string of unfamiliar names. As I pretended to listen, out of the corner of my eye, I noticed the dark-haired guy I'd been waiting for coming down the stairs. I pretended to be engrossed in Jordan's conversation as my peripheral vision sharpened. Brody started in our direction then slowed down when he spotted me. I laughed at one of Jordan's jokes, although I hadn't heard the punch line. I noticed Brody approaching, and my heart raced. Maybe he would join the conversation. He loved baseball. Last fall, we'd gone to a Cubs game when they played the Brewers. Or was it the Cardinals?

As Brody walked by me, his arm brushed against mine.

I took a sip of beer. *It's okay,* I told myself. *You're here with Jordan. He's cool. He's sorta cute. He's kind of funny. He's a good guy. And he's not the son of the doctor that almost killed your sister.*

I smiled when Jordan responded with a sarcastic remark to his smart-ass friend. He elbowed me. "Hey, need a refill?"

"No, I'm good," I said as I nonchalantly scanned the room and spotted Brody talking to Jennifer Kirkpatrick. *Slut.* He looked past her and saw me, our eyes meeting for a moment. I turned away. Maybe seeing a movie would have been a better idea. I walked over to Polly, who was stirring a glass of vodka and cranberry juice.

"Oh!" she said when she saw me. "He's here. Did you see him?"

"No, I didn't notice." I tossed the cup of stale beer in the garbage. "Will you make me one of those?"

Polly grabbed another glass and mixed me a drink. "How are you doing? For real?"

I took a few gulps of the drink. "I want to go home."

"So, go home then. Maybe it's too soon for you to go out with another guy."

"Maybe." But I wanted to be stronger than that. I wanted to be able to go out and have fun. Brody seemed to be succeeding at doing that. I lifted my chin and smiled weakly. *Fake it 'til you make it.*

Greg Goldenberg came over to us and distracted me with topics like upcoming summer concerts and *American Idol* contestants. Twenty minutes later, I decided it was a good time to go pee.

The line outside the bathroom in the basement snaked around the corner. I weaved my way through the crowd toward the stairs. There had to be at least three other bathrooms in the house. The party had gotten huge enough to take up the whole first floor, too, so the bathroom off the kitchen also had a line. Someone had turned on the family-room stereo that was connected to surround sound throughout the first floor. The Shins blared through every corner of the house so clearly that they seemed to be playing live in the living room. I downed the rest of my vodka cranberry as I passed through the hallway. Various friends tapped my shoulder or waved as I navigated to the front of the house to find the staircase to the second floor. I wondered if anyone was using the bathroom upstairs—or the bedrooms. As I passed what appeared to be the library, where a group was playing beer pong on a large mahogany desk, Brody was coming from the other direction.

"Looking for the bathroom?" he asked. He was so hot in his grey V-neck T-shirt and faded jeans that I wanted to reach out and hug him.

"Yeah. There's a line outside of the one down here." I waved at a girl walking past us. I watched the guys playing beer pong. Anything to avoid eye contact with my ex-boyfriend.

"Use the master bath," he said. "It's like a spa."

"How do you know that?"

"I just came from there. I can show you where it is."

"I'm sure I can find it," I said, but I followed him up the curved staircase to the quiet second floor.

"This house is so huge," he said, "the master suite is actually in another zip code."

We walked through the dark hallway lined with doors. Brody reached for my hand to guide me, but I pulled it away.

"How many bedrooms do you think they have?" I asked.

"Dunno. Probably five or six."

We came to the end of the hallway, where a smaller staircase led us to the third floor. At the top of the stairs were glass French doors with white curtains. Brody opened them with a grand gesture. The palatial master bedroom took up most of the third floor, and the master bath was about half the size of the bedroom. A giant Jacuzzi tub sat in the middle, with a painted mural above it of trees and sky. To the side of the tub was a double-sided fireplace that cut through to the bedroom. Another door led to a small closet-size room with the toilet and a bidet.

"The master toilet," Brody announced with a wave of the hand.

"Wow, it really is like a spa. Are you sure we're allowed up here?"

"No, but who cares? You'll be done before anyone notices. I'll let you pee in peace." He stepped out of the bathroom, shutting the door.

I exhaled after he left. I had handled it well. I didn't lose control or reach out and pull him to me like I so badly wanted to. His messy hair begged for me to run my fingers through it. And I'd glanced at the bulge between his legs.

After peeing, I checked myself in the mirror. I touched up my lipstick, dusted more powder on my face, and wiped the smudged eyeliner from under my eyes. I bent over and fluffed my hair to give it more volume. Being all the way up there by myself felt creepy, so I wanted to get back to the party.

When I walked out of the bathroom, Brody was still there, sitting on the edge of the massive four-post bed. "I wanted to make sure you got back downstairs okay."

"Liar." I sat down next to him.

"Have you been smoking a lot since... you know..."

"Is it that obvious?"

He laughed. "The dilated pupils gave it away."

"Well, Jordan's a smoker, too, so..."

"How are things with him?"

"You know, we don't have to talk about this. I should get back downstairs."

"Wait." He reached for my arm as I got up. "Don't go yet."

"I have to find Jordan."

"Fuck Jordan." He pulled me down and pressed his mouth against mine. I should've pushed him away or fought to free myself from his arms. But I was right where I wanted to be.

Brody's kisses were a soft, delicious taste of my biggest vice. The familiar place calmed me, like I was home again. I relented. *This can't lead anywhere good,* I thought as I pulled off my top, and he put on a condom. But it was exactly what I needed—validation that he still loved me and missed me as much as I missed him. Letting go of what we had just because of our parents' mess was too much to expect from us.

As he entered me and we found the familiar rhythm we'd perfected together, I felt complete again, and the heaviness in my chest dissolved with each kiss. Brody rested his damp cheek against mine as he thrust against me. I didn't think about what would happen next or how we would deal with it. There was no later tonight, tomorrow, or next week. There was only that moment together.

Chapter 32

JILLIAN

Hannah wasn't in a good mood that Sunday morning. Her eyes were downcast most of the day, and she wouldn't even crack a smile when I sang to her. She barely acknowledged we were there. It was oddly comforting to see her have mood swings like a normal, healthy person. I wanted her to be moody, angry, or sullen—whatever she wanted. She had every right.

Nate slammed his fist on the TV set as if that would improve the reception.

"Nate, we go through this every time," I said. "They don't have cable."

"I know that, Jillian." He shifted the set to the right a bit and played with the rabbit ears. Hannah had been at Misericordia for almost three years, and every week, Nate competed with the TV for a clear picture. "Maybe we should offer to pay for cable. That would be nice, wouldn't it? It would be a tax write-off."

"I think they want families to spend quality time together, not watch television," I said. "Turn it off."

Caroline sighed. "Dad, give it up."

Hannah moaned.

Another lovely Sunday with the Moores.

Nate shut off the TV and mumbled a few choice words about

missing the Bulls game, then sat down next to Caroline on the couch. Caroline ran her fingers through her hair as though she were primping in front of a mirror. She'd worn dark skinny jeans and a teal sweater set. She'd painted soft pink on her eyelids and cheeks and glossed her lips with a berry glaze in an effort to look just right for a Sunday morning with her family—and in case she ran into Brody, who was still volunteering at Misericordia.

I had decided not to have him fired, although I wasn't sure I would've even been able to anyway. But I did talk to the administration, who talked with Brody, and everyone agreed that he would continue to volunteer as long as he wasn't around Hannah. He was transferred to a volunteer position on a different floor, and that solution satisfied everyone.

Caroline didn't tell me much about how she was handling the breakup. She said very little whenever I asked how she was doing. I did manage to get her to tell me about her date with Jordan the night before. She'd told me about the nice dinner I was sure they didn't really have and the hilarious movie I was certain they hadn't seen afterward.

When we arrived in the lobby that morning, she glanced around for Brody while she pretended to be texting on her phone. I had decided to give her time. I knew how hard it was to get over a first love, and I didn't want to make things worse than they already were. Maybe she wanted to look nice to show Brody that she could be happy without him. I remembered playing that game.

"I think Hannah's seizing," Nate said.

Hannah was still gazing down, her eyelids barely fluttering. I stood closely over her, watching as her nostrils flared. She opened her eyes and cocked her head to the side. Her mouth twisted into the eerie smile—the only smile I never wanted to see. I looked at my watch and started counting the seconds.

~

WE TOOK Hannah back upstairs after her second seizure and alerted Claire. We were all used to the routine. Claire administered the anti-seizure medication into Hannah's NG tube with us standing around, waiting until the medicine kicked in and the seizures stopped. Caroline sat next to Hannah and massaged her arms and legs while we waited. Hannah opened her eyes a few times and looked at Caroline. She even cracked a smile while her sister cooed in her ear. Nate and I watched our two daughters together. I took out my cell phone and snapped a perfect picture, one in which Hannah's eyes were actually open. Caroline was smiling at her and touching her arm. I immediately saved it as my cell phone's wallpaper.

The seizures stopped about twenty minutes after she'd had the medicine. Hannah was getting sleepy just as Claire brought in a bag of formula for her lunch. We each kissed Hannah goodbye as she dozed and ate.

When the elevator doors opened to the lobby, Nate, who was checking the game score on his phone, darted out, running right into someone who was waiting to get on. Caroline swore under her breath as Brody stood before us. There was an awkward dance between him and Nate as they each mumbled apologies and stepped around each other. Brody and Caroline exchanged a generic greeting as we stepped out and he got on. But as the doors were about to close, he stuck his hand in between them, and they jerked open again. "Mr. and Mrs. Moore?"

His fists were shoved into his pockets. He tried to make eye contact with me, but his eyes kept shifting to the floor. "I wanted to say I'm sorry for everything." He glanced at me as he spoke. "I didn't mean for any of this to happen. I just wish I could change it all."

No one said anything. He bit his lip and glanced at Caroline, who stood stock-still beside me. Nate jiggled his change in his pocket. Everyone was waiting for me to be the first one to respond.

"Well," I said. "We know it's not your fault, but I'm sure you understand why..." I paused, uncertain what to say next. I didn't want to even mutter any words that described a relationship between him and Caroline. "...you and Caroline can't be together."

"Of course," he said.

"Thank you for respecting my wishes to stay away from my daughter," I said. "Both of them."

"Yeah, sure." He pushed the button to call the elevator back.

Caroline glanced over her shoulder at him as we walked away. I thought I noticed a smirk on her face.

Chapter 33

CAROLINE

Denial is a great thing. It can be your best ally, as long as you don't realize it has become your best ally.

The following Monday morning at school, Brody and I didn't talk about what had happened at Polly's party. We barely talked at all, going about our days as we had been since our breakup. We acknowledged each other in English class or in passing in the hallway, like acquaintances who barely knew each other. But we were acquaintances with a secret.

Jordan had no clue. He'd been getting high with his friends while I was getting busy with Brody. He didn't seem to notice that I had been gone for so long. After my tryst in the master bedroom, I'd joined Jordan in the family room with his friends. He just smiled and handed me the joint they were passing around.

Courtney wanted answers that morning at school. "So, does this mean you're *secretly* back together with Brody?" She spoke with a hint of giddiness in her voice.

"No," I said. "It doesn't mean anything."

"Sex always means something."

"It's..." I thought a moment for the right words. "It's a residual effect from our past relationship."

Courtney laughed. "Are you going to go out with Jordan again?" she asked, like a prosecutor questioning the defendant.

"He hasn't asked me."

"Well, have you given him any signs that you're interested?"

"I haven't given him any signs that I'm not."

Courtney narrowed her eyes. "Hmm. Whatever."

The prosecution rests.

I was determined to move through each day, holding my "residual effect" with Brody deep in my heart, while on the outside, I acted as though it hadn't happened. The night was special, though. We'd lain on the plush king-size bed in a luxury suite far above the revelry of our classmates, feeling so at home with each other, rediscovering each other. I was reassured that he still had feelings for me. And for some strange reason, knowing that his feelings for me still existed gave me confidence to move forward with my life.

Being with him that night had also given me hope that we could get back together someday. I buried that hope deep in my subconscious, far from the surface of reality.

Guilt weighed down on me because I'd ditched Jordan that night and lied to him about it. So when he did ask me out again a few days later, I immediately said yes. This one was a proper dinner date at Mimi's Bistro. Throughout our meal, I kept an open mind and stayed positive. I tried my hardest to see Jordan for who he was and not for who he wasn't. I admired him for trying the escargot. He made me laugh with his impression of our school dean. I found it especially convenient that he liked smoking pot as much as I did. When he dropped me off that night, we fooled around in his car for twenty minutes before I went inside the house.

I wanted to keep my options open without giving Jordan the impression that I wanted to be in a relationship.

I met a guy named Gabe Lindstrom, the son of my parents' church friends, one Sunday after mass. Mom told me he was "a really nice boy." I had talked to him a few times at church functions, and he seemed decent enough. I also wanted to show my mom I was getting over "that Stewart kid."

Gabe picked me up on a Friday night, and we went to dinner at a new sushi bar in town. He was a senior at Glenwood Academy, a Catholic college prep school my mom had tried sending me to, and had just been accepted to the University of Iowa on a football scholarship. He already had a Hawkeyes Football jacket, which he wore with pride and a little arrogance. At the sushi bar, we talked about the typical first date requisites: favorite TV shows, movies, music, and where to hang out on weekends. He talked a lot about how his high school football team consistently beat mine, as if I gave a damn, but I let it slide. Gabe had a fake ID and told me how he and his buddies often went downtown to the Chicago bars in Wrigleyville. He said he could get me in if I wanted, and I'd told him I might want to go someday. When he took me home, we fooled around in his car for a few minutes before we called it a night. He told me he'd call, but he never did.

I didn't care.

Brody still hovered in the back of my mind. I ignored it, and during the times that we spent together—English class, lunch, and in the halls before class—we succeeded at maintaining the charade of being just friends.

But as the weeks went on, Brody and I found ourselves around each other more frequently. It seemed as if we'd just needed a little time to let things cool off and blow over. We were gathering the courage to forget the past. In the mornings, we hung out with our friends in front of our lockers. He would ask about our English homework, and we would compare notes. We started eating lunch together again—not alone, but with all our friends, so it made it feel like we weren't doing anything wrong. My parents had never said we couldn't be friends.

One day, Brody cut study hall to hang with me during my free period. At least I liked to believe I was the sole reason he'd cut study hall. We sat on the benches outside of the cafeteria. I usually spent this time doing homework that was due that afternoon. But on that day, I was easily distracted by Brody's presence.

"Are you going to Turnabout?" he asked.

I'd only been to Turnabout, the dance where the girls ask the guys, my freshman year when I'd asked a boy from my science class. He was sort of cute and really funny, so I thought it would be fun to go with him. But the night of the dance, he turned out to be a huge bore. And the dance itself was lame, so I'd never gone again.

"Nah," I said. "You?"

He shook his head. I wondered if he was expecting me to ask him. I pretended to read my history book. "Don't you have any homework to do?" I asked.

"Of course. But it's for doing at home. Later tonight. Get it?" He made air quotes. "Home work." He rested his head against the wall and closed his eyes.

"How's my sister?" I hadn't seen her in a few weeks. And even though Brody wasn't supposed to be around her, I knew he was still sneaking visits in when he could. Claire turned a blind eye.

"She's fine. Juan is sick. Did you know?"

"No, what's wrong with him."

"I don't know for sure. Probably pneumonia. He's been in the hospital for a few days."

I thought of chubby Juan and his adorable dimpled hands. "Poor guy."

"So, I think I have an idea."

"Yeah? What's that?"

"Why don't we all go to Turnabout together? As a group." He turned to me. "I talked to Travis and Zeke. They don't really feel like going with dates. Trav and Courtney are fighting again anyway."

"I can't keep up with those two." I laughed.

"I know. Too much fucking drama. So what do you think? About going to the dance?"

"My parents won't go for that."

"So we won't tell them. We'll pretend you're going with Zeke. They'll never know."

I shrugged. It could work. I doubted my parents would pay that much attention. I'd pretty much convinced them I was over Brody by going out with other guys.

Courtney and I talked about it, and other than the fact that Travis, whom she hated on that particular day, was going to be there, she agreed the idea was brilliant. "We don't even have to stay at the dance that long. Let's find a cool restaurant to eat at. Then we can hang out at Zeke's."

I told my parents I had asked a guy named Zeke to the dance. They had no idea he was friends with Brody. Mom even offered to buy me another dress, so she wasn't onto me, but I told her I was going shopping with the girls.

"Turnabout is more casual," I told her. "It's not as formal as homecoming. I'll probably buy a new skirt." Gone was my bitter attitude after my breakup with Brody. I needed her to know I was fine. I didn't want to give her any reason to believe otherwise.

The plan all along was to go as one group of friends. No assumed couples. No obligations. No hooking up. Just six friends having a good time. It may not be a repeat of my homecoming with Brody, but spending the evening with him was all that mattered to me.

The night of the dance, Polly Bonner and I went to Courtney's to get ready. I'd bought a black leather skirt that hit above the knee and paired it with a silver sequined tunic. I wore black tights and black knee-high leather boots with a three-inch heel.

The three of us chipped in and hired a chauffeured limo to take us to the dance. Polly stole a bottle of Dom Perignon from her parents.

"Aren't they going to notice an expensive bottle of champagne is gone?" Courtney asked. "Isn't that bottle worth, like, two hundred bucks?"

Polly waved it off. "They have two other bottles. They'll never think it's me. I'll pin it on my brother if they ask."

Courtney filled an ice bucket with ice, and I searched the pantry for plastic cups and a few bags of chips. By the time we picked the boys up at Zeke's, our ride was fully stocked. We decided to drive around town for a while before going to the dance. We held up our red Solo cups in a group toast and pledged a night of fun among friends. Courtney passed a joint, and I didn't hesitate taking a toke.

Brody and I didn't even sit next to each other in the limo. I talked to Zeke about music we'd recently downloaded to our iPods. Brody, Polly, and Travis chatted about random stuff. Courtney and Travis were ignoring each other, while at the same time pathetically trying to get each other's attention. We all had a part to play. This group date thing was convenient for all of us.

We were all buzzed enough when we got to the dance that its lame Under the Sea theme didn't ruin our night. The cafeteria looked as though a whale had vomited metallic blue streamers all over the place, but the DJ was playing great music, and Brody immediately grabbed my hand and pulled me out to the dance floor. He held me close as John Mayer crooned. He whispered in my ear, "Our plan worked."

"It was your idea." I inhaled his scent, a mixture of Axe and fabric softener. He wore a hunter-green cable-knit sweater over a shirt, tie, and black slacks.

He leaned in and kissed me. I let him linger for a moment before pulling away. "No hookups, remember? We're all supposed to be friends."

"We are friends," he said, "with benefits."

I laughed and he kissed me again. We danced for three more songs before taking a break. By then, Courtney and Travis were all over each other by the vending machines. We stayed at the dance for about an hour, which was long enough to make an appearance and get an idea of what it was all about. We left before the Turnabout committee even announced who the Turnabout King and Queen were.

We passed around another joint in the limo on the way to dinner at the Melting Pot, where we devoured chunks of beef tenderloin, lobster, and chicken breast cooked in oil and dipped in melted Emmentaler cheese.

It was the most fun I'd had since the breakup.

Chapter 34

JILLIAN

When Caroline was little, before her belligerent teen years and long before Hannah was born, back when my marriage was a marriage, we had a Sunday morning tradition where we'd attend church together, then come home and cook a big brunch. Caroline would crack the eggs in a large bowl, and I would whip them up with a whisk. Nate would flip the pancakes to a perfect golden brown. I would fry up a big pile of crispy bacon. Every week, we looked forward to it. The time together made Sundays all the more special.

Somewhere along the way, life got in the way. Caroline became less interested in getting out of bed, let alone eating a huge meal, on Sundays. Nate stopped going to church on a regular basis. Then Hannah came into our lives.

I woke up early Sunday morning after a deep sleep, thought about those weekend mornings long ago, and decided the time had come to bring back the brunch tradition.

I had a quick visit with Hannah. Nate was getting over a cold, so we decided he should stay home. On the way home, I stopped at the store and picked up a dozen eggs, bacon, turkey sausage, pancake mix, orange juice, and a loaf of bread. At home, I got the coffee perking, imagining the scent wafting up the stairs and into the bedrooms, rousing my family out of sleep as it did in the commercials. I scrambled the eggs and cooked blueberry pancakes on the griddle, then fried the bacon and sausage and made toast. I put down my grandmother's tablecloth then set the table for three. I poured the orange juice into a carafe and set it on the table, where the sun shone right through it.

"What's going on?" Caroline walked over to the stove and lifted a lid. "Bacon? Pancakes? Who's coming over?"

"No one. It's for us."

She looked at me as though I had snakes coming out of my ears. "All this food for three people? I'm not sure I'm that hungry."

"Well, hungry or not, at least have a bite of something. The pancakes are blueberry—your favorite."

She raised her eyebrows, then pulled out her cell phone and started texting.

I went upstairs to wake Nate. When we came downstairs, Caroline had served the pancakes and the breakfast meat and placed the toast in a basket. She'd brought everything to the table and even set out cups for the coffee along with cream and sugar.

I couldn't remember the last time the three of us had sat around the table together for a meal. It had been weeks since I'd seen Caroline in a good mood. Nate asked her about the dance the night before, and she told us it was lame, but dinner with her date at the fondue restaurant was "crazy," which I believed was a good thing.

She seemed emotionally stable, and I wondered if she was really over Brody. A few months had passed since we'd found out the dirty truth. I knew she still saw him at school; that was unavoidable. The school had about two thousand students, so I didn't know how often she ran into him. Plus, she was dating other guys. I'd taken a lot longer to get over Jesse Hamilton. Maybe she was stronger than I was.

After breakfast, Caroline cleared the table and loaded the dishwasher while Nate and I packed leftovers in plastic containers. Nate's cold was still bothering him, so he lay on the couch to watch TV, and I offered to make him a cup of green tea. I asked Caroline what her plans were for the rest of the day.

"I don't know," she said. "Maybe I'll call Courtney. We'll go see a movie or something."

"You can use my car if you want," I said. "The keys are on the counter."

She thanked me and went upstairs to take a shower.

The teakettle whistled, so I didn't hear the first ping come from Caroline's phone that she had left on the counter. As I poured boiling water over the tea bag, the phone pinged again. I glanced at it more out of habit than curiosity. Like everyone else with a cell phone, I'd been conditioned to look when a phone pings. The name "Brody" caught my eye.

"Gr8 hanging with u last nite." the first text said.

"Miss U," the second one read. *"Call me later."*

I didn't know why I was surprised. Maybe because I wanted so badly to believe she had moved on and that she understood why dating him was wrong. Maybe because we had just finished a peaceful family brunch without any bickering or eye rolling. I wanted to believe that it wasn't all for nothing and that Caroline wasn't really pulling the wool over our eyes.

I didn't have it in me to march upstairs and confront her. I just wanted to keep the peace in the house a little longer. I brought the phone over to Nate and showed him the texts.

He sat up and read the messages, sighed, and ran his hand through his hair. "I had a feeling about this."

"What are we going to do? Should we pull her out of school? Transfer her to Glenwood?"

"You know we can't do that. That's a little extreme." He took a sip of tea. "This is her first love. It's going to take more time. I think she's trying."

"I know she is." I rubbed my temples. We had tried talking to her and explaining our feelings, hoping she would at least respect our wishes and understand when she got older. We'd tried talking to Brody, via Misericordia, by requesting that he stay away from Hannah. Neither of them had respected our decision.

I knew what I had to do next. And I wasn't looking forward to it at all.

~

"You know where he lives?" Nate said from the passenger seat.

I hesitated before answering. "Yeah."

"How the hell do you know where he lives? Have you been there before?"

"No," I said, "not really."

Nate stared at me as I turned onto Timber Ridge. The route had become familiar to me, like the route to an old friend's house.

I felt odd pulling into the paved driveway instead of parking across the street. We stepped onto the front porch. Dying flowers sat in pots on either side of the door. A trio of burnt candles adorned a small, dusty table between two chairs. I imagined Mr. Stewart and his wife sitting there on a mild night after dinner, waving to their neighbors. *Or did Caroline sit out here with Brody?*

Nate rang the doorbell, a majestic tone sounding through the house. I held my breath as the footsteps from the other side of the door got closer. The door swung open, and Dr. Stewart stood in front of us with a look of bewilderment on his stupid face.

For a moment, we just stared at each other in anticipation. I opened my mouth to say something, but I couldn't find the words. Finally, Nate spoke.

"Dr. Stewart, I'm Nathan Moore, Caroline's father. We wanted to talk to you about our children."

He nodded. "Okay." I noticed his thinning, graying hair. Years of guilt were etched into his skin.

"You son is still seeing our daughter," I said, "even after we specifically forbade them to date."

"Oh." He shifted on his feet. "I wasn't aware of that."

"We tried talking to our daughter, but she won't listen to us," Nate said, his voice calmer, less biting than mine, but still clipped with a stern edge. "So maybe your son will listen to you."

He nodded, dropping his arms to his sides. "We, my wife and I, talked to him after the... that night at the police station. I thought we'd made it clear that he wasn't to see Caroline anymore. I'll have another talk with him right away."

"They were together at the dance last night," I said. "Did you know that?"

"No, absolutely not." He folded his arms in front of his chest. "Brody told us he was going with a girl named Polly."

"Caroline told us she was going with someone else, too," Nate said. "Listen, they're going to see each other at school. We can't control that. But maybe you'll have better luck talking to your son."

"There is no way that this *thing*"—I waved my hand—"could ever amount to anything. So they need to stop before it goes any further. It's already gone too far."

He continued to nod as I spoke.

"I don't want to have to move to another state in order to keep her away from him."

"I will talk to him today," he said. "I'm sorry. For everything. I wish there was something I could do to reverse all the trouble I've caused. But all I can do is say I'm sorry."

Nate dropped his head. I glared at Dr. Stewart. "Don't apologize to me." I spoke the words I'd waited so long to tell him. "Apologize to my daughter, Hannah. She's getting her meals through a tube now."

Nate put his hand on my shoulder. "Let's go."

He led me back to the car, but not before I got one last glimpse of Stewart and the look of shame that washed over his face, just as he closed the door.

I wasn't ready to forgive. I wasn't ready to accept Mr. Stewart as a fallible human being like the rest of us. No. He was not like the rest of us. He was an evil monster that didn't deserve a life of abundance. But his words stuck in my head, and his soft, calm voice was unnerving. It was the opposite of what evil should sound like.

Chapter 35

CAROLINE

I hate Shakespeare anyway, I thought as Brody pressed his lips against mine. It had taken all of ten minutes before our Othello paperbacks were cast aside and our bodies were entwined as music played from the radio in the background. During lunch, he'd asked me to his house to study for our English test. I had refused at first, but all I needed was just a little more convincing.

"Tell your mom you're going to Courtney's," he'd said. It was another simple lie, like the one I'd told about going to the dance with Zeke. *Like the lie you're living, pretending to be over Brody and open to dating other guys.* Something in the back of my mind rang. But I ignored the warning signal. *Was it really this easy?* Brody and I were seeing each other again. We just weren't defining it. And not labeling it made what we were doing okay.

Brody dotted soft kisses down my neck and onto my chest. Then he stopped and pulled away.

"What's wrong?" I asked.

He didn't say anything at first. His hair was getting longer, and it just touched his shoulders.

"Why are you looking at me like that?"

He leaned against the wall. "There's actually another reason why I asked you to come over tonight."

"What?"

"I talked to my dad. You know, about what happened."

"What do you mean?"

"To your sister."

I sat up. "Hannah? You talked to your dad about Hannah?"

He nodded and started biting his cuticles. "I guess your parents came by yesterday. They know everything. That we went to the dance together. That we're still seeing each other."

"Wait. My parents were here?"

"They told my dad to talk to me about staying away from you."

I retraced my steps from the day before. *Yesterday?* We had a nice family brunch, the first in years. We got along. We talked. Everything was normal. I went to see a movie with Courtney in the afternoon. Was that when they came over to the Stewarts'?

"I don't understand," I said. "Why didn't you tell me today that they came over?"

"Because then you wouldn't have come over tonight. Dad told me I couldn't hang with you anymore. I told him to fuck off. I wasn't going to stop seeing you. Why should I be punished for his fuckup?" He got up from the bed and turned up the volume on the stereo. "We started fighting. I asked him straight up why he did it, why he ignored your mom like that the day Hannah was born."

I almost didn't hear that part. My mind was still wrapping around the fact that my parents had been there the day before. *Why didn't they say anything to me last night?*

"I wanted to tell you everything. But not at school, you know, with our friends around and classes and shit." Brody sat down next to me. "There's something you should know about the day your sister was born."

~

I SAT at the bottom of the staircase in the darkened foyer of the Stewart home. My mind twisted and turned with all the details I had just been given. I believed every word, but I still needed to process it. I placed my head in my hands.

I had said goodbye to Brody upstairs with a tight hug and a weak kiss full of apprehension and uncertainty.

I heard the shower running upstairs in Brody's bathroom and wondered if he was as confused standing under that hot water as I was sitting on that step. I wanted to curl up, right there on the stairs, and go to sleep. My mind was heavy with new information I wasn't ready to understand. Did my parents know? If they did, why didn't they ever tell me?

I was so lost in thought that I didn't hear the sounds of life coming from the kitchen—the muffled voices and the sound of keys hitting the countertop. Then Mrs. Stewart appeared before me, her white-blond hair beaming in the dark foyer.

"Oh, Caroline, you startled me." Her manicured hand flew to her chest. "What are you doing here in the dark?"

Dr. Stewart walked in and turned on the light. "Caroline, you shouldn't be here. You need to go home."

"I know." I stood up. "I was just on my way out."

He opened the front door for me, but I stopped at the threshold. I believed Brody. He had never lied to me. He wouldn't embellish the details. But I needed to hear it again, straight from the source.

"Dr. Stewart, can I talk to you? In private?"

He glanced at his wife, then at me. "We can go into the study."

I imagined dark oak-paneled walls, a large mahogany desk, and rows of bound books stacked in built-in bookcases. Instead, his study was a small room with beige walls and a glass-top desk pushed against the wall. Stacks of papers and file folders covered the desk. A small bookshelf stuffed with more papers, magazines, and miscellaneous items stood against the wall. Dr. Stewart motioned for me to sit on the chair; then he shut the door behind us.

"You know, I had a talk with your parents yesterday. We had no idea you and Brody were still seeing each other. I wouldn't have allowed it if I had known about it."

"Brody told me they came by." I moved some books that were on the chair to the floor and sat down. "He also told me what happened when Hannah was born." Does he even know my sister is named Hannah?

Dr. Stewart looked away and sat down at the desk. He was quiet for a minute. "I wasn't sure if he was going to tell you or not."

"So it's true?" I asked, even though, at that point, I had no doubt.

He nodded. He picked up a pencil and twirled it. "It was the darkest time of my life. Rock bottom. I hit it hard."

I folded my arms and stared at him. "I want to hear it from you. I want to hear your side of the story."

He avoided eye contact and stared out the window. "If you asked anyone I went to high school with, they'd never believe it was true. I never thought I would be the type of person that would be an addict. That wasn't who I was. I was the smart, dependable one. I didn't drink a lot. I didn't smoke. I don't even know why I'd started in the first place. It was during med school. Everyone was doing it. Even my prim and proper wife. It got us through the long nights of studying. It wasn't a problem at first. I only did it on occasion, like everyone else in my class. After graduation and starting my own practice, I stopped using. I didn't really need it anymore. But then my practice grew. My life got busier. Things got really stressful."

He turned and faced me. "I had it under control, at first, but then I did it more frequently. I couldn't stand the crash. I began neglecting my wife, my sons, my friends. People had to start covering for me at the office. And then the day your sister was born..."

I looked away. I remembered that day. Mom and Dad woke

me up early to go to the hospital with them. I was excited and unsure about what was about to happen. Our lives were going to change that day. I just hadn't realized how much.

"The night before had been a long one," he continued. "I think I delivered five or six babies. The last one was around four in the morning. By the time your mother came in, I was exhausted. No one else was around to cover for me. And since I'd known your mom for so long, I knew I had to be there for her. But I wasn't. I only intended on leaving for an hour. I just needed a bump to get me through the next few hours. I went back to my office. Then one bump led to another..."

He paused and picked up a paper clip and started untwisting it. "Before I knew it, six hours had gone by. I rushed back to the hospital. By then, I knew it was too late."

His story matched exactly what Brody had told me. So Hannah was permanently brain damaged because of someone's drug addiction. *What would the AMA think? Wouldn't he be fired? Wouldn't they take away his license to practice?*

As if he knew what I was thinking, he said, "No one knew. I made up some story about being tied up at the office with someone who was cramping and spotting. The nurses at my office suspected. I'm sure the ones at the hospital did, too. But they'd never blow the whistle. No one would ever listen to them anyway."

He didn't say anything for a few minutes. I think he was waiting for me to reply, but I said nothing.

"I never told anyone," he continued. "Except for the people in NA. And then Brody. And now you. I think my wife suspects, but she doesn't like talking about it."

NA. Narcotics Anonymous. Courtney's cousin went to NA meetings because of a heroin addiction. He fell off the wagon a few times. Courtney said that was to be expected, but he just had to pick himself back up and start over again. I wondered if Dr. Stewart had ever relapsed.

"After what happened with your sister, I knew I needed help. I started going to NA. At first, two or three times a week. Now I go every Saturday. I have a sponsor and have been following the steps."

Dr. Stewart got up from his desk and went to the window. "Several months ago, I finally reached the step that I dreaded the most. Step Nine. Make direct amends to such people wherever possible, except when to do so would injure them or others. I knew I had to apologize to your mother. I thought about going to your house. But I thought that would be rude, or that she'd call the police. When I saw your mother at the coffee shop, I knew it was the right opportunity. I had to tell her then."

"You saw my mom?"

"Yes, didn't she tell you? It was a while ago. I got the chance to apologize for all the pain I caused her and your family. I don't know whether she accepted or not. But that's up to her."

I should have been angry with Dr. Stewart. He ruined my sister's life. I should've reported him and had him sent to jail. But that would only have ruined things for Brody and his family. I couldn't do that, not that anyone would believe me anyway. His addiction had nearly ruined his life, and he'd done what he needed to do to recover. I didn't know what it felt like to have an addiction like that. I loved smoking pot, but it had never threatened to take over my life or interfere with my responsibilities. I guessed having an addiction made people feel in control while everything around them spiraled out of control.

"I'm sorry, Caroline," Dr. Stewart continued. "I'm deeply, deeply sorry for everything that I have done."

I found a cuticle on my index finger to chew on. I would've done anything to avoid seeing the pain in his eyes. There was no deep festering anger inside me like there should have been. My mind was still trying to sort out all the details of this twisted plot. I thought of my parents, my baby sister, and her difficult future. I should be angry. I should scream at him and describe the life

Hannah has to live. He didn't deserve my forgiveness. But I felt empty and numb, like I wanted to bury all the feelings I was supposed to feel and just move forward.

Denial was still my best friend.

Chapter 36

JILLIAN

It was the perfect time for a smoke. I told Nate I was going out on the patio to call Abbie. Caroline was still at Courtney's. The storm clouds were moving in from the west, so I pulled up a lawn chair on the patio and sat under the umbrella, in case it started drizzling.

How could I have been so naïve? I thought as I lit up. Of course Caroline would go behind our backs and continue to see Brody. Why wouldn't she? Knowing how belligerent she'd been, I never should have believed she would get over him in just a handful of months. She was a sensitive and impressionable girl, insecure and desperate. Letting go of her first love was going to take a lot longer than I had anticipated.

She wasn't going to listen to us. Brody seemed to be a well-mannered, disciplined boy. Maybe he would respect our wishes and break up with her.

I stubbed out the cigarette and immediately lit a new one. The storm clouds were overhead. Thunder rumbled in the distance.

It's come to this. My wanting—needing—my daughter's heart to be broken again by her first boyfriend. All for what? Empty justice for Hannah?

"You smoke?"

I looked up and saw Caroline standing behind me. I waved my hand to disperse the cloud of smoke hanging in front of my face, as if I still had time to hide my nasty habit.

"When did you get home?" I asked, stubbing out the cigarette.

"Now. Since when do you smoke?"

"Oh, I don't smoke. Well, I mean, not often. Just once in a while."

Caroline stared at me, her arms crossed across her chest. Then she took a cigarette out of the pack on the patio table and lit it. She pulled up a chair beside me while taking a long drag, then handed me the cigarette. "We can share. I won't tell Dad."

I hesitated, but didn't really see the point in lecturing her on the dangers of smoking when she'd just caught me red-handed. I took the cigarette and inhaled. "Did you get a lot of studying done at Courtney's?"

"I wasn't at Courtney's." She took the cigarette from me and took a long drag. "I was at Brody's." She held the cigarette out to me, studying my face, but I sat emotionless. Neither of us spoke until the cigarette was down to the filter.

"I don't know what to feel anymore," she said as she stubbed out the butt. "I don't feel anger, sadness, anxiety. Just emptiness."

I nodded, understanding that overwhelming sense of all those conflicting feelings coexisted inside, fighting for the spotlight. Eventually, the mind and heart shut down.

"Do you know what happened the day Hannah was born? Where Dr. Stewart was all day?"

I sat up and turned to her. "No. Do you?"

She paused, nodded, and reached for the pack of cigarettes. This time, she took one out for herself and one for me. For the first time, as she lit each cigarette, she looked like a young woman to me, not the little girl I'd always thought she was. She handed me a cigarette and waited for me to take a few drags before she told me everything she knew.

The cocaine. The all-day bingeing. The trip to rehab months

after Hannah was born. Narcotics Anonymous meetings. The effect on his family. The effect on *our* family.

I stared into the distance as each word absorbed into my mind. The final pieces of the puzzle that had been incomplete for years finally fell into place. For a moment, I felt peace in finally getting the explanation I had wanted all along. I relished that moment because I knew it was going to be short lived. And as the moment slowly passed and the picture became clear, reality hit me. Anger pulsed through my body as I jumped up from the table, and the lawn chair fell backward with a large crash.

And then I screamed.

THE STORM HIT around nine o'clock, just as the information I had waited so long for settled into my bones. Loud cracks of lightning followed by a burst of thunder were annoyingly apropos. Nate, Caroline, and I sat in the living room as the rain crashed against the windows.

So that was the reason—a common drug addiction. That was why Hannah was lying in a steel crib, still wearing diapers when she should have been potty trained. It was so pedestrian. So cliché. I wasn't sure what had happened the day she was born. I had assumed Dr. Stewart had a family emergency or an illness.

I suppose it really was an illness, just like alcoholism was my father's illness.

"Mom, I'm sorry," Caroline said, sitting beside me. Her eyes filled with tears. "I mean, I'm sorry I didn't listen to you. I'm sorry I still love Brody. I do. I still love him. But I don't know anymore. Everything has gotten so messed up. I don't know what to think anymore. I feel so numb."

She was so young, and her life had been so unfair. It was unfair for all of us. But we had expected Caroline to understand so much more than someone her age should. I remembered how full of life she was when she was little. She loved to go grocery shopping with me. While sitting in the seat of the cart, she counted each piece of produce as she dropped it into the plastic bag that I held. She would march right up to kids on the playground and introduce herself. She would suggest things like spaghetti with hot dogs and peanut butter tacos for dinner.

I actually made the peanut butter tacos once. When she'd first suggested it, I thought she was just being silly. But then I heated a corn tortilla in a frying pan until it was crispy, added a spoonful of peanut butter, and folded it into a taco. Caroline gobbled it up like it was a regular menu item in our household. I tried one myself. The warm peanut butter melted and spread across the crisp tortilla. With a glass of milk, it made a nice simple meal. I couldn't remember the last time I'd made one for Caroline.

I looked at her now, the same little girl who had grown into a woman much too soon. I wiped her cheeks. "No one meant for any of this to happen." *Not even Dr. Stewart,* I thought. I didn't dare say the words, though. Saying them for my family to hear would be like accepting what had happened. Like my father, he had an addiction. People with addictions didn't have any control. The drug controlled them. Being so young and naïve, I had tried to help my father. I'd thought my love for him would give him the strength to quit drinking. I wondered if Mrs. Stewart was as co-dependent with her husband as my mother was with my dad.

I wasn't ready to forgive Dr. Stewart. I still wanted to be angry and to hate him with every muscle in my body. He had done this to us, to Hannah. His addiction resulted in my being neglected the day of Hannah's birth. And in Hannah's life being forever ruined. That was very different from Dad's situation.

Nate swore under his breath. He sat on the loveseat, his elbows resting on his knees, his eyes fixed on the floor, a vein pulsing in his temple. He turned to me. "I'm sorry, too."

"For what?"

"For being in denial. For not dealing with my anger. For not being there for you when you were angry. I guess... I didn't want to deal with it."

For the first time in a long while, I reached out and rested my hand on his. We had all handled Hannah's illness in our own ways. My way was more evident on the outside—arguing with my family and confronting Dr. Stewart. Nate had suffered in silence by keeping his anger packaged up inside for fear that if he too expressed himself, our whole lives would implode. Caroline had also suffered in silence, but in a different way. She reluctantly accepted her new role as an older sister. She stayed out of our way as we learned how to be parents to a child with special needs. Then she inadvertently fell in love with the one person she shouldn't have fallen in love with.

The last three years felt like a decade. I looked back on the family we had been before Hannah was born and wondered who those strangers were. Our life had been a well-oiled machine on autopilot. Then God threw a wrench into it. I suppose he thought we could handle it.

I guess he was right, because there we were, sitting on the couch, listening to the rain subside. We had survived. We were still a family. That day felt like a bittersweet breakthrough. I was still angry, but for the first time, we were all in this together.

"How about peanut butter tacos for dinner?" I asked.

Caroline's face lit up. She laughed lightly. "I can't remember the last time I had one of those."

"I'll get the milk," Nate said.

"After dinner," Caroline said, "maybe we can go see Hannah?"

"This late?" Nate asked.

Caroline nodded and smiled through her tears. "I want to see my baby sister."

I reached out and pulled her to me. "Sounds like a plan."

Chapter 37

CAROLINE

I opened my eyes the next morning, feeling like I'd slept for days. I could see things differently. The picture was still blurry, like seeing the world without contact lenses. I sat up in bed and thought about Brody, from the time we'd met to our relationship as it blossomed into love. A few days ago, thinking about us would have filled me with warmth and hope. That morning, it felt as though it had been an act.

I didn't blame Brody for anything. But knowing the truth about what had happened to Hannah, I saw everything in a new light. For the first time, I was seeing things through my mother's eyes.

My phone buzzed. Brody's name was displayed on the screen, and I let it go to voice mail. I knew I was going to have to face him in school that morning. But I still needed time to clear the cobwebs from my mind and sort out my feelings. As I got ready for school, my mind weeded through the details.

I still loved Brody. That I knew for sure. I didn't hate his dad, and I felt guilty about that. I had always assumed there was a valid reason, and sooner or later we would find out.

Knowing the truth, I wasn't sure I could still be with Brody.

I walked slowly through the halls at school, still processing the facts in my head. My baby sister's life had been forever damaged because of the recklessness of my boyfriend's dad. I didn't know what to do with that, or if my relationship with Brody could continue. I turned the corner and saw Brody leaning against his locker, talking to Laura Mattingly. For a brief but strange moment, I was relieved to see him talking with another girl. *Maybe he's done with me. Then I won't be forced to make a difficult decision about our relationship.* Or maybe I wasn't done with us yet.

I turned around and headed back toward my locker before he saw me.

I blew off English class.

Where are U? Brody's text read, but I didn't respond. I rerouted my normal course between classes to avoid running into him. At lunch, I didn't hide out in the library, because I knew he would find me there. Instead, I left campus and spent my lunch period, plus the next two periods, sitting at McDonald's. Brody texted several more times. Courtney also messaged me, wondering where I was. I didn't even know what to say to her. I sat in that McDonald's until my butt was numb from the hard plastic chair. At two thirty, I walked home.

Chapter 38

JILLIAN

Friday morning, I dragged myself out of bed at seven o'clock to check on Caroline. She had missed the last two days of school by faking an illness I knew she had only in her heart. I didn't blame her. I'd spent the week roaming the house, processing my emotions that went from anger to sadness to resignation and back to anger. Abbie convinced me to come into the bakery on Wednesday and help her bake the latest batch of Twilight cookies to help keep myself occupied. She'd offered me a part-time job, telling me a few days a week in the bakery would be good for me. It was a tempting offer, especially since my freelance marketing projects had dwindled, and I was ready for a change. I'd told her I would think about it. I went to see Hannah almost every day that week. I held her and watched as she blinked and gazed around her world.

I opened the door to Caroline's room and stuck my head in. She was burrowed under the blankets, her ponytail sticking out at the top. I stepped over the piles of clothes and textbooks on the floor and pulled open the blinds.

"Are you going to school today?" I asked. "You've already missed two quizzes and a test."

"I don't care," she mumbled.

"You can't avoid him forever." I climbed into bed next to her and pulled the covers up to our chins. "How many times has he called?"

She had sheet lines on her face and sleep in her eyes. "I don't know. I turned my phone off Wednesday night."

"The sooner you face him, the better," I said.

"I don't know what to say to him yet."

"Maybe you just don't want to tell him it's over," I said gently.

"Maybe I don't want to hear it from him that it's over." She rubbed her eyes and yawned. "Mom?"

"Yes, baby?"

"Do you hate Dr. Stewart?"

I'd never bothered to ask myself that simple question in all those years. Of course I was angry. And I'd wanted something bad to happen to him. I'd wanted him to feel the same pain I felt. I suppose all those emotions added up to hate, although I'd never said the words to myself. *I hate Dr. Stewart.* I didn't want to hate him. My father had always told me hate was a waste of energy.

"You can dislike someone," he'd told me, "or not care about them. But never hate them."

I never hated my dad for everything he'd put my mother and me through. Of course, *he* hadn't almost killed my baby.

"I don't know what I feel anymore. He was obviously sick, like Grandpa was. But that shouldn't excuse what he did. If he were driving drunk and killed someone, he'd go to jail. Why isn't he in jail for what he did to us?" I couldn't bring myself to say that I hated him. I guess that meant I didn't. Even though I had every right to. "I'm so tired of feeling anything," I said.

"Me, too," she said. "What are you doing today?"

I sighed. "Oh, I don't know. Maybe I'll see if Abbie needs help at the bakery today. Or maybe I'll have lunch with Kate. I'll call my recruiter and see if there are any freelance projects available. The house needs cleaning. And I have to pay the car insurance. I take it you're not going to school today?"

She smiled. "Just one more day. Please?"

I threw an arm around her and closed my eyes. "Let's take a long nap and go get our nails done. How's that sound?"

"Perfect."

Chapter 39

CAROLINE

Saturday morning, Dad enticed me out of bed with a promise of Walker Brothers' blueberry pancakes. Normally, with the funk I was in, nothing could get me out of bed, but after a few days of wallowing, I was ready to take a small step forward, with or without clarity. Plus, I was starving.

On the way to the restaurant, I turned on my phone for the first time in two days. It took a few moments to reboot. Then it beeped and vibrated with notifications. Seventeen missed texts. The voicemail icon blazed. I scrolled down to the first of several messages from Brody:

WEDNESDAY 10:30 A.M.

I know u talked w/my dad. Hope u don't give up on us cause he fucked up. this isn't our fault. never was. Why should we be punished? U and ur family suffered enough cause of my dad. Don't throw away what we had because of it. Please call me.

WEDNESDAY 6:37 P.M.

I hate his fucking guts for doing this to us. I think he's using again!

its the same shit he did when I was a kid. wish I could find a way to throw his ass in jail. He's a worthless piece of shit. Please please call me! I need you right now.

WEDNESDAY 11:30 P.M.
I will never give up on us.

THURSDAY 9:02 A.M.
why aren't u in school? getting worried. hope ur ok. love u.

THURSDAY 12:41 P.M.
schools not the same w/o u. call me. want to know ur ok.

THURSDAY 7:12 P.M.
hope ur not mad at me. all dads fault. hes a motherfucking junkie. hope he dies with his next hit.

FRIDAY 11:30 A.M.
I understand if you need space. dont shut me out. call me please. we can fix this. I LOVE YOU!!!

FRIDAY 8:25 P.M.
We have to talk about this. please please call me. I need to see you. I love you. You and me 4ever.

BY THE TIME we got to the restaurant, I'd lost my appetite. The growing desperation in Brody's texts made him sound like a different person. Was his dad really using again? What other family is going to suffer from his actions like we did? I forced two bites of pancake before telling Dad I wasn't hungry and asking him to take me home.

"You barely ate anything," he said. "What's going on?"

"I'm full."

"I've never seen you turn down blueberry pancakes," Dad said with a skeptical look. "It's Brody, isn't it?" He motioned toward my phone, and I reluctantly nodded.

"He's understandably upset," he said. "I know this is hard for both of you. It's hard for all of us. It's a messed-up twist of fate, and I hate that you have to go through this."

"Brody needs me."

"Care-Bear," he said, "I won't tell you some cliché phrase to make you feel better, like there are other fish in the sea or something lame like that. But I will promise you that the pain of not being with him will go away. You won't feel this anxiety forever. And neither will he."

I stared down at the pancakes absorbing maple syrup on my plate.

"You know what you need to do," he continued. "Let's box up those pancakes to go. Mom will eat them."

When we pulled into the driveway, I asked Dad if I could borrow the car. "Courtney texted me. She wants to meet at the mall."

"Now, we both know that's not true," Dad said. "Go to him. Better to do it now and get it over with." He got out of the driver's seat and left the car running for me.

THE FRONT DOOR SWUNG open at the Stewart's house before I had the car in park. Brody came out, wearing faded jeans and a wrinkled Ferndale West Soccer T-shirt.

"Where are your parents?" I asked.

"Out." He pulled me to him and kissed me hard. His tongue

tasted like black coffee. For the first time, I tensed up when he touched me. "How are you? I was so worried."

"I'm fine. Just needed time to think." I pulled away and looked into his bloodshot eyes. "How do you know he's using again?"

"I walked in on him." He grabbed my hand and led me inside.

"You saw him snorting coke?"

He nodded. "And he knows I saw him, too."

"Did you tell your mom?"

"No." We sat on the couch in the living room, a gaudy room that Brody's mom had attempted to decorate in French country style, but it looked more like Moulin Rouge. "I missed you."

I avoided his eyes and focused on the blue toile wallpaper of a farmer plowing a field.

He leaned into me again, but I pushed him away.

"What?" he asked. "We didn't let this bother us before. Nothing has changed."

"Everything has changed."

"How?"

"I don't know. It just has. I see your dad differently now."

"Fuck him. He's not me. He's a worthless asshole."

I turned my body away from Brody. "I guess I always thought he'd have a good reason for doing what he did. Now I know he doesn't."

"But I'm still the same person," he pleaded. "I haven't changed."

I thought of the texts he'd sent. The anger. The desperation. Was he the same? What effect had the truth really had on him?

"I need more time," I said, running my hands through my hair. "I still can't understand it all. It's all too much. This is too intense." I jumped up and started pacing.

"We're still us. We haven't changed. Don't let what he did ruin us." His voice cracked as he spoke and his eyes were damp and dark. He held out his hand and motioned for me to come back to him. Brody was as much a victim as I was.

We were all victims. All in a different way. I noticed his

disheveled appearance, his tousled hair, and his tired eyes filling with tears. A physical pain throbbed in my chest as I slowly walked back and sat down next to him.

He leaned into me again, and I didn't stop him this time. I let him kiss me, gently and tenderly at first, the way I'd always known his kisses to be. Then his kiss became more intense and desperate. He pushed me down and climbed on top of me, pinning my arms with his hands and shoving his tongue into my mouth.

At first I wanted to push him off me. But as he pulled up my skirt and yanked down my panties, something inside of me stirred. It was an unfamiliar emotion. Not anger, not fear, not happiness.

His thrusts were angry, but I didn't push him away. Nor did I wrap my arms around him to pull him toward me. I just closed my eyes and lay there, letting the ambivalence run through my heart and mind.

Chapter 40

JILLIAN

A bbie unlocked the front door to Jacob's Crumbles and let me in. "You could've come through the back. You're an employee now."

"I guess that's true," I said as I walked into the warm storefront and inhaled the scent of a fresh batch of sugar cookies.

I'd called Abbie the night before and told her I was ready to come work for her. I wanted something less stressful and with less responsibility than the marketing industry. And something about flooding those cookies with sugary icing was therapeutic. Abbie scheduled me to work Tuesdays and Thursdays, but if all went well, I'd probably show up more often whether she paid me or not.

"I have an idea," I said as I took off my jacket and hung it in the back room.

"Ideas already? I love it!"

"You mind if I make a sample first? It'll be like a test of the skills you taught me."

Abbie laughed. "I can only teach so much. The rest is talent. Have at it." She tossed me an apron. "I'm going to get started on some more red stilettos."

I dug through the drawer of cookie cutters until I found the shape I was looking for. I went to the fridge and pulled out a small batch of leftover sugar cookie dough that Abbie kept on hand for testing cookie ideas. I floured the marble surface and rolled out the dough to about ten inches in diameter, large enough to make about four cookies. I pressed the cookie cutter into the dough, laid the cookies on the cookie sheet, and shoved them in the oven. While they were baking, I whipped up red frosting and scooped it into a piping bag. I didn't even wait for the cookies to cool completely before I started decorating them, which made the red frosting a little runny, but I was sure Abbie would get the idea. I used white frosting to pipe on the remaining details then placed them on a plate to show Abbie.

When I approached, she looked up from rolling out chocolate cookie dough. I placed the plate on the counter in front of her and showed her my creation: cookies in the shape of the Misericordia logo—a red heart with a white cross cutting through the center of it. "We sell them and donate twenty percent of the sales to Misericordia. It can be an ongoing campaign."

Abbie surveyed my work. "You were so eager that you couldn't even wait for them to cool?" She swiped some red frosting that had run off the cookie and licked it off her finger.

"Well, what do you think?"

"I'm wondering why the hell I haven't thought of this earlier." She reached out and hugged me. "You know the North Shore mommies love a good charity. But twenty percent is a little steep. Gotta pay the bills, you know. Let's start with ten percent."

"Okay."

"I'll call Misericordia and let them know and to make sure we have permission to use their logo. I'm sure they'll be okay with it."

"Should I get started on the first batch? We can send a couple dozen to them as a gift."

She smiled and nodded. "Get to work."

The bell above the front door dinged, and Kate walked in wearing a neon-green jumpsuit and red loafers. "I didn't think my ass was big enough, so I thought I'd have cookies for breakfast."

"You know we don't open for another hour." Abbie laughed. "And the cookies are still baking. I can offer you some of yesterday's leftovers."

"Hey, I'm not picky," Kate said. "A cup of coffee would be nice, too. Preferably not leftover."

Abbie smiled and pointed to the coffee pot. "Help yourself."

"What a nice surprise," I said to Kate, pulling her into a hug. "What are you doing up so early?"

"I wanted to see how your first day on the job was going," she said. "And I was bored."

As Abbie put out a plate of broken cookies for Kate to munch on, I showed Kate my Misericordia cookies and told her our fundraising idea.

"Brilliant. I'll buy a few dozen. See, Abbie? I told you she'd be good for more than just baking," Kate said and then winked at me.

Chapter 41

CAROLINE

B rody and I barely spoke throughout the following week at school. I didn't know if he was embarrassed, or if he was just giving me the space I wanted. We acknowledged each other in English class with a reluctant nod. During lunch, our friends acted as a buffer, an excuse not to talk to each other. There wasn't any hostility, just a mutual understanding to keep a distance from each other.

I wasn't sure how, when, or even if I was going to talk to Brody again. I went through the week, taking each day in stride, getting comfortable in the numbness that had taken over my body. I knew there was a possibility that our relationship was finally over for good. Maybe there wasn't going to be a dramatic breakup, just a neglected relationship slowly fading into the past. A few weeks before, I would have crumbled in despair over the end of our relationship. I wasn't sure what I was feeling anymore. I kind of hoped it would just fade out of my mind, like a bad dream.

As the days went by, I busied myself with other things. I focused more on school. I spent time with my parents, even if that meant just watching TV together or sitting down for a family dinner in the kitchen. I hung out with Courtney and my other girlfriends, doing what normal teenage girls do: shopping, going to movies, and getting pedicures at the salon. These distractions made it easier to ignore making any decisions about my lingering relationship with Brody.

But I knew I couldn't escape it for long.

THAT FOLLOWING SATURDAY, I was actually bored. For the first time in months, I didn't have anything to do. Normally, I would have been at Misericordia with Brody. But I wasn't even sure if Brody was still volunteering there. I curled up on the couch and switched on the TV, resigned to having a lazy day watching Lifetime movies and eating leftover fried chicken from the fridge. Mom was at the bakery. Dad was at a Cubs game. I had the place to myself.

I took a nap on the couch while the TV acted as background noise, lulling me to sleep. I chatted on Facebook with Courtney, who was stuck at home with the flu. I even cleaned the house a little.

At around two o'clock, my phone dinged. I assumed it was Courtney again, but when I saw Brody's name across the top, my heart leaped.

Please come over, the first text read, followed immediately by another: *My dad is dead.*

I shot up so quickly that my head spun. I steadied myself as I reread the text three times before I grabbed the car keys and headed out the door.

As I raced to Brody's house, various grim thoughts raced through my mind. *Car accident? Heart attack? Is it a cruel lie to get me to come over?*

The obvious was furthest from my mind.

An ambulance was stopped in front of the Stewarts' house. Its spinning lights swept across the yellow colonial. A squad car was also on the street. The coroner's van was parked in the driveway, behind Dr. Stewart's silver Mercedes. Neighbors had gathered, trying to catch a glimpse of anything happening in the house. Her face crumpled in anguish, Mrs. Stewart stood in the foyer, talking to a cop.

I found Brody in his father's study, talking to a stocky woman wearing latex gloves and an ID badge marking her as the coroner. His face was blank, and his arms were folded across his chest. "He's been an addict for years," he said to the coroner.

Dr. Stewart was at his desk, sitting in the same spot where he'd been not long ago, when he'd informed me of the details that had changed the course of everything. He was slumped over, his head resting on its side, his eyes open slightly. A trickle of blood ran from each white-dusted nostril and into a small pool covering the desk calendar. The crimson puddle seeped into his schedule for next week. He looked strangely peaceful.

Brody reached for me. I held him tightly. When I tried to pull away, he wouldn't let me go.

He eventually stepped back, and we both looked at his dad.

"Was it...Do you think it was intentional?" I asked.

"Suicide?" He scoffed. "Doubt it. Son of a bitch wouldn't do us a favor by killing himself."

He led me by the hand out of the study and into the family room. Brody sat on the couch and pulled me down next to him.

"Thanks for coming over," he said with a faint smile. "I'm glad you're here."

"What happened?" I asked.

His eyes were on his mother in the foyer, watching her as she grieved. "Mom and I were out." His voice was low, almost a whisper. "We came home, and I found him at his desk, freaking out."

"Freaking out? What do you mean?"

"He was, I don't know, convulsing."

"Oh my God." It brought me back to the time a few years back when I'd found Hannah not breathing in her crib. Brody resented his dad for causing our relationship to crumble. To feel that much anger toward someone, then find them in a helpless state —that blend of emotions was all too familiar to me. I pulled him into another hug, held him tightly, and told him I was sorry he had to go through that. "Did you try giving him CPR?"

He pulled away. "No."

"What did the 9-1-1 operator tell you to do?"

"I didn't call 9-1-1. Not right away." His jaw was clenched. His eyes, dark and cold like they had been the other night, looked past me. For the first time, I noticed how much he resembled his dad. Then he met my eyes, and his expression softened. "He was... I don't know... seizing, I guess. I just watched him while he freaked. His eyes rolled back in his head. But before... right before they did, he looked right at me. And we stared at each other for what seemed like several minutes. I just watched him, Caroline. He was so pathetic. I couldn't move. I didn't want to move. And then he was gone."

I tried to read his face. He'd been so distant the last couple of times I'd seen him. I wasn't sure who or where he was anymore.

"Brody, why didn't you call the paramedics? Didn't you try to help him?"

He looked at me with the same cold, blank expression that was starting to give me chills. "I couldn't help him, Caroline. No one could."

Brody's mom sobbed from the foyer. A woman came over and embraced Mrs. Stewart then whispered something to her.

I jumped up from the couch, shaking Brody's arm from my shoulder, and went back into the study. The coroner was still taking notes. I hesitated, not wanting to interrupt her work. But I had to see Dr. Stewart again to really grasp the reality. I took a few tentative steps toward the desk. His eyes were turned downward, toward the pool of blood, as though he were reviewing what he had done. After our talk the other day, after his own son had confronted him, everything had returned to the surface. He'd had to face what he had buried for so long. And maybe he couldn't face it anymore.

Someone from the coroner's office wheeled in the gurney with a black body bag on top. I left the room while they loaded the body, but Brody insisted on staying. Mrs. Stewart was sitting at the kitchen table with her friend. I went to her, told her how sorry I was, and gave her a sincere hug. *"I think my wife suspects, but she doesn't like talking about it."* I recalled Dr. Stewart's words and wondered how much she knew. Or was she in denial like I had been?

The coroners wheeled the body out of the house. Brody followed slowly, just like he would when he trailed his father's casket at the funeral. But his energy was different. I felt it all the way from the kitchen. I followed him outside and observed him as he stood, his arms crossed, watching them load his father's body into the coroner's van. The police car pulled away from the house and down the street. The ambulance shut off its lights and drove away. Neighbors returned to their homes. The street was quiet again.

Brody pivoted and walked back to the house nonchalantly, as if he had just emptied the trash. He sat on the porch swing and pushed it back and forth with his foot, making an eerie creaking noise.

"Brody, why didn't you call 9-1-1?"

"I did call them."

"After he died." I added. "Why didn't you call before?"

"After everything he did, after everything he put us through, everything he put you and your family through. And poor Hannah." His voice was deep and unfamiliar, like a stranger's. "I neglected him the same way he neglected your mom."

A chill embraced me. I wrapped my arms around myself even though the evening was mild. I looked into his empty eyes and tried to recognize him. I couldn't see where he had gone. He wasn't Brody anymore. He wasn't the guy I'd fallen in love with, who'd treated me like his princess, who'd wanted nothing but to be with me at all times. At any cost.

Seeing how quickly things could change was unnerving. How I'd come to be the person I was all because of Hannah. How Brody could go from a caring and sensitive soul too a vengeful, twisted person because he loved me. My heart raced, and my breaths became shallow.

Brody was watching me. He reached out to me, his mouth turned up in a faint smile. He whispered that he loved me.

My eyes filled as I let him take my hand. I looked at his beautiful face one last time and studied his features that I never wanted to forget. I watched as his smile faded and his expression changed from satisfaction, to acceptance, and then to sadness. And without another word, I let his hand go.

Chapter 42

HANNAH

When I open my eyes, the sunshine is streaming through the blinds next to my bed. I squint, and my eyes begin to water. It happens every morning, but I don't mind. I love the sunshine on my face. I don't get to experience it too often, except through a window.

I turn my head and exhale loudly to let Claire know I'm awake and patiently waiting for her. She comes to me right away and greets me with her big, toothy smile. Every few days, she changes her hair. Today, it's blond and comes down to her shoulders. Her booming voice shakes loose whatever sleepiness is left in me.

"Mamma's coming today," she says as she dresses me and combs my hair into two side ponytails.

I hope Daddy and Caroline come, too. It wasn't often the three of them came together. But the last few visits, they did, and we were all together. One happy family. We don't do much when they're here. Mamma holds me and rocks me like I'm still a little baby. Daddy covers my face with kisses, but mostly watches TV. Caroline whispers things in my ear like, "I'm sorry" and "Don't be mad at me" and "I always loved you."

Caroline's friend used to come and visit me a lot when my

family wasn't here. He would take me for long walks in the sunshine and talk to me about Caroline, school, and soccer. He once brought me a soft and squishy teddy bear. I loved to hug it, but it made me sneeze and made it hard to breathe, so Claire took it away. I haven't seen Caroline's friend in a long time. I wonder if he's sick or if he and Caroline had a fight like Mamma and Daddy fight sometimes.

My family arrives after I finish my breakfast and takes me outside for a walk. Mamma tries to put sunglasses and a hat on me, but I squirm and whine, so she takes them off.

Mamma's happier now. I can tell by her face. It's softer and more relaxed. She hums nice songs as we walk around campus. I can also tell by the way she looks at Daddy now. It's different than how she used to look at him. Daddy's more relaxed, too. I think when Mamma's happy, Daddy's happy. I like seeing them hold hands.

Caroline doesn't seem as happy. But she's not mad, either. Just a little sad, I guess. Maybe because her friend isn't here with us. But she tries. She smiles at me and wipes the drool from my chin. She brushes my pigtails and tells me I'm pretty. She's doing her best. At least she's not fighting with Mamma anymore.

Mamma parks my chair in the garden, where the flowers are all the different colors of the rainbow. She asks a nice man who is walking by if he will take our picture and hands him the camera. They stand around my chair, Daddy to my right, Mamma to my left, and Caroline right above me. I lift my head in an effort to face the camera. I can feel my family smile as the man snaps a picture.

I can still feel them smile as Mamma unpacks a picnic lunch. And when they laugh at a silly joke Daddy tells. And when Caroline picks me up out of my chair and cuddles me. And when I feel them smile, it makes me smile too, knowing that they're all happy when they visit.

They're happy. All because of me.

AUTHOR'S NOTE

All Because of Hannah is a work of fiction, but, like many works of fiction, a lot of my personal life has been woven into the story. Regardless, all the characters in this book are fictional, and any similarities to real people are just a coincidence.

Misericordia, however, is a real place in Chicago. It's a wonderful facility for children and adults with developmental disabilities. If you'd like to learn more about Misericordia, or make a generous donation, please visit www.Misericordia.com

ABOUT THE AUTHOR

Danielle Patarazzi was born and raised in the Chicago area, and currently lives in San Luis Obispo, California. This is her debut novel.

www.daniellepatarazzi.com

98988515R00171

Made in the USA
Columbia, SC
05 July 2018